GLITTERING DEATH

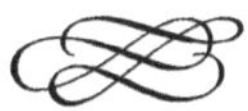

CARMEN RADTKE

ISBN 978-1-9162410-2-2

 Created with Vellum

The Case of the Missing Bride (An Alyssa Chalmers mystery)

False Play at the Christmas Party (A Jack Sullivan mystery)

A Matter of Love and Death (A Jack and Frances mystery)

CHAPTER 1

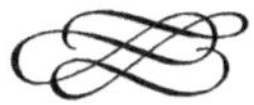

29 July 1862

Hammer-blows startled the birds into protesting flights. Five men slid freshly sawn planks three boards wide into an orderly row, wedging each one in good and proper. Half the men in town had found excuses not to leave for too long since they'd had word that their brides should arrive in Canada any day now. Nobody wanted to miss that moment when the first females ever to set foot in this place came ashore.

They'd waited almost a year since their late pastor came up with the crazy idea of shipping over a gaggle of poor, hard-working girls from Australia. A fever had gripped them back then, with big plans for a proper town, to call home instead of moving on wherever there was gold. It separated the men into two groups, the homebodies who readily parted with their cash to stake their claim, and those who feared for the freedom of their ways, once females moved in, and joined the next pack train into the wilderness. A handful of men stayed out of the discussion, kept what was theirs and waited to see what happened.

Money. It had taken a lot of money to pay for the skirts' passages, and to spruce up Run's End. But then, everything did. All you needed was patience. Patience, and luck. Or, in his case, a good plan and a cool head. A few more months, that was all he needed to make his luck. Or let the others make it for him.

The evening bell interrupted his thoughts. The men downed their tools, slapping each other on the back in unbridled happiness.

Land, after all these endless months at sea. Alyssa Chalmers hurried down the wooden gangway, but her knees gave in after two steps on firm ground. A firm hand grasped her waist at the last moment.

'Steady,' said Mr Kendrick, first officer of the 'Artemis Delight', the ship that had carried them from Melbourne. 'That goes for all of you ladies.'

Indeed, most of the girls had by now made the same discovery as Alyssa, that their legs betrayed them. Nancy and Susanna clung together with a little cry that turned to laughter when they found themselves unceremoniously sitting on the rock-hard earth. Grey dust swivelled around them in a shimmery column.

Alyssa smiled, too. Canada! After all the storms and seasickness, they'd arrived.

She sucked the salty air deep into her lungs. It carried the crisp tanginess that she'd grown accustomed to, but instead of being mixed with the stink of burning coal there was an almost forgotten scent at its heart. It smelt of life, and hope, of a fresh start. She gazed around, rapt. A cluster of trees appeared as dark silhouettes against the backdrop of a long warehouse.

Someone blocked the sun.

Mark Bryson, the ship's surgeon, made his way towards her, with barely a glance for anyone else.

Mr Kendrick let go of Alyssa with flattering slowness. She'd barely noticed his presence any longer in her excitement to see trees again. To her surprise, the doctor gave them a regretful shrug and walked on.

By now all twenty-one girls stood more or less firmly on the sun-bleached ground. Their chaperone, Matron McKenzie, fished a list out of her reticule, and with a sigh of relief ticked off name after name. Her task as a stern guardian, nurse and moral guide, was almost over. Beside her stood the second officer, Mr Wainwright. Every so often Matron would glance at him from under her bonnet, and meet his slow smile.

Laughter rose in Alyssa's throat. How wonderful to stand on a pier again, free from the confinements of the ship and the tyranny of wind and waves.

She stretched her arms as wide as she could and let out a happy little cry.

'Alyssa,' her friend Hannah said. 'People are staring at you.'

Alyssa sighed as she dropped her arms. 'Aren't you happy?'

'Yeah, but you know how upset Matron gets when you do odd things.'

Not just Matron, Alyssa thought. Although Mrs McKenzie

had readily accepted Alyssa's assistance, and let her teach the other brides how to read and write properly, and do their sums, she still fretted over Alyssa's too free behaviour. A young, well-educated lady of good family, was someone she could not treat the same way as Matron would a girl like Rosie, who with her loose morals and meanness was a constant burden.

Alyssa's friendship with the doctor and the first officer on the other hand was a fact that Matron readily accepted as the logical outcome of a sea-voyage where Alyssa's nursing skills had been tested when seasickness laid low half the brides, most of the male first class passengers, and several crew members.

Hannah prodded her. 'Stop daydreaming. Matron's finished.'

'Sorry.'

Alyssa waited for a sign of what to expect now.

The five male passengers still stood on deck, while all the luggage sat in the hold or cabins.

The sun's warmth seeped into her bones. A few more hours until dusk. Where would they sleep tonight?

Matron must have wondered too, because she beckoned Mr Kendrick. She whispered into his ear with an unaccustomed urgency, but his answer seemed to please her.

She clapped into her hands for attention.

'Girls,' she said, 'Mr Kendrick has informed me that we are all invited to a celebratory dinner in Fort Victoria.'

Loud gasps interrupted her. She clapped again.

'If you will follow Mr Kendrick in an orderly fashion, he will take us to the hotel.'

'A hotel?' red-haired Susanna asked. 'But our dresses – I sat in the dirt.'

She craned her slender neck in dismay to survey the bedraggled appearance of her skirt.

'Let me help you,' Alyssa said. She patted the faded material until a small dust cloud rose from it.

Susanna wrinkled her nose. 'I've never been in a hotel before. If Matron had told us we'd have put on our good dresses.'

'There'll be more opportunities to dress up,' Alyssa said. 'Besides, no-one will notice a speck of dirt on your skirt.' Especially if they looked at her face, with its sparkling blue eyes and the dimples in her cheeks.

'Yeah.' Susanna's mood lifted. 'Imagine, food that we don't have to cook ourselves.'

She linked her arm with Alyssa's, decidedly upbeat. Heavy footsteps fell in behind them.

Alyssa turned her head and smiled. The gentlemen passengers had come to join the party, with the ship's boy, Davies, bringing up the rear. She wondered whose idea the dinner invitation was.

Some of the girls already limped a little, after less than a quarter of a mile. They hadn't been able to walk much during their long sea voyage in cramped conditions.

At least this path was smooth, with the solid earth baked hard. A few buildings made of rough timber or stone lined the port, probably the workspace of clerks, or for the storage of goods, Alyssa guessed.

She wished that she could stroll around and explore this new place.

Mr Kendrick and Matron stopped in front of a low-slung building, with a porch running along one side.

It appeared new, with the timber barely weathered.

While her friends entered the hotel in silent awe, Alyssa took stock of her surroundings.

It was rustic, but pleasant, she decided. She noticed with delight the dancing fingers of light on the scrubbed floor boards. The window panes gleamed, and the brass lantern fittings shone. The main bar offered space for at least two dozen men side by side, while half a dozen small tables with chairs scattered around them waited for custom.

Mr Kendrick led them through a door into another room, this one with a large unlit fireplace at the end and a chandelier furnished with a dozen tallow candles.

Two long tables were already awaiting them, with Captain Moore at the head of one. The gentlemen sat down next to him.

Mr Kendrick led Matron to the other table and installed himself at the head.

Alyssa craned her neck. Where was the doctor?

'Your beau is missing,' Susanna said.

'The doctor is not my beau.'

'Then how come you know who I meant?' Susanna winked at her. 'Everyone can see that he likes you. Too bad for our Canadian friends.'

She lifted her skirt to sit down, with Alyssa next to her.

Alyssa couldn't suppress a smile. Susanna didn't know Alyssa's secret, that she'd never intended to marry one of the men who awaited them several days' travel up the Fraser river. For her new friends, this opportunity to exchange poverty in Melbourne for a prosperous life in Canada offered everything they wished for. But Alyssa, with her private means as the orphaned daughter of a high-ranking civil servant, had other plans with her life. All she wanted was a chance to secure a passage to go back home, to the England she'd left as a two-year old. As much as she hated lying to everyone, this bridal voyage had been her only opportunity to secure a berth. No shipping agent would have sold a ticket to a single lady, without a proper chaperone.

At least now she'd halved the distance, and as soon as the girls were settled in, she and Matron McKenzie would book two berths on the next ocean-going ship. With Matron as her companion, no-one would deny her the ticket that a single lady could not obtain. A tiny doubt crept up in her mind that the pretty young widow might have other plans, but she shut it out.

Susanna nudged her and nodded towards the entrance. Dr Bryson stood there, with a heavy leather brief-case in one hand, the other smoothing his dark blond hair.

He strolled over to Alyssa's table.

'Over here, Bryson,' Mr Kendrick said.

The doctor gave Alyssa an apologetic shrug that she ignored for her companion's sake.

'Sorry it took me so long, Captain Moore.' He put the brief-case next to him on the bench as he took his place.

The captain gave him a curt nod. 'That's alright. Is everyone here?'

'Mr Wainwright is still missing,' Mr Kendrick said.

A faint tinge of colour spread over Matron's cheeks.

Rosie, who as usual was made to sit beside Matron to be kept in check, sniggered. The second officer's affection for Matron and her feelings towards him had long since ceased to be a secret, but only Rosie would make fun of it. Matron slapped her hand with her fan. Her brittle blonde charge poked out her tongue.

'She's getting meaner and meaner every day,' waif-like Nancy, at not yet eighteen the youngest of the girls, said. 'She should be thankful the Captain didn't clap her beau in irons when he caught them together.'

'She told me they'll leave here,' said Nellie, the closest to a friend that Rosie possessed. 'She said he's going to marry her and she'll live in a fancy house.'

'And I'll be the queen,' Hannah said. The other girls laughed. They'd all suffered under Rosie's vicious tongue.

Alyssa hoped, for Rosie's sake, that the stoker kept his word and regularised the relationship, but she had her doubts.

Two boys entered through a swing door behind a wooden bar and set down platters with ham, fish, boiled potatoes, and freshly baked bread. A plump woman in a spotless cotton frock with a starched pinafore supervised their effort. Alyssa took her for their mother.

The door swung open and Mr Wainwright rushed in, a small bouquet of wildflowers in his hands.

'Please excuse my tardiness, Captain,' he said as he motioned Rosie to give up her place to him. She did so with her customary scowl, but surprisingly no protest.

The captain lifted his bushy eyebrows. 'I'm sure you had a reason. Now let's say grace.'

The food disappeared in record time, but the two boys competed to replace empty platters at a staggering speed.

They ate like they hadn't done in weeks, since the last fresh victuals arrived during their stop in San Francisco. After all the salted meat and hard biscuits on board, it was heaven to have meat, crusty bread, pale yellow butter, creamy and shaped in a mould, fish from the very day's catch and a pie bursting with apple, with cream slathered on top. Even the gentlemen concentrated on their plates.

The landlady beamed in good humour as she watched them enjoy every morsel of her home cooking.

After the pie, a reverent silence set in, until Mr Wainwright tapped his spoon against his glass – beer for the men, water for the girls - and stood up.

He picked up the bouquet he'd kept in a glass of water all during their dinner, and with his other hand clasped Mrs McKenzie's.

Their gaze met for an exquisitely tender look as she took the wildflowers from him and sniffed their soft fragrance.

'I would like to extend on Captain Moore's well-wishes,' he said. 'Had our kind passengers not beaten me to this celebratory dinner, I would have issued this invitation.' He raised his mug. 'Luckily for me none of them beat me in another matter. I'm happy to tell you that Matron McKenzie has consented to do me the honour to become my wife.'

Mr Kendrick jumped up and clapped him on the shoulder. 'Well done, you sly fox.' He dashed over to Matron, grabbed her by the shoulders and bestowed a hearty kiss on her cheek. Dr Bryson followed suit, to the flustered delight of a blushing Matron and applause from everyone else except the groom. 'That's enough,' he said. 'Please unhand my bride.'

'He's right, Bryson,' said Kendrick. 'When we're on land it's every man for himself.'

The doctor gave Alyssa a quick glance. Susanna nudged her again.

'The wedding will be tomorrow, on board,' said Mr Wainwright, 'before this kind lady and I will escort our other brides to be to their new home.' He bent over Matron's hand and pressed a kiss on it.

Alyssa and the other girls broke into wild applause. Matron blinked away happy tears. She fumbled for her reticule.

Mr Osborne, a shy banker and hobby-astronomer, came to her rescue. He offered her a snowy handkerchief to dab her eyes with. 'I wish you all the happiness in the world,' he said. 'Both of you.'

'Aye.' The captain raised his glass. 'A toast to the best second officer I've sailed with. If you do half as well as a husband, of which I have no doubt, Matron can consider herself a very lucky woman.'

'To Mr Wainwright and Matron,' Mr Kendrick echoed.

Alyssa wished for something a bit more suitable for a toast than water, but she could imagine the scandal had she asked for a bottle of sherry. If hotels in Canada offered sherry at all. She sipped her water, as did the other girls and the bride.

The captain said, 'It's time to return to our chambers.'
Rosie sniggered again, but this time got no reaction.

Matron made a radiant bride, despite the lack of a wedding dress.
Nancy spent all morning trimming Matron's blue woollen

dress with a lace collar that Alyssa had with some prescience purchased in San Francisco as a present, while Hannah brushed the bride's hair and put it up in a bun at the back, with soft ringlets framing the face.

Davies stood by, ready to run any errand needed. Alyssa marvelled at his boundless enthusiasm to pick up a dropped pin or fetch warm water and a heated iron. She also envied him his patience with enforced idleness. He didn't mind standing in wait for half an hour at a time, until he could make himself useful again.

Lucky boy, she thought. Apart from donating the collar, Alyssa found herself for once helpless of assisting any further. She lacked Hannah's hairdressing skills, and her sewing, though adequate, could not match Nancy's.

She finally decided to ask Susanna to help her with the packing of the girls' meagre belongings. But first she needed the lists she had compiled for each of them.

'Davies,' she asked, 'can you spare me a few minutes to accompany me to the office? That is, unless he is needed here, Matron?'

'Don't move, Ma'am.' Hannah curled a strand of hair around a heated tong.

Matron fluttered her hand in a gesture of permission.

'We'll be back as soon as possible,' Alyssa said.

The office was barely a few hundred yards away, but by captain's orders no female was permitted to walk around unaccompanied, to keep them safe from unwanted attention.

Alyssa raised a hand to knock at the office door, but raised voices made her stop at the last instant.

'As soon as the wedding vows have been exchanged I want you off my ship,' Captain Moore said.

A high-pitched voice answered. 'Well, my fiancé and I'll be happy to be rid of this stinking hull and of you and that stupid woman lording it over us.'

Davies and Alyssa drew in their breath in unison. Rosie, of course.

'Out with both of you. I give you ten minutes to collect your sorry things. And if you, my man, expect a character reference from me…'

Alyssa and Davies fled around a corner as Rosie and a stocky man with soot ingrained in his cheeks and hands stomped out of the office.

'Davies!' The captain sounded as he was half-choked.

The boy rushed towards the captain. As did Alyssa, who collided with the doctor as he left his surgery.

'I'm sorry,' she said, but his mind was already on his patient. He grabbed the captain's wrist, counting under his breath. Captain Moore's face was purple with rage, but he already calmed down.

The captain shook the doctor off. 'I'm fine,' he said. 'You, sir, better spend your time looking after Mr Wainwright. Bound to get jittery on such a day. And you, Davies, make sure that those two troublemakers don't take a single thing that doesn't belong to them.'

He spotted Alyssa. 'What is it that you want now?'

'The inventory lists, sir,' she said. 'If Davies and I have those we can assure that Rosie's box contains nothing apart from the items it should.'

The captain nodded. He reached for a ledger.

Alyssa watched with dismay as Rosie stuffed her few shabby clothes into her box. True, she'd caused nothing but trouble, but casting off all her ties to the other brides would leave her at the mercy of the stoker.

Alyssa pulled out her own luggage and dragged it behind a partition, to hide her actions from curious eyes. She opened the secret drawer and took out a velvet pouch. Coins clinked softly as she selected one. She stowed the pouch away, closed the drawer and restored her trunk to its place.

'Rosie?'

The girl scowled at her. 'What do you want, Miss Toffeynose?'

Alyssa's resolve shrunk to pin-head size, but her conscience told her that she couldn't let Rosie go without any means to escape.

'Take this,' she said, holding out a gold half-eagle.

Rosie gaped at the coin. She grabbed it and dropped it inside her shift. 'Five dollars. You must be filthy rich.' A slow, for once real, smile curled up the corners of her mouth. 'You're not such a cow after all, are you.'

'Please take care of yourself, Rosie. And if you're ever in trouble, you know where to find the girls.'

Rosie shrugged. 'I don't think so, I'm sure.' She felt for the coin. 'I'd better be off. The fiancé is waiting.'

She snapped her fingers at Davies. 'You can take my box now.'

'Davies has got other things to do,' Alyssa said. 'But we will see you to your cabin.'

Rosie narrowed her eyes at Alyssa, her moment of gratefulness obviously past. 'I'm not sticking around to see the old trout hitched.'

'If you wish.' It was probably for the best, Alyssa thought. With Rosie gone, nobody would spoil the happiness of this day.

CHAPTER 2

The wind played with Alyssa's hair, teasing a few tendrils out of her formerly neat bun. A large bird swooped down onto the water, reappearing with a silvery fish in its talons. She shaded her eyes against the already dazzling morning sun and looked at Mark and Mr Kendrick who'd joined her at the rail.

'A beautiful creature,' she said. 'I've never seen its kind before.'

Dr Bryson shook his head and grimaced.

'A sea-eagle,' Mr Kendrick said. 'It's a common sight in these waters.' He observed the still wincing doctor. 'I told you you'd regret toasting the newly-weds with the rot-gut from the hotel. Buy in haste, repent in leisure.'

'You had as much as I did.'

'But I possess an iron constitution, and the will-power to know when to stop. But let's not talk about your sorry condition in front of Miss Chalmers, who as always looks the very picture of bloom.'

Alyssa beamed at the men. How she'd miss them both, chivalrous Mr Kendrick and the doctor, who was so much less sure of himself than he believed.

Mr Kendrick still looked at her.

'You flatter me,' she said, 'but if the doctor had been confined to water as I was to toast Mr and Mrs Wainwright, he'd find himself in better health but with lesser enjoyment.'

'Thank you for your vindication,' the doctor said. 'Shall we go in, for a final breakfast on board our trusty vessel?'

'Our last meal together,' she said, hoping for a light tone. 'I hope your next voyage will be less turbulent.'

Both men linked arms with her. 'Our last meal on the *"Artemis' Delight"*,' Mr Kendrick said. 'But you won't get rid of us that easily. We will both accompany you and the other ladies to your final destination, as will Mr Wainwright.' He grimaced. 'It will make an interesting change to travel as a passenger on a boat.'

To describe this as a mere change did injustice to the word, Alyssa decided on their second evening on board the steamboat *Serenity*. Although the girls still had constant supervision, from a dreamy-eyed Matron and her new husband, as well as Mr Kendrick and the doctor, they found themselves for the first time free of any chores.

'Right now, we'd be up to our elbows in dishwater,' Hannah said, interrupting Alyssa's thoughts. 'Or doing the laundry, or sums, or listening to you read to us.' She shot Alyssa a quick grin. 'Not that it isn't lovely, your reading I mean, but this...'

She cupped her ear as the first faint piano notes filled the air, and broke into an improvised dance. The wooden soles of her boots clanged on the wooden floor.

'Stop dawdling, if you don't want us to miss the music,' Susanna said. She whisked Hannah out of the way and regarded her image in the small wall mirror with justified pleasure. Her copper curls shone in the light of the two wall sconces, and her blue eyes sparkled with delight. 'Who else are we waiting for?'

The *Serenity* was almost fully booked, they'd been told. Mr Wainwright and his bride had a small cabin to themselves, but the girls shared their lodgings again, the way they were used to. Although Alyssa longed for the day when she had a room to herself again and her freedom, she appreciated the watch held over them. With so many strangers around them on their way to the Canadian gold-fields, two of the girls had already been forced to fend off unwanted attention, when a couple of fur-traders had cornered them outside the dining room and pulled them into a rough embrace. Luckily their cry for help called Mr Kendrick and half a dozen other defenders to their side.

That was all Alyssa knew, but she gathered from Mr Kendrick's remarks to the doctor that the two assailants were left at the riverside, with a well-deserved forty mile walk to the nearest settlement.

'Ready?' Hannah pulled a strand of Alyssa's hair free on each temple and rolled it over her fingers. 'Not quite as it should look, but it will do.' She nudged Alyssa in front of the mirror. Alyssa smoothed her sleeves. She'd never be a beauty like Susanna, but the strained look on all their faces seemed to have been wiped away, now that the worst of the journey lay behind them.

Humming to herself, Alyssa followed her friends along the well-lit passage. Every four or five yards there hung a kerosene lantern on the walls, low enough to take down if needed but not so low as to bump into them when the ship heaved.

Alyssa marvelled at how still the *Serenity* lay in the water, despite the white squalls that churned the river. A large wheel at the stern propelled the boat forward at a speed that impressed even Mr Kendrick.

The biggest surprise was the saloon at the heart of the *Serenity*, where they were headed now. It held a hundred people with ease, and boasted a piano at one end of the long rectangular room and gaming tables at the other. On one side a bar of polished wood with brass railings reflected the light from the lanterns that hung above each table.

The pianist, a diminutive Irishman with a scar on the left cheek that ran to the corner of his mouth like a permanent grin, broke into a fanfare as the girls made their way to a cluster of tables in the middle of the room. Lighter squares on the floor showed where the table legs usually stood. The legs were fixed with brackets to the floorboards, and a wooden band two inches high, prevented things rolling off.

Matron and her husband sat side by side, in a haze of happiness. Her right hand rested on his. A ruby ring in an old-fashioned setting caught the light with every movement of her left hand. She stared at it in fond rapture.

As did Nancy and Susanna. Their mouths formed perfect circles. Alyssa focussed on the mild-mannered man on Matron's other side, and so did Hannah, whose cheeks turned slightly rosier.

'What a lovely surprise, Mr Osborne. Do you mind if we sit with you?' Alyssa asked as she steered Hannah next to their old shipmate.

'It appears that I shall be able to enjoy your company for a lot longer than anticipated,' said Mr Osborne. His gaze travelled side-wards to Hannah, who looked at him out of the corner of her eyes. 'I received communication from my bank. They have asked me to replace another employee in the very town you are heading to.'

'Permanently?' Alyssa asked, willing for Hannah to break her flustered silence.

'For a reasonable amount of time, I presume.' Mr Osborne straightened his already straight bow-tie. 'With so much gold and paper money coming in ... But let us not talk business.'

The rest of their companions joined them. The pianist did not repeat his fanfare for the men, Alyssa noticed with pleasure. Around her, the girls giggled in hushed tones. A few men, noticeable for their bushy beards, leather waistcoats and wide-brimmed hats worn indoors, stared at them, but mostly the other passengers occupied the bar or lost themselves in card games. Money constantly changed hands, but the stakes were small. Men on their way to the gold-fields were usually cash-strapped or saved their coins for any equipment, or food they needed to buy in a township. Alyssa was grateful for that, because Matron would never allow the girls to stay in the saloon when things got rowdy.

Plates with their dinner were put at the centre of their table. More smoked salmon and ham, as well as bread and cheese. In an impulse Alyssa leant towards Mr Osborne. 'Will you show us the stars after we've eaten? That is, if Matron doesn't mind.'

'I'd be delighted,' he said, his eyes gleaming even more at the mention of his hobby.

'Matron?'

Matron looked at her husband and whispered into his ear. He squeezed her hand.

'How many would like to go?' he asked. Hannah, Alyssa, Susanna and Nancy put up their hands.

Mr Kendrick said, 'In that case it should be enough if I go along as well, and I shall fetch my telescope.'

The deck ran in a narrow oval around the enclosed cabin. The night air had a velvety quality, and the stars appeared like tiny candle-lights in an ocean of deep blue.

Mr Osborne trimmed the telescope, which looked like nothing more than a slim brass tube of ten inches, and held it in front of Hannah's eye. She used one hand to steady it. He put her other hand gently on the moveable ring. 'This is where you adjust your sight with,' he said.

She stood transfixed. 'It's beautiful. It makes one feel so insignificant yet somehow it's comforting, isn't it?'

Alyssa felt a tug at her sleeve. Mr Kendrick motioned her a few steps away from Hannah and Mr Osborne. 'I wanted to show you a few of the constellations but I think the telescope should not change hands right now.'

Susanna and Nancy shared a look of conspiracy. 'We're going back inside,' Susanna said.

Alyssa nodded. She tilted back her head as far as she could. 'I can see – what is it? Venus?'

'She's always the brightest start in the firmament.' He took her hand and traced a pattern across the sky, outlining a flickering cluster of stars. 'That's Orion.'

'Do you mind if I join the lesson?' The doctor's amused gaze wandered from Mr Osborne and Hannah to Mr Kendrick.

'Not at all. You haven't missed much of my learned discourse which will leave both you and Miss Chalmers breathless.'

Osborne and Hannah had fallen silent. Alyssa shivered a little. Her cotton dress offered little protection from the unexpected coolness of the night. She rubbed her arms.

The doctor took off his jacket and wrapped it around her shoulders. It smelt of his medicines and wood smoke, an odd combination but a pleasant one.

Mr Osborne followed his example and enveloped Hannah in his woollen coat, smoothing it over her slim arms.

That night, before they took to their wooden bunks und snuggled under freshly laundered blankets, Hannah gave each of the girls a quick kiss on the cheek. Alyssa smiled to herself. Mr Osborne might not be a dashing figure of romance, but he and Hannah with her common-sense and kindness were well-suited. She hoped that Mr Osborne did not consider himself honour-bound to the unknown Canadians who had paid for the brides' transport.

Her worry proved unnecessary. On their last evening on the water, before they went to dinner, a blushing Hannah showed them a well-worn ring with a square stone in a setting popular in the Regency period. Nancy wiped a tear out of her eye as she hugged Hannah. 'I'm so happy for you.'

'Never mind that,' Nellie said, pulling Nancy off their friend. 'Put it on your finger.'

'It belonged to Mr Osborne's mother.' Hannah held the ring close to the lantern. The artificial light sparked a small rainbow in the depth of the gem.

'Why aren't you wearing it?' Nellie touched the ring with the tip of her index finger with something bordering on awe.

'Mr Osborne asked me to wait until we've met our proper suitors and then make my decision.' Hannah's eyes took on a far-away look.

Alyssa said, 'But what about you? Have you made up your mind yet?'

'Oh yeah. He is such a darling.' Hannah's smile deepened as she slipped the ring into a satin-lined box. 'But enough about me. Tell us, Alyssa, what are you going to do?'

Alyssa felt four pairs of eyes burn into her. Her heart-beat pulsed in her ears as she sank down onto a bunk. 'I don't know. I honestly don't know.' Her voice sounded thin in her ears. So far, she'd refused to think about the change in Matron's circumstances, and what it meant for her own plans. But she'd have to face the facts soon that the new wife might travel with her husband, or be subject to other plans that would not allow her to accompany Alyssa.

Susanna clasped her hands. 'Do you mean they have both declared themselves? The doctor and Mr Kendrick?'

Alyssa shook her head. 'Of course not. Whatever gave you that idea?' She struggled to regain her usual composure.

'Then they've led you on.' Susanna narrowed her eyes. 'I'd like to give them both a piece of my mind.'

'Me too,' said Nellie. 'Men! They're all the same, wherever you go. Bloody useless articles.'

'Thank you,' Alyssa said, 'but you all have misread the situation.'

Hannah snorted. 'You think we're daft? They've both been hanging after you for weeks. Mr Osborne said so himself.'

Nancy kneeled in front of Alyssa and reached up to stroke her cheek in a silent show of support.

Alyssa stifled a groan.

A bell rang to call them for dinner. Nancy got up reluctantly.

'Well, all I can say is serves 'em right if you do marry one of the local men instead.' Susanna jerked the door open and swept out of the room.

At dinner Alyssa knew herself to be under keen and sympathetic observation by her friends. For once she wished they were in forced isolation again instead of having to endure these silent speculations.

She suspended her fork in the air as a new thought hit her. She'd always intended to make it up to the men waiting for them by paying another girl's fare, but how could she do that, unless the church sent out another boatload of brides? She'd promised herself that she'd make sure that all the girls were safe and settled before she left them. And what about unwanted suitors?

The Canadians had been led to believe that they were all available and keen on marriage.

Involuntarily her look shifted to Mr Kendrick and the doctor who sat side by side, engrossed in a quiet conversation. The doctor looked up and caught her glance, as did Mr Kendrick. Susanna winked at her.

Alyssa attacked her boiled pork.

'Alyssa?' Hannah held the box with the ring out to her under the table. 'Can you pass it to Mr Osborne?'

'You haven't changed your mind, have you?'

Hannah shook her head. 'No. I don't feel safe keeping it. It's worth a fortune, Matron says, and there's folks enough who'd kill to get their hands on it. Please? I'd do it myself, but everybody would stare and think I've been stringing him.'

Alyssa took the box and slid it into the pocket hidden in her wide skirt. How odd that everybody trusted her to solve their problems, but she still was at a loss on how to deal with her own.

'You're remarkably quiet,' Kendrick said as he and Mark sat together in their shared cabin for their regular evening drink. 'Something bothering you?'

He took a deep swig of brandy. The liquid filled his body with a welcome warmth.

'Simply a bit of end of the road nostalgia,' Mark said. 'From here on our roads will lead in very different directions. Mine to the battlefields, and yours, God knows where.'

He clinked his glass against Kendrick's.

'Let's drink to smooth sailing from now on,' Kendrick said. 'Your war between the states can't last forever, and then your country will at last be free of the stain of slavery.'

'That's what I tell myself,' Mark said. 'But the news in Port Victoria wasn't good.'

They paused for a moment of sober contemplation. Mark made an effort to tear his thoughts away from the horrors of bodies torn to pieces by musket balls and bayonets that awaited him once he reached the frontlines. 'Do you have any idea about your future?'

Kendrick relaxed into the chair. 'We haven't got a new destination yet, but odds are that we'll be sent down to Portland to await orders.' He deliberately avoided Mark's gaze. 'If the new Mrs Wainwright feels she can leave her young charges by then, the captain might ask for permission to take her and maybe Miss Chalmers home with us to England. If that's where we are heading.'

He swirled the half-inch of brandy still left in his glass. 'That is, provided Miss Chalmers is by then still unattached and wants to return home.'

'I don't think a miner would hold any attraction for that lady.' Did that sound disinterested? Mark certainly hoped so. He'd thought of Alyssa too much already for his peace of mind. He liked her, of course he liked her, he admired her with all his heart, but forming a lasting affection was something he could not afford. A field surgeon could not be shackled with a wife he'd have to leave behind.

'I wasn't thinking of a miner, or prospector as I believe they call themselves in these parts.' Kendrick loosened his collar and smoothed back the dark curls from his forehead.

Mark held his breath for a heartbeat. Kendrick's admiration for Alyssa was something the second officer showed openly. It was equally clear that Alyssa accepted his friendship with gratitude, but he'd never suspected more.

'No?' Mark smiled, a forced effort that peeled his lips away from his teeth.

'You know perfectly well what I'm talking about. Do you intend to propose, or shall I have to save this damsel? We can't let her be stuck like this, with who knows how many men deprived of female company and clamouring for their brides. Unless it's what she wants, and I for one don't believe it.'

'I never thought of that.' Mark massaged his scalp. This was getting uncomfortable.

Kendrick downed the last of his drink. 'Well, now would be a good time to do so.'

Mark woke up blurry-eyed. Kendrick's words echoed in his head, round and round. He splashed cold water in his face and rubbed it vigorously dry with a scratchy flannel. Kendrick had already left the cabin, with his bag waiting to be picked up by the boy.

Mark glanced at his fob-watch. They'd make landfall in about two hours' time. Or was that the wrong term, now that they steamed across a river and not the ocean?

He tapped on a jar containing precious leeches. The creatures curled themselves up into a tight ball, wanting nothing to do with him apart from at feeding time. No surprise there, he thought. If only all relationships where that uncomplicated. I feed you, in return you feed on patients' wounds. The medicinal uses of leeches were boundless, although no-one but a few people had the stomach or the intellectual power to listen to his lectures. Well, two people to be precise. Kendrick and Alyssa.

The ship's bell brought every conversation to a halt. The only other sound was the constant whooshing of the wheel, leaving a trail of white foam in the water.

Mark sought out Alyssa, who stood pressed against the rail, framed by her friends. So far there were no buildings in sight yet, but a gentle bend lay ahead. The sun brought the mountain range on the left side of the river into sharp relief. At the foot of the craggy peaks dark, dense forest ran on for what must be miles.

He wondered what the girls made of this. It took little imagination to populate these woods with wolves, bobcats and other predators of the north.

One of the girls hugged herself, as if she had read his thoughts.

Kendrick stepped up to him. 'Must be eerie in winter. Although you're probably used to this kind of landscape.'

'I'm from Boston,' Mark said. 'A city-dweller, but I spent one or two holidays in the mountains. Beautiful, but only pleasant if you have a good roof over your head, a blazing fire in the grate and plentiful stocks.'

'Let's hope our little Australians here will find all that once winter sets in. Otherwise they will soon regret this voyage.'

Mark remembered the naked red soil, the endless horizon with clusters of gum trees breaking the monotony, and most of all the shimmering heat beating down relentlessly. Even a freezing Melbourne winter would be dismissed as a mild spell here. 'Frontierland.'

'Rough and primeval.' Kendrick rearranged his hair again, obviously missing his naval hat. 'That's probably why the men here applied to the other side of the world for their spouses. Hardy pioneers and all.'

The *Serenity* changed course, moving further away from the riverbanks. She slowed down, too, Mark thought.

Kendrick shaded his eyes against the sun. 'Looks like a bit of driftwood tangled up against the bank. Nothing serious though.'

Mark followed his gaze. A tree trunk the size of a small boat about fifty yards in front of them struggled to break free from roots and rocks that blocked its way.

Kendrick said, 'Nothing to worry about. The water'd put a mill pond to shame.'

'You sound disappointed.'

'On the contrary. In rough situations, I prefer to know the man who steers our fate.'

A steam whistle roared into life, loud enough to reach every living soul within miles. A white plume spiralled into the air.

The passengers hastened to get their bags as the *Serenity* swung around the last bend. Before them lay a wooden landing that sloped all the way up to a wide road.

A handful of men came running up and formed a welcome line.

Mr Wainwright steadied his wife as the *Serenity* inched closer to the landing. Two of the crew members flung thick ropes over the side onto the landing. The men on shore hurried to secure the ropes and lash them around wooden posts.

Mark turned around to make his way to Davies, who was entrusted with looking after all his precious medical supplies and private belongings. The boy gave him a salute. Mark copied that gesture. He'd grown increasingly fond of the eager young

Welsh boy, who performed all his tasks with unwavering good humour.

'Everything accounted for?' he asked the boy.

'All present and correct.' Davies craned his neck to search for the girls. 'If you don't mind, I'll take your luggage first and then I could give the ladies a hand?'

'Excellent idea.'

Davies wasn't the only one keen on assisting Matron's flock. Before Mark and the boy were half-way off the gangway, the Canadian men jostled each other to get on board. Mark's first impression was one of toughness tempered by fairly decent manners.

He joined Kendrick on the landing. The girls stood on the grassy bank, a little further away. They clustered around Matron and Alyssa, but the first shy glances already slid towards the men who hefted luggage boxes as if they were weightless.

Hooves whirled up a small cloud of dust as a fair-haired giant with a waxed moustache and bright blue eyes brought his dappled horse to a halt, ten feet away from the brides.

The rider pulled off his hat and bowed respectfully before he swung himself off the horse. He addressed Matron.

'Mrs McKenzie? Tom Abbott, at your service.'

Matron's cheeks coloured slightly as she sought out her husband. He stood with Osborne and Turnbull just close enough to be within earshot.

'Yes,' she said, 'that is no, I mean I used to...' She reached out for Alyssa's hand.

'Good day, sir,' Alyssa said with suppressed laughter in her voice. 'What Matron is attempting to say is that she has changed her name since she took on our care. She is now Mrs Wainwright, and over there you'll find her most excellent husband, our second officer Mr Wainwright.'

Abbott held out his hand. Alyssa nudged Matron to clasp it. He shook it warmly, with a smile that was meant for all of them. 'Congratulations, to both of you. But now we'd better get you to town.'

Abbott led his horse along the way. The road was wide enough for two wagons, but Mark could see hardly any grooves or ruts in the trampled earth. A walkway of sorts existed next to it, made of still unseasoned, rough wooden planks. It appeared that the town had prepared for the arrival of the brides.

The girls walked arm in arm, growing quiet the closer they came to their new home.

Abbott and Wainwright both measured their steps to match Matron's, but the Canadian kept on glancing back at Susanna and Alyssa, whose impatience with their sedate pace was growing more obvious with every step.

Mark stumbled over his own foot. Stupid clod, he thought, mentally cursing himself. The last thing he needed was an injury to keep him stuck for even longer.

CHAPTER 4

The town stretched out for almost a mile, Alyssa guessed. The size surprised her, given the newish appearance of the pitch-roofed wooden houses dotting the main road, and so did the cleanliness. She'd expected, well, not squalor, but an air of neglect in a community of men devoid of women.

Some of the houses had a small porch tacked to the side, offering shelter from sun and wind. Cabbages and root vegetables sprouted in one large plot, and a large chicken coop stood next to a building that seemed to combine a shop with living quarters. The letters General Store, Prop. W Turner, were carved two inches deep into the front of the building and partly filled with black paint.

A stocky man whom she took to be the proprietor stopped sweeping the floor as they filed past, as did the man next door, at Harper's Hotel.

By now their parade had attracted a dozen spectators, who cheered and whistled but did not follow them.

Mr Abbott tethered his horse to a post outside a wide building. 'Open up, Peg-Leg,' he said.

The door swung wide open, letting daylight stream into the dark room. A man limped outside, a wide grin making his thick moustache curve up to his ears. Contrary to his nickname he appeared to have all his limbs. Probably a sign of the local humour, Alyssa decided.

Peg-Leg ushered them in before doing a complete round of the room, flinging open half a dozen shutters. Sunlight drew patterns on the floor and the bunk-beds that lined the back half. The room itself was spacious enough to still feel roomy despite the beds, tables and chairs. Cupboards to one side stood open, revealing empty shelves.

'We thought it best if you all stay together for a start,' Mr Abbott said. 'That is, we did not prepare a separate accommodation for you and Mr Wainwright, Ma'am.'

'Of course not. But as you can see we have also the first officer and our doctor and the boy with us, although Davies will return with the boat.' Matron rubbed her temple. Several loud bangs made her start.

'I see your luggage has arrived. Put it down at the back, boys.'

The boys all counted at least thirty years and, although shorter than Mr Abbott's six feet, could not be called scrawny. Nancy openly admired the dexterity and care with which the men handled the boxes in their callused hands. One after another they nodded to Matron and said, 'Welcome to Run's End, Ma'am. Ladies.'

Abbott inclined his head a fraction too, as if to signal his approval. They'd probably practiced their welcome. A few of Alyssa's worries melted away. These were good people, who'd take care of her friends.

'If you'd like to freshen up, we have a well out back,' Mr Abbot said. 'Peg-Leg will bring you a bucket full of water.'

'We ain't got a wall mirror yet for you, but if a shaving-mirror'll do you?' Peg-Leg turned a small, wall-hung frame around that Alyssa hadn't noticed before.

Matron smiled at him. 'Lovely, thank you.'

'As for your husband and the other men, they can either stay in the hotel or bunk in an empty cabin. Lodger's not coming back anytime soon,' Mr Abbot said.

A shot rang out. Matron cried in alarm and clung to her husband's arm. The men formed a protective front, but seemed strangely at ease. Another shot. Through the window Alyssa saw a man streaking past, holding on to his brown felt hat. Another man was hard on his heels, cracking a whip. Alyssa's breath eased. Not shots then, alarming as the scene was.

Mr Abbott strode to the door. 'Leave him be, Bert, you're scaring the ladies.' He turned around. 'Sorry about that. Bert has a bit of a temper at times and the boys aren't used to having fair company yet. I'll keep him in check, and the others too.'

'I hope so,' Matron said with new-found resolve. 'Now if you'll excuse us, a bit of peace and quiet should restore our nerves.'

Mr Abbott nodded. 'One moment, please.' He whistled on two fingers, loud enough to startle some of the girls into clinging to each other. 'Bert!'

A man sheepishly poked his head through the door. With his

shaggy brown beard trimmed and in a clean shirt he could be presentable enough, Alyssa thought. His hazel eyes held a twinkle at odds with his contrite manner.

'Sorry, Tom,' he said. 'Ladies. I hope you won't hold this little incident against me.'

The whip was nowhere in sight.

'Do wild chases occur often in this town?' Mr Wainwright asked.

'That? That was nothing serious. Just the stupid ba-, the stupid bloke trying to smuggle his moonshine into my hotel. We're all as peace-loving and friendly as you could find in a day's march.'

'That's right.' Mr Abbott's air of authority matched Mr Wainwright's. 'You'll always find a couple of moochers, or men who can't hold their drink, but I haven't had to throw the book at anyone all year long.'

He noticed their puzzled looks. 'I forgot to mention that I've been appointed constable by the magistrate. Right, Bert?'

'Most important man in town,' the landlord said. 'Postmaster, tax collector –' he shuddered good-naturedly, 'and anything official you can think of. All under one big hat. But now, if you'll excuse me, I better get back home afore that stinking no-gooder sneaks into the hotel again.'

The girls selected their bunks with an unusual amount of chatter. Hannah flung herself down on hers and spread her arms so wide they dangled over the edges. Susanna followed her example. 'No more being cooped in,' she said, wiggling around on the hard mattress. A few dust mites floated up, followed by a few bits of chuff. The mattresses must be stuffed with cobs, Alyssa assumed, but the pillows were soft and bouncy and felt like her hand sank into a cloud when she pressed it.

Susanna turned around to grin at her. 'Feels strange, doesn't it, with everything still under your feet? No slipping, no bruises and best of all no sea-sickness.'

She threw her pillow at Alyssa. One quick look at Matron, who stood in a corner, in what appeared to be an earnest discussion with her husband, and Alyssa flung it back. Hannah grabbed her pillow and threw it at Nellie.

Five minutes later, all the girls lay in a laughing heap on the bunks. Matron shook her head at them, with an indulgent look, until a pillow sailed towards her. Mr Wainwright snatched it in the air.

'That's enough,' he said. 'You can destroy your bedding once you've set up your own households.' He prodded the pillow with an appreciative finger. 'I shall keep this for the time being.'

'You're not going to do that? Matron, please.' Nellie looked so apologetic that Mr Wainwright handed over the pillow, winking at his wife.

'Thank you, sir.'

Matron patted her hand. 'Lovely manners, dear. Well done.' Indeed, Alyssa thought. The girls might be poor and without families, but they had all the skills to succeed in their new lives, and make their future husbands proud of them. With Rosie gone, they hadn't squabbled once.

Alyssa wondered how the errant girl was now, and if she

realised how leniently the captain had treated her and her paramour, when he found out that she had engaged in a forbidden relationship with one of the stokers. Still, good riddance. As for the rest of her friends, things looked very promising.

Fiddle tunes erupted from the hotel while the girls changed into unrumpled skirts and blouses. Alyssa fumbled with a row of buttons at the back of her high-necked dress.

'Keep still.' Hannah slapped her fingers away and hooked the buttons up in record time. 'How do I look?'

She twirled in front of Alyssa in her second-best cotton skirt and blouse. The original yellow had faded to the colour of bleached parchment and the fabric was fast becoming threadbare from washing, but then none of them would be here if poverty hadn't driven them to emigration. All except for herself, Alyssa thought.

Threadbare and plain as their clothes might be, today even the most unassuming girl glowed. They'd made it across the ocean, and two hundred yards away their future husbands counted the minutes until their first proper meeting.

Matron inspected them all one last time. She smoothed down skirts and checked boots for traces of dirt, or the blackening they'd used to cover up scruffs and tears in the leather.

'You'll do,' she finally said. 'Don't forget to talk only if you are spoken to and use your manners at all times. The first impression is of the highest importance.' Her glance flickered to Alyssa.

'Remember, your behaviour will reflect on all of us, so a little bit of restraint is asked for.'

'No gallivanting off to talk to your beaus.' Susanna twinkled at Alyssa. Nancy giggled. Fortunately, she was the only one standing close enough to hear Susanna.

Candle-filled lanterns swung from the massive ceiling beams. Although the daylight would last for another couple of hours, the candles had been lit. A makeshift banner hung across the bar, with the words 'Welcome ladies' painted in ochre onto three yards of hessian. Fresh sawdust covered half the floor.

Behind the bar Bert gave the glasses a final wipe. As Alyssa had expected, he cut an agreeable figure in a white shirt, leather waistcoat and with his beard freshly trimmed.

Their old friends from the *Artemis Delight* sat around a table, looking as gentlemanly as possible in their good suits and with starched collars that belonged more in a salon than in a saloon.

The Canadians stood awkwardly at the back. Alyssa counted less than two dozen of them, ranging in age from their twenties to early forties.

The fiddler, a bow-legged fellow with his brown hair slicked back and a bushy moustache, lowered his instrument as Mr Abbott approached Matron. He bowed with an easy manner that would have charmed the sternest woman.

Matron rewarded him with a dimpled smile.

'Welcome again,' he said. 'I'm sure you will feel right at home in no time at all, and get to know our little town. How about we cut down on the formalities? Gentlemen, you say your bit to Mrs Wainwright here, and then she'll decide if you're fit to talk to her delightful charges.'

Matron turned towards the table with her husband and Mr Kendrick. They both gave an encouraging nod. They could be relied upon to keep a discreet watch on them.

'How about another tune, Little Joe?' the publican asked. The fiddler took up his bow again.

Fifteen minutes later, Matron led the dance with her husband, Susanna floated around the room in the arms of Mr Abbott, Mr Osborne held Hannah with tender care, and Alyssa found herself dancing with Mr Kendrick.

'I beat the doctor to it,' he said between two energetic hops. Alyssa didn't recognise the dance, but she let herself be led by her partner, as the other girls did. 'Let me know if you'd rather mingle with your new town-mates.'

Alyssa shook her head and smiled up at him. 'Thank you for your consideration, but this is perfect.'

'Nice little town,' he said, 'but we'd better save our breath for the dance.'

Feet aching, Alyssa sank onto a rough-hewn bench. Mr Kendrick handed her a glass of water. All around her, faces were flushed but happy. Mr Abbott, who seemed intent on claiming all of Susanna's attention, led her to the table.

'This is wonderful,' she said, her left foot tapping to the music. Alyssa winked at her. From what little they had seen her friend had made an excellent choice.

She peered around discreetly. Mr Osborne and Hannah sat close enough to demonstrate their affection to all the world.

Nancy and Nellie were still dancing with two broad-shouldered men who looked like brothers, with brown hair curling up to their shoulders.

Mr Abbott followed her gaze. 'We may look a bit rough, Miss...'

'It's Chalmers,' Susanna said, before Alyssa could open her mouth. 'Alyssa to her friends. Isn't that right, doctor?'

The doctor broke his silence for the first time that evening. 'Very true, Miss Terry. You both appear to have a talent for making friends easily.'

How odd he sounded, Alyssa thought. He had been acting very distracted lately.

The doctor said, 'It must be pretty hard to keep peace in a place like this.'

'Not more than on board a ship, I'd say.'

'I don't know,' Mr Kendrick said. 'At least we don't have gold lying around, and leaving in a hurry is a bit difficult at sea.'

'We keep the gold safe enough.' Mr Abbott gave a small nod towards Mr Osborne. 'It's waiting to be assayed by your friend here, and until then we have a strongbox in the bank that would take a lot of black powder to open.'

'That shouldn't be too hard to come by, in a prospectors' town,' the doctor said with the first hint of interest in his voice.

'Tempted to try your luck?' Mr Abbott's grin held a challenge.

'Simply wondering. After all, we have promised to look after the safety of the young ladies.'

'Well, I'll have to disappoint you. We don't look for gold by blowing holes into the Rockies. We mostly pan for it, with good success.' He beamed at Susanna. 'That's also why you find us a bit lacking in numbers. More gold's been found further inland, and half our men have cleared out already.'

'No crime at all?' the doctor asked.

'One or two thefts, but that's all. Look around you, doctor, where'd a man go? Take the steamboat back to Port Victoria, when a rider would already have brought word about a crime? Or head up into the Rocky Mountains or deep into the forests, with tribes able to track any white man back to when he was born? Then there's bears and wolves and bobcats. But we don't want to scare the ladies.'

The fiddler played another jaunty tune. Mr Abbott held out his hand to Susanna. 'Care to dance?'

Kendrick looked at the doctor. 'Well, my friend?'

The doctor's nudged him out of the way. 'This one's definitely mine. May I have the honour of this dance, Alyssa?'

'You may.' Happiness bubbled up in her.

CHAPTER 5

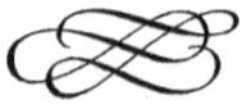

Rosie hurled the tobacco tin at the wall. It fell to the ground with a satisfying thwack. Bloody useless, that man. Sitting around in the bar night after night, and not one job lined up. So much for her grand new life. Yeah, right. She might as well have stuck it out with the other girls. Marrying a man with gold jingling in his pockets instead of ice clinking in his glass sounded better and better.

But she'd blown it. Her skin crawled, thinking of him. The appeal of a clandestine cuddle at sea had quickly worn off on dry land.

He blamed her too, for his not getting work. As if it were her fault that the captain didn't put in a good word for him. As for a former railway and stoker man always getting to pick and choose, ha!

She grabbed her hairbrush and viciously untangled her hair. In the first few days, at least he'd taken her to the bar with him.

But all she ever did now was sit in this crappy room, with its corncob-mattress on the floor, a half-blind mirror, a table and two chairs under a cracked window.

She'd had it better on the *Artemis Delight*, sharing with the other brides. Rosie bit back tears of frustration. Some kind of honeymoon this was. He hadn't even married her yet. Said he needed to find a preacher first.

Her stomach lurched, as if a vice gripped it. She'd had this pain a couple of times lately. Dr Bryson would have looked after her. Alyssa would have seen to it. Alyssa – Rosie put down the brush and picked up the tobacco tin. It showed a satisfying dent in the lid. That's when she noticed the grey envelope that had been pushed under the door. A letter. And a dollar note.

'Going back to Portland with some of the boys. There's work down that way. Room's paid up for the week. When you follow me, ask for me at the station. Be a good girl."

At least he could write. Follow him? How far would she get on a lousy dollar?

Fear seeped into her body. He'd left her. Abandoned her to her fate. What was she going to do?

'What are we going to do?' Matron pressed her head against her husband's comforting shoulder. 'I promised to stay as long as my girls need me, but now that I've found you …'

She peered around. Such a promising little house, she thought. Two good-sized rooms, with a snug fireplace at one end, and fresh sawdust on the floor. Mr Wainwright – Walter, she thought with a new jolt of happiness – had chosen wisely among the dwellings left behind by men lured away by the latest gold finds, further inland. Most men wouldn't have thought twice about a wife's comfort, but Walter had selected the airiest and quietest of places, although they would only stay for a few weeks.

He stroked her cheek. 'You worry too much. They are settling in nicely, and if all goes well, you should be giving your girls away before we've had word about our next voyage.'

The boy, Davies had reluctantly left them to report back for duty on the *Artemis' Delight*. His return, as dear as he was, would be to call her husband away. Matron forbade herself to dwell on that and concentrate on happier thoughts.

'You're right. There's Hannah and Mr Osborne, Susanna and Mr Abbott, Alyssa and –' She paused. Alyssa and who?

Walter dampened the light and silenced her with a kiss. After that, every thought about her duties was forgotten.

Osborne put his books in alphabetical order, by subject. Astronomy first. The shelf looked a bit crowded already. Tomorrow he'd ask who the town's carpenter was. He needed a few more shelves. And a wall cavity to hide the strongbox in. The doors needed bolts in addition to the locks.

This strongbox preyed on his mind. The bank managers had promised the delivery of a proper safe, but until then he had to make do with what this bank offered. It wasn't bad as such – a ten-foot wide building made of the thickest timber he'd seen, with two cosy rooms at the back for the banker to live in.

He'd found the strongbox placed against the wall, visible for anyone gazing through the window. His blood ran cold. Nuggets and coins stowed away in clear sight, in a steel cube that a strong man could lift, behind a door that a crowbar could pry open.

That had been his first act of duty, seeing that the strongbox found its way under his bed, with a blanket falling all the way to the ground to hide it. Kendrick and the doctor had carried it for him. He could count himself lucky to have found such good shipmates, and more.

Tomorrow he'd ask Hannah and Matron to visit his lodgings. He wanted it as well-appointed as possible, so his bride would find her first home lacking in nothing.

'The boat is coming.' The excited yell shattered the early morning peace like a cannon shot. Half the town must be running towards the jetty, Alyssa thought, judging by the deafening trample of feet rushing past.

'What's going on?' Susanna struggled to hook up her skirt.

'Hold still,' Hannah said, doing up the bothersome hooks with ease. 'I can't imagine. They sure weren't that excited when we arrived.'

'Maybe the bar ran out of drinks, and they've got new bottles coming. That'd get the men going.' Nellie chuckled. 'They're all the same.'

Alyssa peered out of the window. 'Not all of them. Mr Wainwright is escorting Matron over to us. Mr Kendrick is with them.'

'They're still honeymooning, aren't they? You wait when he's off to sea again. Can't miss her that much then, can he?' Nellie shrugged.

An icy cold made Alyssa shiver. She'd never thought of Mr Wainwright leaving Matron behind, for long periods of time. No wonder so many of the crew were unmarried. Like Mr Kendrick, a man who could easily win a woman's heart.

Susanna echoed her thoughts. 'He wouldn't go without Matron, would he?'

'He can't take her with him, now can he?' Nellie's stomach rumbled. 'How about our grub?'

A loud rap on the door signalled Matron's arrival. She mustered the girls with a fond, if short-sighted look. Matrimony became her, Alyssa thought. A near constant smile on Matron's lips and a tender look in her eyes bore witness to her happiness. If only it would stay that way.

Mr Wainwright and Mr Kendrick waited on the doorstep, heavy baskets in their arms. 'Do come in,' Matron said. 'We'll all have breakfast here, if you don't mind the gentlemen joining us?'

The girls turned to Alyssa. 'They'll be most welcome,' she said.

Mr Kendrick gave her a small salute before he turned on his heel, obviously to fetch the other men.

Susanna nudged her with her elbow. 'Quick now. Put the kettle on, and then we'll have porridge.'

Hannah blew into the embers of last night's fire and gently brought them back to life. Nancy added kindling, and as soon as the flames engulfed the small sticks, she placed one foot-long log in the middle. That should be ample to last for their cooking.

Alyssa smiled to herself. Here they were, surrounded by an almost primeval forest with a bountiful supply of firewood, but her friends were still as thrifty as they'd been in Australia.

Hannah hung two large pots over the fire, one for the porridge and one with water for their tea.

Susanna set the table and took half a dozen fresh loaves out of the basket. She sniffed them with a blissful look on her face. Fresh bread, without them having to do the kneading and damping!

Mr Osborne's glance constantly slid towards Hannah, whose cheeks were pinker than usual. But that could be attributed to the heat of the cooking.

'Where's the doctor?' Susannah asked. 'Should we keep his breakfast?'

'He's busy. He'll eat at the hotel when he's got time.' Mr Kendrick held out his tin mug for a refill of strong, dark tea that had no resemblance to the fragrant brews Alyssa had grown up with.

'Busy?' she asked. 'Is someone ill?'

'All I know is that Bert, I mean Mr Harper, asked him to come along.' Mr Kendrick helped himself to a generous spoonful of sugar. 'The men should be back soon enough.'

'The ship appears to have caused a stir,' Matron said.

'I still say it's because it carries liquor,' Nellie muttered. Matron shot her a reproachful look.

'She might be right,' Mr Kendrick said and winked at Matron.

'Mr Harper and Peg-Leg had a few words last night behind the bar. Not that I would have listened, but I did hear the word empty.'

Matron frowned. Her husband patted her hand. 'Not to worry, my dear. Mr Abbott has everything admirably under control. I must say, I did except something a bit rowdier.'

Now a faint tinge of pink spread over Susanna's face.

Mr Wainwright pushed away his empty porridge bowl. 'If the ladies would care for a stroll, we would be happy to accompany you.' He shared a meaningful look with the other men.

'Sweet.' Nellie bumped into Nancy's shoulder as she jumped up to pile up bowls and mugs.

'Thank you, Nellie,' Matron said. 'But I'd prefer it if you'd let the rest of us finish.'

They forgot all decorum as soon as they left the main street behind. Alyssa felt Hannah and Susanna link arms with her and almost lift her off her feet as they ran after Nellie and Nancy. Before them lay an open meadow, dotted with flowers they'd never seen before. It was small really, maybe a hundred yards until it vanished into the forest, but it was green and lush, and fragrant with the scent of grass. Pollen-smeared bees flew past, and in the near distance the sound of water cascading over rocks reminded Alyssa of their months at sea.

They tumbled onto the meadow. Nellie let herself fall headlong into the grass.

Alyssa settled on a patch of grass. Susanna ambled around,

picking a handful of long-stemmed flowers. She put one behind her ear, the petals grazing her cheek, and decorated Alyssa's left ear likewise.

Hannah had joined Matron and Mr Osborne. Whatever they talked about, it sent her off in rapture, because she shrieked with delight and hugged Matron with enough force to take a step backwards. Then she took Mr Osborne's hand and gave him a resounding kiss on the cheek.

Nellie's mouth fell open. Susanna walked over to her and pressed her hand under Nellie's chin. 'That's better, before the flies settle in.'

Mr Osborne blinked away a tear.

Mr Kendrick lowered himself into the grass next to Alyssa and hugged his knee to his chest. 'Glad?'

'Yes. Except ...' She plucked a blade of grass and slid it through her fingers. 'It feels unreal, that our journey together is over.'

He motioned towards Hannah and Mr Osborne. 'Looks more like another happy beginning.' She liked that he hadn't said happy ending. It sounded too final. A beginning, that's what they all were looking for.

He lowered his voice. 'How about your own plans? Or are you really intending to settle down here?'

She peered around to make sure no-one else could overhear. 'I'm not sure,' she said. 'Originally I'd hoped that Matron would agree to travel to England as my companion. But now – will she accompany Mr Wainwright? Where will they live?'

'We have no idea when and where our next voyage will take us.' Mr Kendrick smoothed back his dark curls, unconsciously ruffling them. Alyssa resisted an urge to tidy his hair. 'The captain won't be too happy to accommodate females again, but then he could hardly say no to his second officer unless for a very good reason.'

A bell tolled in the distance. Mr Kendrick got up and brushed a few blades off his coat. He raised his voice. 'If the ladies would be good enough to follow me? There will be a surprise waiting for you in the hotel.'

Alyssa had to force her jaw shut. In front of a row of beaming men stood half a dozen trunks stuffed with bolts of cloth. Summery cotton in all colours of the rainbow, kempt wool, and swathes of creamy muslin dazzled their eyes. Another trunk held thick furs. The girls stood in awe, suddenly too shy to do anything but gape.

Mr Abbott broke ranks and ambled over to Matron. 'I hope you don't mind us taking the liberty to get a few supplies in. Winters tend to get perishingly cold in these parts.'

'You're too kind, sir,' Matron said. She fumbled for her handkerchief and dabbed her eyes. 'I hope that none of you will ever regret this generosity.' Her gaze fixed on the creamy fabric. Mr Abbott must have guessed her unspoken question. He said, 'For wedding dresses, on special request. I've also been asked to perform the ceremony, if the lady agrees.'

He held everyone's attention, but instead of divulging a name, he sauntered over to the bar and asked Bert for a beer.

Mr Osborne's gaze searched Hannah's. She lifted her right

hand to straighten her bonnet. On one finger, a ring glinted. She returned Mr Osborne's tender look.

'Next Sunday, my dearest?' he asked in a surprisingly steady voice. Hannah nodded.

One of the men flung his hat in the air. Nellie cheered and clapped, and Bert broke into an impromptu reel. Alyssa craned her neck to see if Dr Bryson was somewhere in the now boisterous crowd. Peg-Leg grabbed a fiddle from behind the bar and played a jaunty tune. Mr Kendrick swept Alyssa into his arms. All around them, couples danced. Susanna's head rested firmly against Mr Abbott's shoulder, while Matron and Mr Wainwright seemed lost in their own world.

A sudden draught cooled Alyssa's hot skin as the hotel door opened. 'Let a fellow have a go, Kendrick,' the doctor said behind her back. 'And I'd appreciate it if you could get me a drink.'

The music broke off. Mr Abbott whistled loud enough to make Alyssa's ear ring. 'Next Sunday, at ten o'clock sharp, we'll celebrate our very first wedding. What do you say boys, shall we make it a few more couples if you're going to bring out the good suits anyway?'

It was hard to tell if any of the men changed colour under their deep tans, but a few of the girls hastily stepped away from their dance partners.

'Goodness me!' Matron's hand flew to her mouth. 'The dresses. If we want Hannah to be dressed properly, we'd better get a march on.'

'Well, boys? Don't be shy. How about going for a stroll and letting Mrs Wainwright know before dinner if she needs to organise a bigger sewing party? Mr Osborne, when do you want us to bring your equipment over?'

Mr Wainwright and Mr Kendrick carried the fabric for the wedding dress over to the cabin, followed by a dazed Hannah who couldn't stop admiring her ring. If Alyssa hadn't steered her, she'd have run straight into matron, who stopped, and moved on again with the same abruptness.

'Are you well, Matron?' Alyssa asked.

'Thank you, I thought for a moment I'd seen – but that's impossible. Never mind.'

They measured Hannah for her wedding dress. The bride to be had firm ideas on the style, but so had the other girls, who one by one returned from their walks with their suitors.

'You want to be able to pass it on to your daughter.' Susanna said. 'Make it so you can let out seams and hem.'

'Or you could keep it simple, and wear it to church on Sundays.' Nellie appraised Hannah with a critical look. 'No need to dye it and make it an everyday dress, with a rich man like that.'

'He's not rich.' Hannah reached for the measuring stick and counted off thirty lengths. 'He works for the bank, but it's not like he gets any of the gold.'

'Hannah will be comfortably off,' Matron said. 'As will be the rest of you, one dare hope. Any more good news?'

Two pink spots appeared on Nancy's cheeks. Susanna nudged her forward.

'My beau proposed.' Nancy swallowed a couple of times. 'I haven't said yes yet, Matron, because –'

'Because we thought you might want to have a word with him.' Susanna grinned. 'He's a bit on the quiet side with us.'

Alyssa thought back. Nancy's admirer had been around her almost as soon as they'd arrived, but she'd be hard pressed to tell if she had ever heard him say a word. He'd looked pleasant enough, with an open face and a ready grin, but she could understand the girl seeking advice.

'I'll ask Mr Wainwright to talk to him tonight. It would be more proper for a man to ask questions.' Matron patted Nancy's shoulder. 'I think he will be perfectly suitable. We better take your measurements too.'

'And mine.' Susanna took a deep breath. 'Come Sunday I'll be Mrs Tom Abbott, and we are invited to an engagement meal at the hotel tomorrow night.'

Three dresses to make! Mr Wainwright had found Joshua Scott as amenable as his face had suggested, so Nancy's engagement was settled too. Alyssa suspected that the other girls would announce their matches soon enough, when they could count on having some attention lavished on their gowns. As it stood, they would have to abandon everything else in favour of sewing.

Hannah as the best seamstress. took charge of the whole operation, and handed out tasks with enough tact that not even Alyssa felt slighted because all she had to do were hooks and buttons – nothing that would be visible if her skills proved inferior.

They worked straight through lunch, until the late afternoon. Alyssa's back ached from bending over her work without as much as a tea break, but none of her friends complained. Hannah hummed to herself as she went around to check on her seamstresses. Nancy couldn't stop smiling, and Susanna sang under her breath as she stitched together sleeves.

A few biscuits and hurried cups of tepid water kept them going, until a bell reminded them to stop for the day.

Alyssa put in the last stitch on a cuff, sat up straight and rubbed her back, happy to be done. Hannah gave her a stern glance.

'I want everything brought over to me separately.' she said. 'We can't afford any mix-ups with the dresses, and we need to wrap them properly. I won't have any dust or dirt on them, do you hear?'

'Yes, Ma'am,' Nellie curtsied. 'No, Ma'am. Thank you, Ma'am.'

'Very funny. Do you want us to send you out looking like something the cat brought in, when it's your turn?'

'I was only funning.' Nelle grinned. 'Ma'am.'

A slow grin spread over Hannah's face. A giggle rose in her throat.

Susanna broke into song as she carried over her finished pieces to Hannah. Alyssa joined in, for once able to enjoy a moment without any worries about the future. If only she could preserve this harmony, she thought. Who knew how long it would last?

~

Two hours later she had her answer. They had put away their sewing following Hannah's exacting instructions, and made themselves as presentable as possible in honour of the engagement party.

Mr Harper and Peg-Leg had done them proud, with polished candle-holders, a few wildflowers on the table, and a fresh layer of sawdust on the floor.

Matron presided over one end of the table, and Mr Abbott, his beaming bride at his side, sat on the other head. Alyssa found herself between Dr Bryson and Mr Kendrick, but for once all her friends were too distracted to pay them any unwanted attention.

Peg-Leg darted back and forth with unsuspected agility, serving roast and potatoes in a quantity ample enough to feed them for a week.

'You looked sad for a moment,' Dr Bryson said.

'I was thinking that there should be a dog, sitting close to the table in case any scraps fall to the floor. My dog – but that's in the past.' She raised her cup in a silent toast to the doctor and Mr Kendrick. 'Today we'll think about nothing but what lies ahead.'

Mr Kendrick touched her glass with his beer mug. 'Wise words. As for me, I foresee music, and a dance, and me beating our doctor as usual when it comes to claiming you for the first hop.'

'You might be surprised,' Dr Bryson said with something resembling a challenge in his voice. 'May the better man –'

'Be prepared. I have asked for proper dance cards to be delivered once the ship runs again.'

'What do you mean, runs again?'

Before she could receive an answer, Mr Abbott rose and raised his glass. 'A toast to our clerical friends in Australia, for sending us the loveliest ladies any man could dream of, and a toast to the ladies themselves, especially Miss Susanna Terry, my bride.'

The men got on their feet as one, stomping and clapping. Mr Abbott hushed them with a shrill whistle. 'And now, pudding and music.'

Peg-Leg came out from behind the bar, his fiddle under his chin. Bert joined him with a harmonica. The music got louder and louder, as the two moved around the whole room.

Two steaming cakes were put next to a stack of tin plates in the middle of the table, their smell heady with sugar and raisins.

Matron handed Mr Wainwright a knife to cut the cake when she looked in confusion at Peg-Leg and then at a female form flitting back into the kitchen.

'Rosie?' Her husband quelled her with a warning glance. 'Not now, dear.' Matron sat back, lips pressed together so firmly they almost disappeared.

The rest of the party hadn't noticed anything. Alyssa would have thought she'd been mistaken about Matron's word, if not for the sudden tenseness in her companions.

'What's happening?' she asked in a low voice.

'Later.' The doctor took a plate and went to get three slices of cake.

For a strange reason neither the doctor nor Mr Kendrick claimed Alyssa's hand for the first dance. Instead they sat back, chatting, while a lanky man with a beard halfway down his chest led her away. A tiny voice in head told her that she was conceited to expect their constant attention, but that increased her disappointment. Then every clear thought fled as her partner swirled her around in a dizzying pace.

Three dances later, she sank onto a chair in sheer exhaustion. Matron too showed signs of tiredness; or maybe she simply longed for some privacy with her husband. Whatever the reason, Mr Wainwright signalled for the music to stop.

Peg-Leg and Bert put down their instruments. The girls fanned themselves, too hot for comfort, but too happy to care.

'If we could get some fresh air? The ladies might also benefit from a stroll before the sun goes down,' Mr Wainwright said.

A few of the men seemed taken aback, but took it with good humour. Those who had been dancing arranged to escort their partner, while the others made a beeline for the few girls who had already been sitting down.

Dr Bryson held Alyssa back, and a flustered Matron also stayed behind. Mr Kendrick, Mr Wainwright and Mr Abbott completed the small circle.

Mr Abbott beckoned Bert over. 'We'll let the others know tomorrow, but for now this will stay among us, right?'

The other men nodded. Alyssa opened her mouth but thought again. Best to hear him out before she spoke.

'Doctor?'

Dr Bryson rubbed his chin, as if stalling for time. 'There won't be a boat running in a while,' he said. 'We should be safe enough, if nobody comes and goes for a bit, but I'm afraid there's been an outbreak of smallpox.'

'Smallpox?' Matron's face drained of colour. 'How close?'

'We don't know. A horseman brought the information this morning.'

Mr Wainwright pulled his wife close and hugged her.

Alyssa shivered. Smallpox epidemics had killed huge numbers of Aboriginals in Australia, and even though white people appeared to be more resistant, the disease had filled more graveyards than she could bear to think of.

'The river traffic has been postponed until further notice, and the pack trains will be stopped along their way. Should anyone get ill, there's nothing we can't handle between you, Miss Chalmers and me, Matron.'

There was something so reassuring about the doctor's manner, and about Mr Kendrick's cheerful calm, that Alyssa's fear abated.

'That brings us to the next issue,' the doctor said. 'Bert Harper has hired a new arrival to help in the kitchen and serve the ladies.'

Matron turned to her husband who shook his head in a silent warning. Kendrick gave the same signal to Alyssa.

'Bert, please call her in.'

Alyssa almost admired Rosie for the sheer cold-bloodedness in marching in here as if nothing had ever happened.

Mr Kendrick squeezed her arm. She nodded at him.

'This is the young lady,' Dr Bryson said. 'Rosie Thatcher.'

Rosie curtsied. 'Pleased to meet you, sir, Ma'am.'

Matron's jaw fell open. Mr Wainwright whispered something into her ear.

'I'm sorry you didn't arrive under better circumstances,' Mr Abbott said, obviously unaware of Rosie's connection to the girls. 'I wonder if it would be more appropriate to offer you a place with the other young ladies.'

'No.' Matron took a deep breath. 'I'm sorry, Rosie, but I cannot agree to that until we are sure that the doctor can give you a clean bill of health. I'm sure you'll understand.'

Rosie curtsied again. 'Sure, Ma'am. I got to sleep here anyway, because of me working late.' Her sweet smile could have fooled most people. 'Besides, I've got my own room here.'

'In the hotel? With the men?' Matron's eyes widened in surprise.

'She'll be perfectly safe,' Mr Abbott said. 'I've looked at the room, and she can lock it from the inside, although I'd vouch for all the men here.'

'Well, in that case, I shall let my girls know that we have a new young lady in our midst.' Matron shot the doctor a dark look, and even gave her husband a reproachful glance.

'Thank you, Ma'am. You won't regret it.' Rosie raised her skirt another inch, although it fell already short of the ground, and twirled around.

'By the way, we have a wedding party on Sunday. Three of my charges. I pray that nothing spoils their special day.' Matron's voice had never sounded as cutting.

Rosie clapped. 'A triple wedding. We'll make it as nice as can be, won't we, Mr Harper?'

'Although, I wonder –' Matron turned to Dr Bryson. 'Should Rosie be quarantined?'

'A commendable thought, but it would be too late. She's already been in contact with too many people, and she's helped prepare the food.'

'Pity.' Matron forced herself to curl up the corners of her mouth. 'Well, I can only wish us all luck.'

'Thank you, Ma'am. And Miss.' Rosie fluttered her lashes at Alyssa. 'Are you one of them brides?'

'No,' Alyssa said as serenely as she could, to hide her anger at Rosie's needling. The girl would never change. 'But thank you for your interest in my future.' She hoped that Rosie would understand the hidden warning. After all, she was the one girl with a reputation she wouldn't want to be made public.

'Maybe the ladies would like to have a private chat?' Mr Kendrick asked. 'Miss –'

'Call me Rosie.' Again the lashes fluttered.

'Miss Rosie. I'm sure Mrs Wainwright will gladly welcome you into her little flock.'

Matron's smile looked strained enough to alert the simplest of man. Alyssa took Matron's arm. 'If the gentlemen will allow, Miss Rosie could accompany us now?'

'But there's the dishes to do,' Rosie said. 'And the sweeping and things.'

'We won't keep you long.' Matron motioned Rosie to follow her. 'I'll send her back as soon as I can, Mr Harper.'

Rosie scrutinised Matron's home. 'Nice,' she said. 'I wouldn't mind this.'

'What are you doing here?' Matron's voice had a sharp edge to it. Rosie had the good grace to avert her gaze.

'Can I sit down?' Rosie asked.

'Answer my questions.'

Rosie nibbled on her lip.

'I'm running out of patience,' Matron said. 'One word from me, and you will find yourself without a single friend.'

'He left me.' Rosie's bottom lip trembled. Her whole body shook as she broke into sobs.

Alyssa took a step closer, holding out a handkerchief. For the first time, she felt a kinship with the wretched girl.

Rosie ignored Alyssa's offering and wiped her nose with her hand.

'Rosie!'

'Sorry, Matron.' Rosie looked at her with tearful eyes, naked fear in them.

'You may sit down. Alyssa, please put the kettle on.'

Alyssa rekindled the fire with newly acquired ease. She filled a pot with tea leaves, all the while keeping an eye on Rosie who squatted on a chair.

'He left you,' Matron said.

'Couldn't find work, could he. All this bosh about how they were going to build all these railroads in Canada, and how he'd be able to pick his own billet.' Rosie's hand shook as she accepted Alyssa's handkerchief. 'Maybe if he'd spent more hours knocking at people's doors instead of knocking back the pints, we'd been in clover.'

'He drank?'

'Like billy-oh. And then I didn't know what to do, and Alyssa said, if anything goes wrong …'

'You did the right thing. Didn't she, Matron?' Alyssa filled the teapot with hot water.

'What lies did you tell Mr Harper?'

Rosie sniffled. 'All I did was say I was on my own, and I needed work. Honest, Matron, I won't cause you any trouble.'

'You didn't say that you belonged to our group?'

Rosie hung her head. 'I thought maybe you'd get angry. And it would've been a bit hard to explain.'

'We'll better leave it at that, then. Alyssa will tell the girls not to give you away. Under one condition.'

'I'll do whatever you want. Honest, I swear.'

Matron poured the tea, with generous amounts of precious sugar for herself and Alyssa and none for Rosie.

Rosie clasped the mug with both hands. She seemed calmer.

'One wrong step, Rosie, and I will no longer shield you. Do you hear that? No fights, no catty remarks, no improper advances towards a man.'

'Yes, Matron.'

'And you'll call me Mrs Wainwright. Drink your tea.'

'She's what?' Susanna plonked down onto a chair. Her arm knocked over a candleholder.

'Careful.' Hannah whisked it out of the way. 'And now tell us everything.'

There wasn't much to tell, but although there were a few satisfied nods at Rosie's downfall, the girls promised to protect the secret. They might not like her overmuch, but she would always be one of them.

Rosie lay awake long after the last noise in the hotel had ceased. She'd done a mountain of dishes, and wiped and polished a seemingly endless supply of beer jugs, but Bert didn't expect her to serve in the bar when it got lively in the evening.

She pummelled the rolled-up towel she used as a pillow and pulled the blanket up to her chin. It was all so bloody unfair. She should have been married by now, with a home like Matron's, or a handsome groom like Susanna's. Instead she'd have to slog out her guts and serve on them. A silent tear rolled down her cheek. Matron would crack the whip whenever she felt like it. All because Rosie didn't act like a sheep. As for Alyssa – she'd been surprisingly nice, but still.

She clasped the gold coin that Alyssa had given to her. She needed a lot more than this, if she wanted to be someone. So many single men, with money in their pockets. Well, Matron had other things to do than watch her all the time.

Rosie rolled over onto her side and fell asleep.

CHAPTER 6

A loud banging against her door woke her up at dawn. She dragged herself out of her bed and washed her face in the enamel bowl on the chest of drawers. This and the narrow bed were the only pieces of furniture.

Rosie propped up her hand-mirror and brushed her hair before braiding and pinning it up. She stroked the wooden frame. At least there was one nice thing the bastard had given her.

Another bang against her door set her teeth on edge.

'Five minutes,' she said.

She pulled her blouse over her head and stepped into her flannel petticoat and skirt. Her wooden-soled boots clanged on the floorboards.

Peg-Leg whistled a song she'd never heard before as Rosie served bowls of porridge and cornbread to a dozen men on their way to the gold fields.

One or two of them gave her a lingering look. She made sure they liked what they saw by inhaling and exhaling as deeply as she could without being obvious. Matron or no matron, she still had a few tricks up her sleeves - or in her blouse.

'Careful with the coffee pot.' Peg-Leg nodded at a square of flannel. 'Handle's hot.'

'Thank you.' She gave him a grateful look. 'Anyone needing some more?'

'Morning. How did the lass do?' Bert yawned as he buttoned his waistcoat. He'd trimmed his beard and his hair, Rosie noticed as she piled up the empty bowls.

'Not too bad.' Peg-Leg flicked a checked cloth over the bar. 'Bit slow, but if I train her she'll do.'

'Good. Breakfast?'

Rosie should have been hungry, but lately she couldn't stomach anything before she'd had a cup of tea.

Bert reached for the coffeepot. Peg-Leg shoved three mugs over to him.

'You do drink coffee?' he asked her.

Rosie nodded. 'Unless you've got tea.'

'Sorry, lass, we're saving that for paying customers. The lord knows when the next ship will arrive.' Bert gave her a critical look. 'You're a bit pale. Sure you haven't picked up anything?'

She faked a laugh. 'Matron said I'm fine, and the doctor didn't worry about me.' She helped herself to coffee, willing it to stay down. 'I'll get the porridge.'

She let the kitchen heat wash over her. A huge cast-iron oven raised the temperature to a level that reminded her of Melbourne. They'd had a coal-fired oven on the *'Artemis' Delight'*, so she knew how to use it. A pot with porridge still bubbled away, although she'd dampened the fire more than an hour ago.

Frying pans the size of wagon wheels dangled from hooks screwed into low beams. She needed to climb on a low stool to get one down, but Peg-Leg's face had been a scream when she lifted the pan as easy as he did.

Her stomach settled down. Proper meals, that was all she needed. Like they used to cook for themselves on the ship.

Peg-Leg pushed himself off his stool as soon as he'd eaten the last spoonful. He belched. Bert glared at him. Peg-Leg shook his shoulders.

'Manners, Peg-Leg.'

'What've I done?'

'I don't mind,' Rosie said.

'I wouldn't have hired you if you did. But others might be a bit more –'

'Prissy?' Peg-Leg snorted.

'That's enough. Off you go. Them animals don't feed themselves.'

'I could do it,' Rosie said. She'd be the most pleasant girl he'd ever met, if she had to muck out the pig-sty.

'You'll look after the bar. Can you read and write?'

'And do my sums. Aly – All that you want me to, I'll take care of.'

'Good.' Peg-Leg gave her a grin that revealed three or four missing teeth in his lower jaw. 'There's half a ton of spuds to peel.' He limped out with a defiant swagger.

'Did I do anything?' Rosie asked.

'He's not used to having a skirt around. He'll get used to it.' Bert motioned her over behind the bar. 'We got tabs for everyone who comes in here, and end of the month they pay up. Cash or gold.'

Rosie blinked at the long list of names. Bert chuckled. 'You ain't seen half of them yet, and the rest will come soon enough, once word gets out it's a pretty lass and not Peg-Leg pulling the beer.'

'But how can I be sure they give me their real name?'

Bert opened a box and took out a tobacco pouch and a pipe. He prepared his smoke without spilling a single thread of tobacco.

It took several puffs to set it properly alight. The smell reminded Rosie of old socks, but she'd expected it to be worse.

Bert said, 'Peg-Leg or I will be around, and it's a pretty honest bunch of fellows. If not –' He reached under the counter and pulled out a thin, coiled whip. One flick of his wrist, and it cracked. 'I'm handy enough with my little friend here.'

He puffed again on his pipe. 'You do your job, and I'll keep the fellows straight. You don't have to handle money either. Any more questions?'

She shook her head and returned to the kitchen, and the spuds.

The day went fast enough, with Rosie cooking gallons of beans with salt pork and potatoes. From the bar came snippets of conversation, and occasionally laughter. She could stick with this for a while, she thought, when Mr Wainwright and his wife entered through the back door.

Matron inspected the kitchen with something close to envy. Her gaze lingered on the range.

Rosie bent down to open the hinged door and flung in a shovel-full of coal. She banged the door shut and wiped her hands on the sack she'd tied around her waist.

'Yeah?'

'Good day to you too, Rosie.' Matron peered over her shoulder to make sure no one could hear them.

'How are you getting on?'

'Fine.' She bared her teeth at her visitors, in what could be interpreted as a smile.

'Two of my young charges will come over tomorrow, to do some baking, with Mr Harper's permission.' Matron narrowed her eyes at her. 'We thought you might feel lonely, but it doesn't seem likely, does it?'

Rosie shrugged her shoulders, before she remembered that she intended to be nice as pie to Matron. 'It'll be good to have a proper natter. Thank you.'

'That's better. But we mustn't keep you.' She peered into a pot. 'At least you haven't forgotten your cooking lessons.'

Mr Wainwright cleared his throat. The cat hadn't got his tongue after all. 'Don't forget that you can come to us if here's any trouble.'

Rosie dug her fingernails into her palms to stop herself from making a curt reply. Honestly, did that man realise how pompous he sounded? And Matron, with her constant clucking and nagging and those stupid ruffled bonnets?

'Thank you, sir. Ma'am.'

'We'll see you for dinner.'

The first prospectors came in as Matron's group was half-way through their food. One of them, a stocky man with flaming-red sideburns who winked at Nellie, slammed his hand on the counter. 'I've got something to put away for me, Bert.'

The publican looked up from his beer barrel and wiped his hands on his leather apron. 'Now, Dave?'

Dave nodded and shoved over a small leather pouch. Bert peeked inside and whistled softly. 'I'll put it in the box. Peg-Leg? I need you here.'

His assistant put down a basket full of cornbread and stepped behind the bar. Bert disappeared into the private part at the back, where a staircase led to the rooms.

Rosie went around with the stew, ladling second helpings into bowls. Nancy gave her a shy smile, and Hannah winked at her, fluttering the hand on which she wore a fancy ring.

Rosie grinned. Fancy marrying a prissy old maid like Osborne. Why, he'd faint if she so much as flashed her ankles at him. But Hannah could easily run rings around him.

'Can I have some more?'

'Sure, Doctor.' She slapped a ladle full of stew into his bowl. 'And you. Mr Kendrick?' She'd never understand how they both could be sweet on Alyssa. Not that she was bad-looking, in her way, but no man would really want a bossy wife who spoke like a duchess, would they?

'No, thanks. Excellent food.' Mr Kendrick congenially flashed his teeth. Rosie swayed her hips a little as she moved on, until she found Matron glaring at her.

A dozen men burst through the doors as Bert returned, and clamoured for beer and whisky.

'Last two bottles, fellows,' Bert said as he filled the shot glasses. 'No more than one shot per man until the ship service runs again.'

One of the men downed his whisky in one go and wiped his mouth with his hand, before he strode over to the diners. Alyssa recognised Nellie's admirer.

'You the banker?' he asked Mr Osborne.

'Mr Osborne, at your service. Banker and asseyor.'

'George Potter. When are you open for business?'

'I hope to have the furnace at the ready for testing gold mid next week.'

Peg-Leg dropped a glass. Rosie smirked. *Clumsy fool.*

George rubbed his hands. 'Hear that, boys? No more having to accept Bert's price here.'

'What do you mean?' Bert's tone silenced them all. He brought up his whip, ready to lash out.

'Nothing. I don't mean anything. Only that you can't tell what our nuggets are worth. Mr Osborne here can.'

'If you don't trust me, I can get you your stash anytime, George.'

'Nah, I mean …' George's left eye twitched.

'Good.' Bert hid the whip again. 'Drinks, anyone?'

CHAPTER 7

Alyssa and Nellie knocked on the open back door to the kitchen. 'May we come in, Miss?' Nellie asked loud enough for anyone to understand that they were strangers. 'We wouldn't want to be in the way.'

Rosie stopped scrubbing the large table, wiped her hands on her apron and motioned them inside. She shut the door with a loud thump.

Nellie put a basket on the floor.

Rosie picked it up and plonked it onto the table. 'Flour, raisins, eggs, a bag of sugar. A full bag!'

'It's for the wedding cake.' Alyssa saw Rosie's hungry look. 'Don't you have any sugar here?'

'Peg-Leg's got the key to the larder.'

'But surely –' Alyssa interrupted herself. 'Do you have a small tin that we could fill? One that you can keep for yourself?'

Rosie shook her head. Her blonde hair slipped out of its pins. She grabbed it in a vain effort to tidy it up.

'Let me do it,' Nellie said. 'Honestly, you're getting as useless with your hands as Alyssa.'

'Thank you very much.' Alyssa's lips curled up at the corners. Rosie grinned, too, while Nellie pinned up her slightly grubby tresses.

'Do you need anything? Soap, or hair pins?'

'As if her highness Mrs Wainwright would let you waste things on me.' Rosie's mood soured.

'She covered for you, didn't she? You can't ask for nicer than that, after everything.' Nellie rammed home the last pin. 'There. Now you look decent again. And now let's crack on with the baking.'

'How come it's only you two?'

'Everyone else is busy with the dress-making,' Alyssa said.

Nellie rolled her eyes. 'It was more like Hannah trying to get Alyssa out from under her feet, after she dropped a button and stepped on it. It was mother-of-pearl, too. Broke into pieces.'

They worked in surprising harmony. Alyssa had never seen Rosie this cheerful before, without having an ulterior motive.

When two cake tins were in the oven, they sat down for a cup of tea. Heavily sugared, in Rosie's case.

'Your bloke was no good then?' Nellie said with a lack of tact that made Alyssa wince. Rosie shrugged. 'Lot more where he came from.'

Peg-Leg pushed the swing doors to the hotel area open. Rosie jumped up and pushed the sugar bag over to Alyssa, who dropped it into the basket.

Peg-Leg bowed his bare head. 'Afternoon, ladies.'

Alyssa smiled. 'Good afternoon, Mr. I'm sorry, I didn't catch your name.'

'Peg-Leg'll do.' He scratched the few patches of cheek not covered by his bristly beard. 'How you getting on? We gotta feed a whole bunch of folks tonight.'

'I'm so sorry to take up Rosie's time, but Mrs Wainwright insisted that we make up for it, Mr Peg-Leg.' Alyssa pointed at the crisp apron that covered her skirt. 'We will stay here and assist Rosie, so you don't have to go to even more trouble on our behalf.'

'See you later.' Rosie fluttered her fingers at him.

'You shouldn't tease the man,' Alyssa said as soon as Peg-Leg was out of earshot.

'Good-oh. I won't. Now tell me all about the girls. Who's snatched herself a man then?'

Nellie lowered her eyes. Rosie gave her a playful punch. 'Spill.'

'You've seen him. George Potter.'

'The one that Bert got upset with?' Rosie whistled under her breath. 'You could do worse, I guess. At least he's got something stashed away.'

'We're going to start a farm.' Nellie's voice grew soft. 'He'll build us a house, with a big fireplace, and we'll have lots of chickens and cattle, and a fat pig for ourselves, and I'll never go hungry again.'

'And you, Alyssa?'

'I'll make sure that we don't go hungry tonight. If you hand me a knife, I'll peel the turnips.'

~

The sight of the three brides entering the hotel caused the same awed silence that Alyssa remembered from the Christmas services she'd attended as a child.

Matron let a happy tear roll unhindered down her cheek as she clasped her husband's hand.

The three grooms gaped in open admiration at Susanna, Hannah and Nancy in their tight-fitting creamy dresses. The brides held their sweeping skirts a few inches above the floor. Hannah, practical as ever, had decided against trains that would get filthy before a single vow was exchanged.

Although Peg-Leg or Rosie swept the hotel floor every single day and exchanged the sawdust, a fine layer of dust and sand settled down as soon as they turned their back, because the publican kept the windows open at all hours while the weather allowed it, to get rid of the stink of stale beer and tobacco smoke.

Mr Osborne adjusted his bow-tie. His face shone with a sincere happiness that led distinction to his otherwise unassuming person.

Nancy's groom stood stock still in his dark woollen suit that looked too hot for a scorching summer day, and probably had been sent for months ago, with approximate measurements, because sleeves and legs were slightly too short. But his happiness made up of for any shortcomings in his attire, and Nancy looked at him with the same tenderness.

Normally Mr Abbott and his bride would have outshone the other two couples without even trying, but today Susanna's red-haired beauty and the golden-haired giant seemed to be simply be part of one big picture.

Behind her back, Alyssa heard the rustling of skirts. The doctor made his way up to her, a cumbersome box in his hands. Mr Kendrick followed, a large tripod under his arms.

Alyssa felt a surge of excitement. A photographic camera! She'd had her picture taken before. Her father had been one of the founding members of a photographic society, that possessed no less than three daguerreotype cameras, but this model seemed even more advanced.

'Sorry to disturb you,' Mr Kendrick said. 'We thought a few pictures would be welcome mementos of this day.' He turned to Matron. 'We'd have used it for your wedding if it hadn't been stowed away. But I'm sure you won't mind having your wedding picture taken with a slight delay.'

Matron clasped her hand in front of her mouth. 'Oh Walter,' she said. 'A wedding picture.'

'Excellent.' Mr Kendrick rested the tripod legs on the floor. 'We'll set the equipment up outdoors once the ceremony is finished. But we won't keep you any longer. Mr Abbott?'

Susanna's groom stopped forward, a bible in his hands. Of course, as the constable he performed most official acts.

'I wonder how he is going to marry himself,' Dr Bryson whispered into Alyssa's ear.

'Yes. But quiet now.'

Half an hour later, Mr Kendrick accepted a temporary transfer of powers invested in him by Mr Abbott, lifted his right hand in a solemn oath and read out the marriage vows with so much heartfelt sympathy that Matron shed more tears, and all the girls except for Alyssa and Rosie, who'd been invited as a guest, fumbled for their handkerchiefs.

Mr Kendrick's gaze met Alyssa's as Susanna said her final 'I will' to Mr Abbott. Alyssa suddenly discovered an urge to stare at the floor, which was increased by the feeling that the doctor's eyes too, were on her.

The first officer gently closed the bible as he said, 'I herewith declare you husband and wife. You may now kiss the bride.'

Mr Abbott had no problem following this suggestion. He kissed his bride with so much enthusiasm that Mr Kendrick had to clear his throat twice before he could return bible and official powers.

The photographic images took all afternoon. Mr Kendrick insisted on arranging each couple in various poses, with the bride sitting and the husband standing behind her, or both sitting next to each other, holding hands, or standing up.

Alyssa grew restless after a bit and returned to their lodging. Harriet and Nellie must have had the same idea, for they already took turns in front of the mirror, preparing for that evening's party.

Three boxes stood ready packed next to their owners' beds. Mr Wainwright had promised to supervise their transport later, to the new homes of Mrs Abbott, Mrs Osborne and Mrs Scott.

Alyssa opened her own trunk and lifted out three parcels carefully wrapped in muslin. They contained lace collars and cuffs similar to those she'd given Matron as a wedding present.

She slipped one parcel each into the boxes.

Nellie peered over her shoulder. 'What are you doing?'

'Every bride should get a gift, don't you think?'

Nellie's face brightened. 'I'll get something too?'

'It wouldn't be fair otherwise, would it?'

'What about Rosie?' Harriet frowned. 'I mean, she almost, I mean, she probably ...' She broke off, red-faced and tongue-tied.

'Who knows what's going to happen?' Alyssa took out her brush and tried to recreate the ringlets that Hannah could form with ease.

'What on earth are you doing?' Nellie took the brush out of Alyssa's hand. 'You do it like that, and a bird will think he's found a walking nest.'

She pressed Alyssa onto her bed. 'I'm not as good as Hannah, but it'll do.' Alyssa sat still while Nellie brushed her hair, braided and pinned it up and pulled out a few strands on each side of the parting. 'What do you think, good enough for your admirers?' She dragged Alyssa in front of the mirror.

'Thanks, Nellie.'

Alyssa remembered something else. She opened her trunk again and took out one of the tins that she used to keep boiled sweets in. The tins were long since empty.

'I'll see you later,' she said as she headed for the door. It still gave her the most satisfying thrill to step out onto the street unguarded. It wouldn't do to stroll around on her own in the dark, but during the day, in full view of other residents, it gave her back a sense of the freedom she'd missed sorely during their voyage.

She found Rosie in the kitchen, staring daggers at her employer. He gave Alyssa a curt nod.

'I'm sorry if I intrude,' Alyssa said.

Rosie rushed over to her and clung to her arm. 'Tell him that you gave me the sugar.'

'What?'

'Peg-Leg found the girl shovelling the stuff into her mug.' Bert Harper crossed his arms over his chest. 'He said he'd not given her any.'

'Because he didn't have to.' Rosie stomped her feet.

Alyssa gave her an encouraging pat on the back. 'It's perfectly alright, Mr Harper,' she said, lifting the tin. 'I came to bring Rosie this, to keep the sugar in that we had left over from the baking.'

'See? I'm not a thief.' Rosie snivelled.

'In that case, you better get back to work, lass. We got a wedding party on.' He stalked off.

'Thanks, Alyssa.' Rosie took a sip of tea. 'Honestly, I think that Peg-Leg is plain jealous because he thinks that Bert might become sweet on me.'

Alyssa thought that unlikely, but kept her tongue.

'Is there anything else I can help you with?' she asked instead.

'Make sure that Matron doesn't spoil things for me. Please? She's always had it in for me.'

Alyssa took a deep breath. 'She's backed you up, and the last thing any of us want it to be caught out on an untruthfulness.'

Rosie's eyes lit up. 'That's right. Course not.' She dusted the flour off the apron and pulled her blouse as tight as possible. 'How do I look?'

'Aren't you going to get changed for the party?'

'As if. I'm playing the blimmin' maid, ain't I.'

Rosie appeared happy enough that night, flirting with several of the prospectors as soon as Peg-Leg fiddled and Mr Wainwright swept his wife onto the dance floor.

All the tables had been pushed to the wall after the meal, with chairs lined up in front. The cake was to be served last, after the dance had ended.

Susanna seemed to float on air as her husband waltzed her around the room. Nancy and her Joshua had already retired, amongst a few ribald remarks that made Mr Kendrick take a few of the men aside for a quiet talk.

Mr Osborne and his bride stood outside, watching the night sky in companionable silence from what Alyssa could see.

She'd have liked to get some fresh air too, but was loath to disturb them. She fanned herself. The air had cooled down in the evening, but with only a light breeze coming in through the open windows, an hour's dancing left her feel sticky. The ringlets Nellie had teased out of her hair hung limp.

Hannah turned around and waved at her. Her husband picked up a kerosene lantern and led her away.

Alyssa waved back although Hannah no longer faced her.

'You've got a wistful look,' Mr Kendrick said.

'I'm going to miss them,' Alyssa said.

'They'll still be in the same town.'

'Yes, but they've got their own lives now. Finally.'

'As do you.' He held out his hand. 'May I once again ask for a dance?'

'This one is mine.' Dr Bryson nudged his friend aside. 'You haven't forgotten you promised the next waltz to me?'

Alyssa was about to protest when he winked at her. Mr Kendrick shrugged. 'In this case I'll rest my weary feet until this overbearing fellow relinquishes you again.'

Their steps were as well-matched as Alyssa remembered. 'I've hardly seen you in days,' he said.

'I haven't been this busy in weeks,' Alyssa agreed. 'The last time was after the hurricane.'

'I hope wedding preparations are slightly more agreeable than nursing sea-sick people.'

'Both have their challenges.'

They danced in silence for a few heartbeats.

'What about you?' she asked. 'Any new patients?'

He shook his head. 'If we're lucky, the smallpox will pass us by, and I can soon be on my way.'

She missed a beat, and he trod on her left foot. 'Sorry,' he said.

'It was my fault.'

Rosie swayed past, brushing a little against a prospector with a thick scar bisecting his left eyebrow.

Dr Bryson shook his head in good-natured resignation. 'Rosie is –'

She kicked his shin. 'A delightful young woman. I was very happy to make her acquaintance.'

He pulled her closer. 'Ouch.'

'Surely you as a medical man know that one can't help one's reflexes?'

'You win. Can I get you a refreshment?'

The moon hung almost full in the sky, shining bright enough to find the way without a lantern. Alyssa smiled. How typical of Mr Osborne to still secure a light to see his bride safely home.

She undid the hooks on her dress, fighting off sleep long enough to change into a nightdress and wash her face. The wake-up call would come soon enough.

CHAPTER 8

A stampede woke her, followed by angry yells. All around her, the girls roused themselves from their sleep. Loud bangs against their door made Alyssa catch her breath as she went to open.

Nellie pressed her blanket against her chest, her eyes wide with fear.

Outside stood Mr Kendrick and Mr Wainwright. Matron rushed past them and hugged Alyssa.

'What is wrong? Is it the smallpox?' Alyssa asked.

The men exchanged a nervous glance. 'There's been a fatality.' Mr Kendrick took a deep breath. 'Bert Harper was found dead. And Rosie's in trouble.'

Matron and Alyssa had to hurry to keep up with Mr Kendrick. A small group of prospectors clustered outside the hotel. Mr Abbott barred the door, his hand on a pistol – the first firearm Alyssa had seen in this town – and his face a forbidding mask.

Poor man; instead of enjoying his first day as a married man he had to keep these men in check. Alyssa's stomach lurched. There had to be a simple explanation. And what did Mr Kendrick mean, that Rosie was in trouble? Had she been found enjoying male attention again?

The men parted to let them pass, but otherwise seemed intent on standing their ground.

Mr Kendrick led them upstairs, to a wide hallway with three doors leading off it on either side. He knocked on the first door. 'Open up, Rosie.'

'No.'

Matron rapped against the door. 'Rosie, you will do what Mr Kendrick says. Do you hear me?'

A key scratched in the lock. Rosie opened the door wide enough to let Matron squeeze through. Alyssa gasped as she saw the girl. Her eyes were blotchy, and a slap had left angry marks on her cheek.

She slipped inside the room. A broom leant against the wall. A fine layer of dust sat on the sparse furniture, but the floorboards were clean enough apart from a few shavings of sawdust that must have clung to Rosie's boots.

Matron sat on the bed with Rosie and touched her cheek. Rosie winced.

'How did that happen?'

Rosie shook her head.

'Did you have a fight?' Alyssa asked. The foolish girl really needed to learn how to keep her temper.

Tears formed in Rosie's eyes. 'I haven't done nothing.'

'Anything,' Alyssa said out of habit. 'Sorry. Can you tell us what is going on?'

'I don't know noth – anything. Peg-Leg wouldn't let me out of my room, so I locked myself in, and I just sat here and sat.'

She grabbed Alyssa's hand. 'You'll find out what's wrong. Please?'

Alyssa said, 'You stay here with Matron, and lock the door again until I come back.'

Mr Kendrick leant against the hallway wall. 'I assume you want to see the doctor.' He rapped against the door at the end of the hallway. 'Can we come in? Unless -' He stopped Alyssa. 'You'd probably rather not see.'

'Thank you.'

'I've got Alyssa with me, doctor.'

Dr Bryson poked his head out. 'I'm finished here. Nothing much to see anyway. I've covered the body.'

Nothing in his voice or demeanour indicated the slightest discomfort. Alyssa shivered. Of course, death was nothing new to the doctor, but still she'd expected some sign that it affected him to see someone so full of life only last night, passed away.

Behind him she glimpsed a chair, with a shirt and waistcoat draped over it, and a dusty floor with footmarks all over it, except for an uneven trail about two feet wide that appeared to have been swept clean.

A sheet covered a prone figure on the bed, or at least the few inches that Alyssa saw indicated that.

Dr Bryson came out and closed the door behind him. He turned a key and pocketed it.

'You look pale. Have you had anything to eat?' he asked. She shook her head. 'We could all do with a bite.'

He took her by the elbow and led her down the staircase.

'What about Matron and Rosie?' Alyssa thought she heard weeping coming from Rosie's room.

Kendrick put a finger on his lips. She fell silent.

Peg-Leg sat in the main room, staring at the entrance door. His jaw worked as he turned around to face the doctor.

'How much longer are you going to keep me cooped up in here?' He took a grubby plug of chewing tobacco, sliced off a portion with his fingernail and stuffed it between cheek and gum.

'I'm sure you can wait a little bit longer, until we can all have a chat with Mr Abbott.' The doctor gave Peg-Leg a brief pat on the shoulder. 'Would you care for a coffee?'

'I'll do it myself.' Peg-Leg heaved himself off the stool.

'No need.' Mr Kendrick flashed his white teeth at the morose man. 'I'm a handy man when it comes to making a decent brew.'

They gathered around the table, the way Alyssa and Nellie had done with Rosie for their baking. They'd been happy that day, carefree. And now a man lay dead, while his assistant sat in the bar, grieving.

Mr Kendrick filled a pan with water from a butt and put it on to boil. He lowered his voice. 'What have you found out, Doctor?'

Dr Bryson ruffled his brown hair. 'Bert Harper died sometime during the night. He'd already started to stiffen, but not completely.' He shot Alyssa an apologetic glance.

She said, 'Don't mind, unless you'd rather not include me.'

'Not at all.' He touched her hand for a warm, comforting moment. 'The party broke up about midnight, and Rosie and Peg-Leg cleared away the glasses. They're still sitting unwashed in the bar. Rosie says that Bert told her and Peg-Leg they could clean up in the morning. Peg-Leg confirms that.'

Kendrick rummaged between the tins until he found the coffee, spooned it into a pot and filled it with water.

'Anyway,' the doctor said, 'Bert was usually the first down. He'd fill the butt with fresh water from the well outside, wash, and rouse Peg-Leg. Rosie would always be the last.'

Alyssa nodded to herself. She could imagine Rosie clinging to her bed for a few more precious minutes.

'This morning though, Bert wasn't up. Peg-Leg knocked on the door, it swung open, and there he was.'

Mr Kendrick put a steaming mug in front of Alyssa and filled another one that he took to Peg-Leg.

The doctor helped himself to coffee and waited until Kendrick had returned.

'What did Peg-Leg find?' Alyssa asked. 'I didn't see any blood.'

'There wasn't any. Bert had been knocked out with one of his giant frying pans, and then the murderer shoved a pillow over his face and smothered him. I found bite marks in the pillow, and a few feathers in Bert's mouth. The frying pan lay next to the bed.'

'What does that have to do with Rosie?'

'Peg-Leg claims that she did it.' The doctor gave her a helpless shrug.

'That's nonsense.' Alyssa wondered why she was so convinced of this, but she was. 'She's trouble, but she's not a murderess.'

'That's why I came to collect you,' Mr Kendrick said. 'We both hope that she's innocent, but we'll see what Mr Abbott has to contribute.'

Alyssa nodded. 'Can I bring Matron and Rosie some coffee? I assume you don't want them to run into Peg-Leg, if the marks on Rosie's cheek are anything to go by.'

'I've asked Mr Wainwright to come and take his wife and Rosie back to our lodging,' Mr Kendrick said. 'They should be gone by now.'

'But we would have seen them.'

'There's another staircase leading to the upper storey, from the outside. It opens into one of the unused rooms.' He and the Doctor shared a weary glance.

'That means anybody could have entered the hotel.'

The doctor paused. 'Except that nobody had a reason.'

'That we know of yet.' Alyssa reached out both her hands to the men. 'Gentlemen, please. Surely you don't believe that Rosie is guilty. I ask you to help me.'

Mr Abbott was taken aback when he saw Alyssa next to her friends, but at least he didn't send her away.

'How is your wife?' she asked.

'Fine. And I don't intend to worry her over this.' He slapped his hat on his thigh. 'Bad business, this.'

'Have you ever had trouble of this kind?' Mr Kendrick asked.

'No. And I've been here for going on five years. I know the boys. A drunken fight, when somebody gets a bit cocky, maybe. But not like this.' He had the decency to appear pained. 'It must have been the girl, but then that pan must have weighed a good twenty-five pounds. That's a lot to get off the hook, lug upstairs and knock a man over the head with.'

Dr Bryson and Mr Kendrick's faces lit up. Alyssa hated herself as she said, 'Rosie is stronger than she looks. Most of us are; including Mrs Abbott. Ask her if she could wield that pan.'

A fly buzzed in, circling the table. Mr Abbott's left hand shot out and caught it in his fist.

'Bert Harper, killed just like this.' He pressed his fingers together hard enough to make his knuckles turn white.

'But what reason could she have had?' Dr Bryson asked.

'That's what I'm going to find out.' Mr Abbott dropped the dead fly onto the floor. 'If you'll come up with me to the girl's room? I'll have a nosey. Miss Chalmers can make sure that we don't put a foot wrong. Coming?'

Mr Abbott unclipped a key-ring from his belt and unlocked Rosie's door. Alyssa frowned. The man had been standing guard outside when Mr Wainwright spirited Rosie and his wife away, using the staircase out back. Where did he get the key?

Rosie's room was as Alyssa had left it earlier. Her few belongings sat in her box. Mr Abbott flipped the lid open. At the bottom of a small clothes pile rested a crumpled cotton dress, with dust and a few sawdust shavings on its hem.

Mr Abbott held it up into the light and handed it to Mr Kendrick. He searched the rest of the clothes, but they all were clean, and neatly folded.

He said, 'You mentioned a trail in Bert's room, as if somebody had swept part of it.'

The doctor nodded.

'Well, gentlemen, it looks like we found what was used to do the sweeping. Rosie's dress trailed over the floorboards as she crept up to the sleeping man and banged the pan onto his head.'

'How did she get in?' Alyssa forced herself to stay calm, despite the panic that had been bubbling away under the surface since she'd first heard the news.

'Bert didn't bother to lock his door, Peg-Leg says. He didn't keep any money in his bedroom anyway.'

'Where did he keep it?' Mr Kendrick gave Alyssa a quick nod. She breathed easier. He at least was on her side.

'He had a strong-box in one of the rooms.' Mr Abbott stared at the stained shift. 'We'll have a look at it, but first I need to figure out what to do with the girl. I don't want any of the boys getting too riled up. Bert had a lot of friends, and we don't have a prison.'

'Mr and Mrs Wainwright will watch over her for the moment,' Mr Kendrick said. 'Until we've found a better solution.'

Mr Abbott jiggled the keys. 'You hold onto that dress, doctor. It's evidence. And now let's have a look at Bert's strong-box.'

The name barely did it justice, Alyssa thought. The box measured about twenty-five inches square, but the hinges couldn't have put up much resistance to the crowbar next to it. Inside sat a mountain of leather pouches, all with initials on them.

'She broke into here, jemmied the strong-box open, and Bert must have caught her. No. That's wrong.' Mr Abbott pressed his hand against his head as if to aid his thought process.

'He was asleep when she swung the pan. She killed him, then she came over here and - why didn't she steal the gold and the money? Right. Maybe she saw it was too heavy to carry, or Peg-Leg woke up, or there was another noise, or she kind of lost her nerve.' He blew out his breath. 'We'll get it out of her later.'

'How can you be sure that nothing is missing?' Alyssa tried to find a flaw in his reasoning. 'And why would she bring a crowbar and a frying pan? Where would she even get a crowbar?'

'All in good time. But you're right, we need to find Bert's ledger. He wrote down every single nugget and every cent that he'd earned or stored for the boys. More honest than a judge, was Bert.'

CHAPTER 9

The three men emptied the strong-box and went down the outside staircase, lugging the pouches between them, in hessian sacks.

To Alyssa's surprise they avoided the main street and took the back route to the bank. Hannah opened the back door, a becoming glow in her face. She stepped aside to let them in without a question.

Her husband jumped up from his chair by the unlit fire. 'Is it true?' he asked.

'I'm afraid so,' Mr Abbott said. 'We need your help.'

'Of course. Would you like tea, or coffee? I'm afraid we don't have any beer, and – what is going to happen to the hotel?'

'I'll let Peg-Leg open it up again as soon as possible.' Mr Abbott gave Hannah a rueful shrug. 'Coffee would be fine. Sorry you didn't get a better start to married life.'

Hannah put a hand on her husband's forearm. 'I won't complain. How's Mrs Abbott?'

'Good, although she'll not be happy to hear about this sad affair. Right. Mr Osborne, you've got a proper safe now, do you?

Mr Osborne insisted on weighing every single pouch and registering the receipt before he stowed them away in the safe.

A furnace in the back room of the bank was almost finished, and on shelves stood rows and rows of bone ash containers he called crucibles.

Hannah drew Alyssa away from the men as soon as she could. 'Tell me what you have to do with this.'

Alyssa bit her lip. 'Mr Abbott thinks it was Rosie.'

Hannah dropped the sugar tong. 'Never!'

'You don't believe it, do you?' Alyssa found her knees grow weak.

'Have you had any bite at all? You're all peaky.' Hannah cut a thick slab of bread and spread jam on it. 'Here.'

'Where did you get jam?'

'Mr Osborne sent for it, as soon as we'd made landfall. But that doesn't matter.'

She watched Alyssa eat. 'And I know that Rosie's a real cow and could do with a good clip around the ear but she wouldn't kill a man.'

'That's what I figured.'

'Mind you, there's enough what would believe it. Especially if a man's involved.' Hannah put a hand on Alyssa's arm. 'You're going to help her, right?'

Alyssa nodded.

'Good-oh. Just tell me what I can do.'

The men must have overheard this as they filed back into the living quarters, because they shared a sheepish glance.

Mr Osborne wet his lips with his tongue. 'I realise it's a lot to ask from you, my dear, but we wondered – I wondered ...'

Hannah gave him an encouraging smile, 'Yes, dear?'

'It's not proper to keep the poor girl in men's quarters, and although I am sure that Mrs Wainwright would offer her a space ...'

'Rosie'd drive her to distraction,' Alyssa said.

'Yes. And there's her safety to consider. If anybody thinks that she had anything to do with that poor man's demise ...' Mr Osborne really should stop letting his sentences peter out, Alyssa thought, but Hannah didn't appear to mind.

She said, 'You want us to take Rosie in.' She glanced at the door to what might be her bedroom, because she blushed slightly.

'There's the small storage room,' Mr Osborne said. 'It's got a strong door, and we could put up bolts from the inside.'

'We better clear it out then.' Hannah pushed up her sleeves, ready to tackle whatever lay in front of her.

'Thank you,' Mr Abbott said. 'That is, if you really don't mind. We'll make sure that one of us is close by, in case you need any help with the prisoner.'

Hannah grinned, an impish gleam in her dark eyes. 'Don't

you fret about me, Mr Abbott. If that girl steps out of line with me, I'll be the one doing the slapping.'

Mr Abbott hesitated. 'I'm sorry to ask this from you. Don't forget that she might look fragile, but she's still dangerous and could be desperate enough to escape.'

'Then take away her boots,' Hannah said. 'She's not going to run on naked feet into the wilderness.'

'She could steal your shoes,' Mr Kendrick said.

Hannah lifted her dainty left foot. 'If she can squeeze her clodhoppers into these, I'll be the Queen.'

'We'll bring her over as soon as we can, without being seen,' Mr Abbott said. 'Thank you both.'

Mr Kendrick and Dr Bryson accompanied Alyssa to their own quarters. The doctor had been uncharacteristically quiet the whole time, Alyssa thought. Surely he could not think Rosie guilty?

Matron's relief was palpable when she heard that Rosie would soon be taken off her hands. The girl cowered in a corner, red-eyed and frightened.

Alyssa sat next to her and said, 'We'll get you out of this.'

Rosie flung herself into Alyssa's lap and sobbed her heart out. Alyssa couldn't tell if the tears were for herself, for the dead man, or regret for all the mistakes that had led her to be in this situation. She stroked Rosie's hair and let her cry.

'Hannah will look after you,' Alyssa said. 'We will all look after you.'

~

Getting Rosie over to the Osborne's proved surprisingly easy, once Matron grudgingly agreed to lend her cloak and bonnet to disguise the girl.

The gallant Mr Wainwright took her arm and strolled with her along the back lane, ostensibly chatting to Mr Abbott.

Matron marched around the room, hands clasped behind her back. 'What have I done wrong?'

'Nothing, Ma'am.'

'Thank you, Alyssa, but I have failed in my duty. Had I let Mr Harper know the truth about Rosie, he'd have sent her away, and he'd still be alive.' She let out a wail of anguish. 'Lies and deceit, and this is what has come of it.'

'You believe Rosie is guilty?' Alyssa took a step closer to the doctor and Mr Kendrick.

'I don't know what to believe.' Matron's shoulders slumped. 'If only the wretched girl had stayed where she belonged.'

The doctor clasped her by the shoulders. 'This despair is so unlike you that I think a medicinal drop of brandy would be beneficial. For all of us.'

Mr Kendrick promptly set a bottle on the table and produced three glasses. 'I'm afraid that's all we have,' he said. 'And with the hotel closed, I would have to sneak in through the back to procure another glass.'

'I don't need a drink,' Alyssa said, her mind on something else. 'Wouldn't the back door be locked anyway?'

'Not on the upper level. I didn't see a lock on that door.'

'Anybody could have entered the hotel?'

'I could be mistaken, but Mr Abbott would be able to tell. But first I think Mrs Wainwright needs support.'

Matron cut a sorry figure. She held the brandy glass in her hand and stared into the amber liquid as if it were poison.

Alyssa touched her arm. 'It will be alright,' she said. 'You have nothing to reproach yourself for.'

'I should have warned Mr Harper. I should have warned everyone. That girl is beyond redemption.'

'You mustn't think that.' Dr Bryson took a stoppered bottle with white pills out of his medical bag and placed two into Matron's palm. 'Can we have some water?'

'What are those pills?' Matron turned them over in her hand.

'A mild sedative. You need to rest, and then we'll return you to your house.'

Matron popped the pills into her mouth and swallowed them dry. Alyssa propped up all the pillows she could find and piled them behind Matron's head.

'Mrs Wainwright?' The doctor chafed her hand as slowly the colour returned to Matron's face and her breath became regular again. Her eyelids drooped.

Alyssa took a blanket from one of the beds and draped it over Matron's legs.

The doctor pulled Alyssa away. 'She'll do for a bit.'

'Maybe we should have taken her home before giving her the pills.' Alyssa said.

'We can't. Not before Abbott brings back her cloak and bonnet, if we want to keep Rosie's whereabouts quiet.'

Mr Abbott brought the garments, and a hefty ledger which he presented with a flourish. 'I found this under Bert's mattress, once we'd removed the body.' He noticed Alyssa. 'Sorry to be so blunt, Miss.'

'Miss Chalmers is not the squeamish sort.' Dr Bryson reached for the ledger. 'Have you read the entries? Is anything missing?'

'I haven't checked with Mr Osborne yet but it looks alright to me. Unless there's one or more of the pouches with nuggets missing. I also found a wallet with fifty-two dollars in notes stuffed under the mattress. She probably didn't know the money was there, or couldn't get at it with Bert's dead weight on the bed.'

'You seem to be convinced of Rosie's guilt.'

Mr Abbott gave her a pitying look. 'I'd do somersaults if there's another solution. I'd hate to see a young woman convicted of murder, but what else am I to think?' 'Everybody in town would know where to find Mr Harper,' Alyssa said.

'Listen, it's hard for you to believe. I understand that. I dread telling my wife, but facts are facts. Why should any of the boys harm him?'

'Greed is as good a motive for any of the men.' Mr Kendrick gave Alyssa an encouraging look.

'I'd believe that if I'd found one of the boys gone, but no-one's that stupid, with smallpox out there, and the bears and wolves hard on your trail.'

'But the men go out on their own to their claims or their preferred stretch of river,' Dr Bryson said.

'Mostly it's two or three of us together. Safer that way.'

'I thought you'd hung up your gold pan, with all the jobs the Crown has entrusted you with.'

'That's very recent, Doctor. But yeah, my days in the wilderness are done. I promised Mrs Abbott as much.'

'Did Mr Harper store everyone's nuggets?'

'He did it for most of the boys, leastways until they got an itch to take the boat and blow some of their wealth.'

'Cards? Or company?' Mr Kendrick gave Matron a quick glance, but she slept soundly.

'I'm not asking and I'm not judging, but mostly cards. Or crap games. I won't have any hard gambling going on here, and sometimes you need to blow off steam.'

He slapped his hat on. 'I'll make sure that Peg-Leg doesn't mouth off about Rosie, and we'll see tomorrow what Mr Osborne says.'

'Why the wait?' Mr Kendrick asked.

'Because he's still busy with that furnace of his. A few more hours won't hurt, and the boys are excited about having a proper fire assay done here to find out if they're in clover yet.'

Matron moved. Her eyes slowly opened.

'How are you feeling?' Alyssa lifted the blanket off Matron's legs and folded it.

'Fully restored, thank you.' Matron bit her lip. 'I'm sorry I lost my calm.'

'Don't think about it,' Dr Bryson said. 'Justice will prevail. But now I'll escort you home, and make sure that your husband won't be far behind.'

He held Matron's cloak for her. She pressed her lips together as she slipped into it. The bonnet, she carried stiff-armed in her hand, as if Rosie had polluted it.

'Ma'am?'

'Yes, Alyssa?'

'Please don't let anybody see that you suspect Rosie. We're all strangers here, and it is too easy to arouse strong emotions.'

Matron blinked, uncomprehendingly.

Mr Kendrick understood. 'Abbott has his work cut out if he wants to prevent a few of the men seeking revenge. We'll do our best not to add fuel to the fire. Doctor?'

'Let's hope that Mr Abbott succeeds in silencing Peg-Leg.'

With Matron safely ensconced in her house, Alyssa insisted on seeing Rosie. Mr Wainwright let them in, with a worried Hannah peeking out behind his back. He and Mr Kendrick exchanged a few whispered words, before the second officer made his good-byes.

The door to the small storage room was locked. Hannah lifted a piece of string, holding a key, over her head, and handed it to the doctor.

He knocked on the door and unlocked it. 'It's Dr Bryson, Rosie.'

'What do you want?'

Alyssa said, 'We want to talk to you.'

From the other side of the door came a scraping noise, as if a bar was lifted. Rosie's eyes were swollen, and the red marks on her cheek stood out in every detail on her pale skin.

Hannah busied herself slicing bread and making tea.

The doctor examined the wide bar inside the storage room that allowed Rosie to keep out intruders even if they got hold of the key.

'Mr Wainwright did that,' Rosie said. 'Just in case.'

'Excellent idea.' He frowned as he gently probed her cheek. 'Any more injuries?'

She shook her head. Hannah poured almost black tea into five mugs. A saucer held a few lumps of sugar. Rosie took two, but stopped her hand half an inch from her mug. 'Do you mind, Hannah?'

'Course not. But leave enough for Mr Osborne, will you.' She dropped a lump into one of the mugs and knocked on the door to the bank part of the building. Her husband called out, 'One moment, dear.'

Several keys clanged before he opened. Beads of sweat shone on his face, but he inhaled the steaming tea as if he felt the need to warm himself. Behind him, the furnace glowed.

'Give me half an hour,' he said before he disappeared again.

Rosie sat huddled onto her chair, as far removed from the shuttered window as possible.

'Nobody is aware that you're here,' the doctor said. 'You're safe.'

Her hand shook as she lifted the mug to her lips.

'What can you tell us?' Pity surged in Alyssa as she contemplated Rosie's sorry state.

'I didn't do it. I didn't do anything.' Rosie wiped her nose with her hand.

Hannah slapped it automatically. 'Mind your manners in my house.' She handed Rosie a handkerchief.

'You're getting as bossy as Alyssa,' Rosie said with the first hint of animation she'd displayed since the morning.

Hannah grinned. 'You wait and see.'

'Last night.' Alyssa said.

The facts were few, but then there wasn't much to tell. After the party broke up, a few drinkers stayed behind for half an hour, but with Bert rationing the alcohol, the men remained sober enough and left peacefully.

Bert had tallied the tabs, Peg-Leg cleaned the glasses and Rosie scrubbed tables and bar counter and swept the floor.

'I was going to do upstairs this morning, so I took up the broom.' Rosie sighed wearily. 'Bert – Mr Harper – always kept windows open, and the dirt blows in before you know it. I told him I'd keep everything nice and clean.'

A touch of the old Rosie shone through as she fluttered her lashes, recalling the conversation. 'That's the last I knew before Peg-Leg knocked on my door. I put on my old blouse and skirt, and when I opened the door he slapped me and pushed me back in.' She covered her cheek with one hand. 'I locked the door and I sat there until you came. I had no idea that Bert's dead.'

She put down her mug and clasped Alyssa's hands. 'Why would I hurt him? That's stupid.'

'His strong-box was broken into,' Mr Kendrick said.

'I never!'

'But you knew where it was?' Dr Bryson strained his ears as if to make sure there was no-one outside.

'Peg-Leg told me the first day. He said, don't go in there, do you hear me?'

'You weren't curious?'

'Doctor, I was that run off my feet I had no time to be curious. Rosie, peel the spuds, Rosie, another pot of porridge, Rosie, the dishes need washing and the bar needs sweeping. Honestly, how they ever got by without me is a miracle.' A dry sob escaped her. 'Why don't things ever go right for me?'

'They will.' Alyssa rubbed Rosie's back. 'Leave it to us. Meanwhile, Hannah will look after you.'

Hannah said, 'Mind you, I'll still have you peel the spuds in your chamber if you act up.' She winked. 'It's going to be alright.'

'Thank you,' Rosie said without her usual truculence. 'It's really kind of you and Mr Osborne.'

'Like it or not, you're one of us, and he would hate to see you deserted.' Hannah twisted her wedding band. 'He's a good man.'

'As are we all.' Mr Kendrick rose and offered Alyssa his arm. 'We should escort you home now.'

Alyssa shook her head. 'I appreciate that, although I can manage a few hundred yards on my own.'

'With a possible murderer on the lose?' Dr Bryson shook his head. 'You, my dear, will have to accept our company.' He looked at Rosie. 'If you could hide in your room and bolt the door while we leave? No-one must see you.'

Rosie's eyes widened in panic. She practically hurled herself into her small room, swishing skirt revealing half an inch of bare skin between hem and top of her ankle boots.

'We would ask you in for a few minutes,' Mr Kendrick said on the way, 'but Matron would object.'

'Thank you,' Alyssa said. 'I'll be happy to fetch the smelling salts for her.' She spoke louder than usual in case somebody overheard them. She couldn't shake off the sensation that they were being watched.

A dozen men hung outside Mr Abbott's office, which luckily was situated in a log cabin, a hundred yards from his house. At least Susanna wouldn't have to deal with angry neighbours at home.

Alyssa stopped. 'If you don't mind, we should look in on Mrs Abbott. She must be scared for Rosie.'

'I didn't realise they were close,' the doctor said.

'We had all just met her, if you remember, but it's not a situation any of us would wish on a female.'

Susanna enveloped Alyssa in a vice-like hug. Worry lines furrowed her forehead. 'What on earth is going on? Tom hasn't been home since somebody banged on our door this morning.'

'He hasn't told you anything?'

'Only to lock the door and wait for him.' She let go of Alyssa and picked up a duster. 'I've been driving myself crazy, cleaning and scrubbing simply to keep me busy.'

Her living room showed the effort. Alyssa admired the carved walnut and oak furniture shining with beeswax polish, the spotless rug and the neatly arranged books on a whatnot corner shelf. Mr Abbott had obviously spared no effort, or money, to create a home for himself and his bride.

Susanna lowered herself into an armchair, placing her hands into her lap. 'Something bad has happened, right?'

Alyssa sat down on the leather button sofa that reminded her of her family home in Melbourne. Mr Kendrick and Mr Bryson flanked her.

'Mr Harper has been found dead,' she said. 'Murdered.'

Susanna's left hand flew to her mouth.

'And your husband suspects Rosie.'

'He does what?' Susanna's skin grew white enough to be almost translucent, making her reddish-gold hair stand out even more.

'There is certain evidence pointing towards her.' Dr Bryson gave Alyssa and Susanna an apologetic look.

'Fiddlesticks.' Susanna snorted. 'What's she supposed to have done?'

'Knocked him over the head with a frying pan,' Mr Kendrick said.

'Oh.' Susanna sank back in her armchair. 'That's different, if she got into a fight with him in the kitchen.'

'He died in his bed. He was knocked out and then smothered.' Dr Bryson rubbed his clean-shaven chin, uncomfortable with what he said.

'In his bed?' A spot of colour returned to Susanna's face. 'You mean that Rosie -'

'No.' Alyssa crossed her arms across her chest. 'Rosie knew that she couldn't put a foot wrong, or else Matron would speak up about her past. And do you see her smothering a man?'

Susanna shook her head.

'But there is the dirt-covered dress, that swept over Mr Harper's bedroom floor,' Mr Kendrick said.

Alyssa smiled. 'I hoped you'd noticed that. You do admit that Rosie may be cunning, but she's not smart enough to create fake evidence against herself that we in return disprove?'

Dr Bryson and Mr Kendrick exchanged a baffled glance.

Alyssa rose from the sofa and motioned to Susanna to get up, too.

'Well, gentlemen? What do you notice?'

There was no response.

'Look at our skirts, or rather the hems.'

Mr Kendrick whistled through his teeth. 'They don't touch the ground.'

'Exactly. You won't see any female here with floor-length dresses, because they'd be impossible to keep even remotely clean, or else we would always walk around with our hands full, lifting them up an inch. Like Susanna did at her wedding.'

Alyssa let the information sink in. 'This, my dear gentlemen, means that whoever murdered Mr Harper had planned the deed in advance and stolen the dress from Rosie's trunk.'

'And returned it while we were all gone.' Mr Kendrick furrowed his brows. 'Practically anyone had access to the rooms.'

'Yes. The only thing that we do know about our man is that he is bold, plans ahead, and he's either shy or not interested in females at all,' Alyssa said.

'The first part I agree with, but the latter?' Dr Bryson rubbed his chin again.

Susanna said, 'I see. Anyone looking us over properly or

trying to catch a glimpse of bare skin would have noticed the dress-length.'

'We didn't,' Mr Kendrick said, 'and I will assure you that the doctor and I both count among your admirers – all of yours.'

Susanna chuckled. 'But you haven't been starved of our company for a long time.'

Mr Kendrick nodded. 'I'm inclined to believe Alyssa's reasoning.'

'Thank you.' Alyssa squeezed his hand, until Dr Bryson's look made her pull her hand away. 'And you, Doctor. Now we need to make Mr Abbott see sense. If only we could be absolutely sure why Mr Harper had to die.'

CHAPTER 10

Mr Osborne rubbed his tired eyes. The furnace made the room stuffy. He sat down on a desk pushed hard against the wall to make space for his shelves full of crucibles. Mr Abbott handed him Bert Harper's ledger. They worked in silence, comparing each entry with the initialled pouches. Alyssa, Mr Kendrick and Dr Bryson held their breath.

She probably had to thank Susanna for the permission to be present, but she hadn't asked and Mr Abbott hadn't mentioned it.

He closed the ledger. 'It's all there. She –'

'Or he,' Dr Bryson said. Alyssa gave him a grateful look.

'He or she was probably disturbed before she –'

Dr Bryson cleared his throat.

'Or he could make off with any of the gold.' Mr Abbott scratched his head.

'That also shows Rosie's innocence. Where would she have been able to hide the gold?'

Mr Abbott answered her without hesitation. 'Her room, bury it outside, hide it in the kitchen, until the boat arrives.'

'But nobody knows when that will be,' Alyssa said. 'That's what's bothering me. The murder was planned, but why not wait until an escape would have been easy? Or are there other ways except for the steamer?'

'My horse is the last one left in town, except that it wouldn't let a stranger ride it. We've also got a pack train station outside the town, but all that's left in the stables now are a couple of half-knackered mules. There used to be a dozen horses, but one half is still on the way East, and the others have been taken up into the Rockies about a month ago.'

He must have noticed Alyssa's confusion. 'A pack train's a group of horses or mules that carry heavy stuff everywhere boats or wagons can't go. That's why you find all these empty log-houses here. Folks hear of new claims, and off they go, following the gold.'

'But you're staying?' Mr Kendrick said.

'I've hung up gold-pan and sluice-box a while back.' Mr Abbott grinned, in the same open, easy way that had won Susanna's heart as soon as they'd arrived. 'As have a few others of the boys. You can't drag a wife and kiddies around the gold fields. Besides, it's a lot harder to hang on to the money if you don't settle down.'

The doctor nodded. 'Lot of gambling and drinking going on?'

'Not here, but you've seen the card tables on the *Serenity* yourself. And that's on the way to the fields, when most prospectors save their cash for equipment. Then imagine them let loose with their pockets full.'

'I used to practice in gold-mining towns in Australia until I heard that war with the South had broken out back home,' Dr Bryson said.

'Then I needn't tell you.'

As fascinating as the glimpse into the male psyche was, it did not help with their investigation. Alyssa steered the conversation back to important matters.

'That means, there are men out and about who usually live here.'

Mr Abbott agreed.

'Which also means, they are well acquainted with the hotel and Mr Harper's habits.'

'Sure.' Mr Abbott picked up a few of the leather pouches. 'These here belong to the Michaels' brothers. They're your neighbours when they're in town, Doctor.' He weighed them in his hand. 'Not bad. I wonder how much that is in dollars.'

Mr Osborne reached for one of the pouches and said, 'If you give me a few days, I should be able to give you an estimate.'

'You're on.' Mr Abbott picked up one of the bone-ash containers. 'I've never seen a fire assay done before.'

'It's easier than it sounds, if you know what you're doing.' Mr Osborne's voice took on an eager note. Metallurgy must be another passion of his, like astronomy, Alyssa thought.

'You're a man of many hidden talents,' Mr Kendrick said.

Mr Osborne gave him a rueful half-smile. 'I tend not to talk about these things. There's enough people believe that a bank assayor might have some gold in his possession.'

He opened a tin trunk and took out beakers, jars full of powdery substances and iron molds.

'It's quite a simple ancient method,' he said, He picked out a small bone-ash container. 'This is the crucible, and when I put in fluxes – they are the stuff that helps make ore fluid and removes impurities from the slag – in this case ground charcoal and powdered lead oxide, and add the crushed rock, this will separate in the furnace. The lead will alloy with the precious metals and the rock will combine with the fluxes and form a slag. I tip everything into the mould, and the slag will float to the top, leaving a button at the bottom.'

Alyssa tried to follow him, but judging by Mr Kendrick's and Mr Abbott's glazed expressions they had their problems, too.

'I thought we were already talking about gold nuggets,' Mr Kendrick said. 'Wouldn't gold washed from the rivers be already separated from the rocks?'

'It depends.' Mr Osborne opened a pouch and shook out some of the contents into a tin bowl. His eyes narrowed. He held up the bowl to the lamp. Amidst a few greyish lumps, two bright-yellow clumps gleamed in the bright light.

Mr Osborne put down the bowl and selected a pocket knife and a small hammer from the trunk. His mouth took on a grim line starkly at odds with his usual kind and effusive manner.

He picked up a piece of the gold and shaved off a slice with the knife.

'Pyrite,' he said. 'Fool's gold. This stuff is worthless.'

CHAPTER 11

'Impossible.' Mr Abbott grabbed the gleaming nugget and held it under the light.

'May I?' Mr Osborne took the doubtful object, laid it onto the table and whacked it with the hammer. It crumbled. 'I'm sorry,' he said.

Mr Abbott groaned.

'There could be a perfectly reasonable explanation,' Mr Kendrick said. 'What do you say, doctor? Don't I recollect you regaling us one night with stories about men with metallurgical experience who lugged home hundredweights of the stuff in the conviction they'd struck gold?'

'Is there any real gold in the pouch?' Mr Abbott recovered from his initial shock.

The banker scrutinised the greyish lumps. 'These appear genuine enough. I'll do a proper assay later. After we've sorted out the pyrite.'

The results were disheartening. In each of the dozen pouches they opened were at least two lumps of fool's gold, more than a pound altogether. Mr Abbott's face grew graver and graver.

'You don't have any gold here yourself, Abbott?' Mr Kendrick made the final entry against Bert's ledger, as dictated by Mr Osborne.

'I took mine down river to Victoria and put it in the bank.'

'That's a long trip,' Dr Bryson said. 'Why didn't you use the bank here?'

'What bank? All your predecessor did, Mr Osborne, was stuff everything into a pitiful excuse for a strongbox and saunter down to the hotel until he finally chucked it in after the last winter. Why do you think Bert stored so many valuables?' He gave the pile of pyrite a disgusted flick. 'Or what we thought were valuables.'

'Well, it's a very young Crown colony,' Mr Kendrick said. 'Institutions don't grow overnight.'

'Don't get me wrong; I'm not complaining. Simply saying.'

'Has anyone found fool's gold hereabouts before?' Alyssa asked.

Mr Abbott shook his head in a manner that allowed for no doubt.

'That's what's changed, then.' She picked up a piece of pyrite. 'For the first time, somebody would be able to tell real gold from worthless bits of – what is it made of?'

'It's a mineral.' Mr Osborne sighed. 'And if you're sure it hasn't been known to occur along here –'

'That's why Mr Harper had to die. The murderer must have

exchanged real gold for these lumps before Mr Osborne opened for business. It was the last opportunity.'

The silence was so complete they could hear Hannah walk around in the adjoining room.

'It could still have been Rosie.' Mr Abbott slammed his hand on the pile of fool's gold, smashing another piece in the process.

'Where would she get pyrite?' Alyssa looked around for support. Mr Osborne gave her a brief pat on the hand. Hannah had chosen well.

Mr Abbott said, 'She could have gotten it from anyone between leaving your company and arriving in town.'

'We didn't mean to deceive anyone.' Alyssa's face grew hot.

'Look here, it's fine. I understand why you all pretended not to know her from Adam, but that doesn't change the fact that she's got a bit of a history, and she could have done it.'

'No. And I'll prove it.' Alyssa selected the biggest lump of pyrite. 'If I may?'

Rosie sidled out of her room. Alyssa found no other word to describe it; almost as if the usually so cock-sure girl found herself afraid of every step.

'Mr Abbott has got a few questions,' Alyssa said, dropping the pyrite behind her back. 'Don't worry.'

She stepped aside, allowing Rosie's gaze to fall onto the yellow nugget. Hannah noticed it too, but Mr Kendrick held her back.

Rosie stooped and picked it up, awe spreading on her face.

She looked at it with naked longing as she handed it over to Hannah.

Mr Osborne winked at his wife.

'Thanks, Rosie.' Hannah handed the pyrite to her husband. 'I don't know about you, but I could do with a cup of tea and a few biscuits. We didn't want to have anything without you.'

They sat down as if this were a perfectly normal social visit. Rosie clung to Hannah's side as she nibbled a biscuit.

'Your questions, Mr Abbott,' Alyssa reminded him.

'Yes. How did you come here?'

'Same as everyone. On the boat.'

'And how did you pay for your fare?'

Rosie looked to Alyssa for support. Alyssa signalled her that she should answer.

'I got a dollar, and I said that I'd work for my trip if it ain't enough.'

'And did you?'

'Work? Yeah, pretty much. I helped in the kitchen, same as here. I ain't done nothing wrong!' She broke into a wail. 'Alyssa, you tell him.'

'Shh.' Alyssa rubbed Rosie's thin shoulder. 'Stay calm, and it'll all be good.'

'How can I be sure you're not lying? Again?' Mr Abbott made a forceful interrogator, so much so that Mr Kendrick stepped in. 'The girl's been through enough already.'

'That's as it may be, but I'm in charge of this investigation. It's my duty as the constable, and I intend to do right by the Queen and the people of this town.'

He addressed Rosie again. 'I'm aware that you used to be part of this group, but decided to search your luck elsewhere, until you changed your mind.'

Rosie's bottom lip wobbled. 'I already said to Matron that I'm sorry. I've been stupid, but that's not a crime.'

'Have you seen any gambling on the ship? Or played at cards yourself, or acted as a mascot?' Rosie's confusion was palpable.

Alyssa said,' What Mr Abbott wants to establish is, have you seen anyone flaunting gold?'

Rosie's gaze went to the pyrite that Mr Osborne had placed on the mantel, underneath the portrait of Queen Victoria.

'A couple of coins is all,' she said. 'I got out of the saloon right after dinner. I didn't like some of the looks the fellows gave me.' A reddish tinge spread over her throat. 'No offense if they're your friends, Mr Abbott.'

'None taken.' He brushed a biscuit crumb of his jacket. 'That'll be all for now. If you'd go to your room, we'll all leave Mr and Mrs Osborne in peace.'

Rosie almost pushed Alyssa off her chair in her haste to obey. Alyssa chuckled and motioned Mr Abbott to observe Rosie's dress hem. It fell a good inch short of the floor. There was no way it would have caught any dirt on the ground, and the stained dress was no longer than this.

Susanna must have waited with bated breath for her husband, because the door flew open before he could turn the handle.

Alyssa felt like an intruder when she saw Susanna's face light up as Mr Abbott hugged her and pressed a kiss onto her hair.

Mr Kendrick and the doctor both had the grace to turn their backs to the couple.

'Are you staying for dinner?' Susanna patted her hair back into place.

'Thank you, but your husband asked us in for a quick chat before we'll all be on our way,' Mr Kendrick said.

'But where are you going to eat if the hotel is closed?'

'You're as considerate as you are kind, but the doctor and I will be able to fend for ourselves for a bit, and I'm sure Mrs Wainwright has taken care of everything else.'

'We'll search the premises properly in the morning, and after that I don't see why the hotel couldn't be reopened, if we find someone willing to assist Peg-Leg.' Mr Abbott pulled a face. 'It's been tough enough keeping him away. The hotel's been his life since he had that accident.'

'I did wonder about that,' Mr Bryson said.

'It's not a secret. He and Bert were prospecting up north, where the mountains start, and Peg-Leg slipped and bust his knee. He'd have been a goner out there in the wilderness if Bert hadn't carried him all the way to their pack horses.' He rubbed his forehead. 'It's been hitting him mighty hard.'

'Poor Peg-Leg.' Susanna's blue eyes darkened in sympathy. 'But what about Rosie?'

'I'm inclined to believe Miss Chalmers. I watched her when she picked up the useless piece of rubbish. No way did she realise what it was, so she wouldn't have switched the nuggets.'

Susanna clapped her hands. 'You'll let her go?'

He nodded, just as Alyssa said, 'No. You can't do that.'

'Why not, if she's innocent?'

'Simply because she's innocent it doesn't mean that everybody else will think so. What about Peg-Leg? You said yourself how close he and Mr Harper were. Rosie's a stranger, and it's much easier to believe in the guilt of somebody who's not close to you.' Alyssa glanced at Mr Kendrick and Dr Bryson, who both moved up to her as if to support her claim.

'It also means that the real murderer will think himself safe, and that his infamous ploy has worked.'

Mr Abbott's brow clouded over. 'I hate the thought of that girl being thought of as a common criminal.'

Susanna stroked his cheek. 'She won't mind, not if it keeps her safe. You leave the rest to Aly – to all of us, and together we will make sure that we get to the bottom of this.'

Alyssa caught her wink, and the clever way Susanna had masked her slip of the tongue. Newlywed as she was, she'd clearly mastered the gentle steering of her husband.

'Good-night,' she said. 'And thank you for your fairness and understanding.'

The next morning, Mr Wainwright fetched Alyssa after breakfast. Thin worry-lines crisscrossed his forehead. His wife stayed behind, to organise a few things. She looked fit to drop. She'd always taken her duties very seriously, and even though she had officially fulfilled her original task of delivering the girls safely to their new home, she'd only consider her job done once every girl was settled.

Nevertheless, she bore up well, Alyssa thought. Before she and Mr Wainwright were out of the door, Mrs Wainwright already sketched out a plan on how to take over the hotel kitchen.

Mr Abbott unlocked the hotel door. A burly man tried to push inside after him, but Mr Kendrick and the doctor managed to hold him back. He struggled to break free, his greasy hat shadowing his face.

Alyssa had seen him before, but where?

'Let go of me, you dirty rotters.' The man spat on the ground.

Mr Abbott half-turned. 'What do you want, Fred?'

'What's rightfully mine, that's what.' Fred glanced furtively around. 'Bert had something he kept for me.'

'Is that right? Last time I saw you he came darn close to catching you with his whip-end.'

Now Alyssa remembered. Fred was the man they'd seen being chased by the publican.

'Tell your fellows to let go.'

Mr Abbott nodded, and Mr Kendrick and the doctor unhanded the man, obviously glad to step back from Fred, who reeked of stale beer, sweat and horse-stable.

Alyssa sniffed the pungent air and fanned herself. Yes, the stench was unmistakable. She made a mental note to visit the pack train station and find out if Fred had anything to do with it. Or if anyone else apart from Mr Abbott had a horse. It would have been no problem for a man who knew his way around, to come to town under the cover of darkness, tether his horse in a safe distance, murder Bert, and ride off again. The waning moon still gave off enough light for a man.

'Tell me what of yours Bert had, and I'll have a look for you,' Mr Abbott said. 'My best offer.'

Fred pushed a piece of chewing tobacco between gum and cheek. 'A bottle. It's got my initials on it. Ask Peg-Leg if you don't believe me.'

'Right. If I find it, I'll let you know. And now get a move on.'

Mr Abbott locked and bolted the door behind them. The hotel already looked unkempt and forlorn, Alyssa thought, with patches of beer-soaked sawdust and the stuffiness of a room in desperate need of airing. She longed to fling open the windows, to hear Rosie complaining in the kitchen, and to see Bert leaning against the counter. Most of all she longed for normalcy. Instead, they lived with a murderer in their midst.

Mr Abbott squatted behind the bar. He put an unopened whisky bottle on the counter. The second bottle contained less than an inch of alcohol. He reached behind a beer barrel. Another bottle, with a half-peeled off label and the initials F K on it. He pulled out the cork, sniffed it and made a grimace. 'Jeez.'

'Moonshine?' the doctor asked. He caught a whiff and coughed. 'That stuff could make you go blind. I didn't take Bert for stupid enough to deal in this.'

'He wouldn't. Fred either hid it here himself, because he bunks with other fellows, and he didn't feel like sharing, or Peg-Leg kept it for him. Can't say no, can Peg-Leg.'

He corked the bottle again. 'Now, for the rooms.'

The third step from the top squeaked as Alyssa trod in it. She stood still, listening while the doctor and Mr Kendrick followed her. The other steps of the staircase were silent. She'd have to ask Rosie if she had heard anything during the night, although the murderer most likely used the outside staircase. The door leading to it came as a surprise. It was solid enough, with its tightly fitted oak boards, but it had no lock, only two bolts from the inside.

Alyssa pushed them upright. They moved with ease, and noiselessly. Had the door been bolted when she first saw it? She couldn't remember. One more thing to find out.

Bert's room held no secrets. A wardrobe, with a couple of shirts, pants and the too tight suit he'd worn to the wedding. A pair of scarlet suspenders was stuffed in a drawer, on top of a vest. Alyssa averted her gaze as Mr Abbot searched through the drawer, to spare him any embarrassment should he uncover something not deemed suitable for female eyes.

Rosie's room contained only her wooden box, with its few garments, and to Alyssa's surprise, a rag-doll wrapped in a shift. The men stood aside as Alyssa took out each garment, spread it on the bed and folded it again. The rag-doll she set aside. Its fabric had turned grey with age, and thinned where small hands might have clutched it tightly each night.

Alyssa blinked back sudden tears. Poor Rosie; pushing everyone away, gaining her comfort from this pathetic little doll. She would take it to her, as soon as she could.

The last garment went back into the box. Mr Kendrick looked under the table. He lifted the mattress. On one of the slats in the centre, a yellowish lump rested. Pyrite.

Alyssa snatched it off the slat, and Mr Kendrick let the

mattress fall into place. Mr Abbott looked puzzled. 'That doesn't make sense.'

'Why?' Dr Bryson finally broke his silence. His behaviour these last few days had been trying, as if he wasn't there half of the time. But this sounded like her old friend; interested, alert, and most of all, on her side.

'We know it's not gold. Why place it there? Or did she do it herself, because she was taken in?'

'Whoever did this, put the fool's gold here after Rosie moved out of the room,' Alyssa said.

'You can't be sure.' Mr Abbott twisted his wedding band.

'Remember how easily Mr Osborne crushed the other sample? And we're to believe that Rosie, who flings herself into her bed, could land with her full weight on this nugget and not at least chip it? Even if the mattress cushioned it?'

'That's easy enough to test,' the doctor said.

'What's important is, how did the person get in? Was the upstairs door bolted when we left?'

They stared at each other, in growing frustration. Nobody felt sure enough to speak out.

'Which means, anybody could have entered. Or they could have come in through the kitchen door, if that was also unbolted.'

'I checked that one.' Mr Abbott sounded remorseful. 'We're not used to dealing with these things, and I –'

'You probably had other thing on your mind, the morning after your wedding.' Mr Kendrick slapped him on the back. 'We are all equally to blame.'

'But at least we have found out little bit more.' Alyssa lifted her thumb. 'The murderer came back, to implicate Rosie even further.' Her forefinger went up. 'He didn't pay her or any of us enough attention to realise that our dresses are too short to touch the floor.' The third, fourth and fifth finger followed. 'He possessed a bag full of pyrite which he probably did not find in his gold pan. He took Rosie's dress to make the tracks in Mr Harper's room while Rosie was downstairs, working, and hid it in her box before the murder. Mr Harper wouldn't have paid any attention to the floorboards. And he's level-headed enough to have planned all this after finding out that Mr Osborne intended to assay the gold.'

Peg-Leg's door was locked. Mr Abbott shrugged his shoulders. 'I can ask him for the key if any of you thinks that searching his premises will do any good?'

None of them could.

The kitchen itself delivered one interesting clue, from Alyssa's point of view. Its back door also was closed with two bolts. Proper locks appeared to be rare in this town. That meant that the murderer had crept up the outside staircase, because Rosie would never have left the door unsecured, with so many precious foodstuffs around.

'Why?' Mr Abbott asked. 'Most folks here came to Bert's for food and only had a few sides of bacon and some bread at home. Much easier that way.'

'Yes, but it wouldn't have been like that when Rosie grew up. And if you'd seen the spectacle that Bert made when he thought that Rosie had helped herself to sugar you'd understand why she would never forget to bolt that door.'

'There's of course another explanation.'

Alyssa waited for Mr Abbott to continue. He tugged at his

moustache. 'Rosie could have opened it for someone else. She was pretty, well, friendly with the men.'

'But she was also constantly working, and Matron made it exceedingly clear that she'd watch her.' Dr Bryson frowned. 'Unless – did someone else travel on the steamer with Rosie? Some of your men?'

'One or two,' Mr Abbott said. 'I'll make sure.'

'Good. I wouldn't put it past Rosie to sneak out for a moonlight meeting, and giving someone else the chance to enter the hotel unseen.'

Alyssa glared at the doctor. 'In which case she'd also be an innocent pawn. But I will ask her, privately.'

He returned her gaze with a mixture of warmth and sadness. 'I'm sorry if I offended your sensibilities, but we can't ignore any possibility.'

He accompanied Alyssa to the train pack station. For once, Mr Kendrick had excused himself with other tasks he'd already agree to assist Mr Abbott with.

The doctor adjusted her steps so they matched hers, but their usual harmony was gone, and it had nothing to do with Rosie.

Alyssa waited for him to break the silence. She stole a sideways glance at his troubled face.

The grass rustled as her skirt skimmed the long blades. Insects buzzed from flower to flower, and far over their heads two eagles circled. Apart from that, everything was so quiet that Alyssa could hear her own heartbeat in her ears.

'Have I done something wrong?' she asked.

He stopped mid-stride. 'I'm sorry?'

'You barely talk to me. You barely talk to anyone. If it's not me, is it because you are stuck here, instead of travelling onwards? Do these few days really make such a big difference after all those long months at sea?' She crossed her arms across her chest, intent on clearing the air between them for good, or at least stop holding on to a friendship that no longer existed.

'It's got nothing to do with you.' He turned away, facing the distant mountains. 'But what good am I, here? There's people out there dying of smallpox, and I'm of no help. In my own country, soldiers tear each other apart on the battlefields, and I'm of no help. I left Australia to serve as a field surgeon. Instead I'm here, twiddling my thumbs.'

'You're helping Rosie.'

'But you don't need me for that.' He made a half-turn, looking her straight into the eyes. There was no twinkle left, no sign of good humour, only unfiltered pain. 'Mr Kendrick would be of just as much assistance, and don't tell me that's not true.'

'Why don't you leave?' she asked. 'No-one here is ill. Why don't you secure one of the mules that we're supposed to find in the stables and leave? Somebody will surely be able to give you a rough map.' She took great trouble to avoid any wobble in her voice. If he wanted to leave, so be it.

'Yes.' He reached for her hand but stopped an inch away from touching her. 'Except that I'd be crazy to venture out on my own.'

'The steamer must run again very soon,' she said, her voice still remarkably level. 'From Port Victoria it should be easy to reach one of the towns on the American side of the border. You told me yourself that huge parts of your native country are well-connected with railways.'

'Not huge parts, but yes.' He chuckled, but his chirpiness didn't reach his eyes. 'You appear to be keen on getting rid of me.'

'No, but I'd rather see you leave than watch you suffer.'

This time his hand did clasp hers, and for a fleeting moment all was well.

They'd reached the station, which consisted of two large paddocks which held three mules grazing in the sunshine, and a couple of long wooden buildings, with a covered porch in front of one of them. On the porch, a grizzled man rocked in his chair, a corncob-pipe in his mouth.

Alyssa and the doctor stood less than three feet away, when the man brought his chair to a standstill.

'You must be the new folks,' he said, scratching his chest. Two buttons were missing from his faded green shirt, and Alyssa saw grey hairs poking out through his greyish vest. She gave him a smile and a small curtsy, doing her best to look elsewhere.

'I'm Dr Bryson, and this lady is Miss Chalmers.'

'Yeah?'

'Mr Abbott sends his regards. He asked me to go over a few things with you.'

The man guffawed. 'Too busy with his bit of petticoat to pay good old Barry a visit, eh?'

The affable expression vanished from the doctor's face in the blink of an eye. 'I'd prefer you keep a civil tongue in your mouth when you are talking about Mrs Abbott.'

'Sweet on her yourself, eh? What you doing with this piece of muslin then?'

'I would also prefer it if you could keep a civil tongue when you talk about Miss Chalmers. Or any other lady.'

Barry scratched himself again, with a rasping noise that made Alyssa itch.

'No harm meant, Doc. Maybe I don't talk fancy like you, especially with the ladies. Sorry, Miss, if I hurt your delicate soul.'

Despite herself, she felt her lips twitch. 'Don't think about it.'

Barry pushed himself off his chair and made an exaggerated bow. 'What can I do for you folks?'

'You've heard what happened?'

Barry's eyes narrowed. 'Bert? Yeah. Shame that. Is it a true that it's a skirt who did him in? Pardon me, a lady?'

'Mr Abbott is still looking into the business.' Dr Bryson shaded his eyes against the dazzling sun. He should wear a hat, Alyssa thought, for once glad of the protection her bonnet afforded her.

'What's it got to do with me?' Barry drew on his pipe, blowing out a series of perfect circles. 'I haven't set foot into town in at least a fortnight.'

'Why?' Alyssa asked.

'Because I didn't want to watch my mates go all silly over a bit of petti – a few ladies. This bride business had nothing to do with me, and anyway, I had to send off the last pack train.'

'When did that set off?' The doctor leant against the porch railing, as if he couldn't have asked for anything better than a chat. 'And how does it work? I've never seen a pack train.'

Barry shook his head in disbelief. 'You haven't? What do they do in Australia?'

'I'm from Boston.'

'Is that so.' He shrugged. 'It's horses, and men. Sometimes a few mules, but they're harder to steer. You pack your things onto the horse – tent canvas, bedroll, panning equipment, and then you go into the wilderness. Last time it was twenty men all heading for the Cariboo.'

Alyssa was all but forgotten as he warmed to his theme. 'It's a sight to behold, I'm telling you. The horses prancing, and the men all willing to test their mettle against storms and bitter cold, grizzly bears as big as two men, black bears that can outrun you any given day.' He shook his head in admiration. 'If I were ten years younger, I'd be off like a shot, too. But as it is, I'm stuck here.'

'How do you get the horses back?' The doctor winked at Alyssa. She strolled over to the paddock fence. One of the mules lifted its head, and slowly made its way towards her.

Barry said, 'The team leader and his partner take care of that, mostly. You can never be too sure, because it's a risky trip, but we don't lose that many horses.'

'How often do the pack trains set off?'

'Depends on what's going on with the gold.' Barry sucked on his pipe. 'See, Mister –'

'Bryson, Dr Bryson.'

'Doc. We're not the first stop, right. There's the big pack train station a few days' ride between here and Port Victoria. A few men start out there, take along some spare horses, and on they go, picking up more men and horses along the way.'

The mule ambled up to the fence. Alyssa stretched out her hand. The animal nuzzled it. She stroked the rough fur on its nose. The mule blew out soft, hot air and rubbed its head on Alyssa's hand.

'Where does the train end?'

'Wherever the latest gold finds are. Or if the terrain gets too rough for the horses.'

'And the team leader leaves the men without a single horse? What about the tribes? What do they say?'

'They mostly keep themselves to themselves. Sometimes they hawk a few wares, or hire themselves out as scouts, but usually they stay out of the way.' Barry pointed backwards. A rifle hung under the sloping roof of the building, easy enough for him to reach. 'You never know who's coming after you in these parts, and a man might easily make a mistake at night, when something scarpers through the woods.'

His voice had turned sly, as if he wanted to see their reaction.

Alyssa rubbed the mule's stubbly mane. She wouldn't say a single word, although Barry's implications made her angry. Dr Bryson might not understand the meaning, but to her it was obvious that the prospectors would kill any native who stood in their way.

Dr Bryson half-turned towards her and gave her a warning signal not to interfere. She concentrated on her new four-legged friend instead.

'Do the men ever return?'

'Sure, some of them. You got to cash in your gold somewhere.'

'How do they get back?'

'Wait for new arrivals and return with the horses. Easiest that way, when you can ride because the horse doesn't carry anything. Or they do what they've always done, use their own two legs.'

Dr Bryson shaded his eyes again.

'You ought to get yourself a decent hat,' Barry said.

'But how? The steamer won't run until the smallpox danger is over.'

'I'm not afraid of any pox. It's usually the tribes get it. Us whites have someone watching over us. And the store has most things you need.'

'Anyone returning from the gold fields lately?'

'A few men, after the spring thaw.' Barry pulled a disgusted face. 'A man loses his taste for adventure, next thing you know he's shackled himself to home and hearth. Take Abbott. Now he was someone. Good shot, clear head, and afraid of nothing. Less than a year later, he's taken to wearing a fob-watch on a gold-chain, pushing paper in the name of the Queen, and next thing he'll be having babies crawling all over the place.'

'Was Bert like that?'

Barry fished a spoon-like scraper out of his shirt pocket and broke up the ash in the pipe-bowl. 'Too smart to be caught out.' He banged the pipe against the arm of his rocking-chair. Ash flew out and settled next to his feet, with a few bits drifting onto his boot. He scraped out the remaining plug of tobacco.

'He might have had an eye for a bit of petticoat once in a while, but he'd stay clear of the priest. Clever man, was Bert. You open a hotel, and the gold comes to you instead of you going after the gold.'

The mule spread its hind legs. Half a dozen steaming pats plonked onto the grass. The whole paddock was generously dotted with them. Barry certainly did not seem to bother to get rid of the manure, although a decent fertiliser would do wonders if one wanted to increase a harvest. She'd talk to Nellie, about her and her beau's ideas for a farm.

'Did Bert have any sense of adventure left?' the doctor asked.

'You bet he did. But he always knew when to stop. It was a sign, was Peg-Leg's accident.'

'That's when they opened the hotel?'

'He did, Bert. Hired a few men to help him build the place, got in a few dozen barrels of beer before he started to brew his own, and never looked back. Mind, he did it as much for Peg-Leg. Give him a job when he could walk again.'

'That was kind,' Alyssa said.

'Damn right it was.' Barry fished a strand of tobacco out of his mouth. A few more strands dotted his beard. 'Makes my blood boil to think of someone doing him in.'

'What do you think is going to happen to the hotel? Will Peg-Leg take over?'

'One of Bert's brothers might run it. Peg-Leg ain't got no money. Never could hold on to it, could he, with his bad luck at cards.'

The doctor stretched and rolled back his shoulders. 'Do you have any saddles for the mules? It's been a long time since I had the chance for a ride.'

Barry pushed open the door and beckoned the doctor to follow him. Alyssa stayed away; the man clearly did not enjoy female company.

In the dim light of the long stable building, Alyssa saw several horse bits, ropes, blankets and three saddles. A long row of boxes stood empty, but the smell of manure and damp straw still lingered in the air. Barry probably saw no reason to hurry with mucking out the stables once the animals were gone.

Inside the stench must be suffocating. Out here, she could bear it; it certainly was no worse than the reek of that man who had tried to get into the hotel. Fred, that was the name.

The doctor pressed a coin into Barry's hand and patted him on the back. 'Tomorrow, then,' he said. Barry winked at Alyssa and tapped his nose.

'What was that all about?'

'You and I, my dear Alyssa, are going for a mule-ride.'

She bit her lip. It would be fun, to get away from the town and explore the woods, or venture along the riverside, but the girls' tongues already wagged about her, and the doctor, and Mr Kendrick.

'I've hired all three mules, if you don't feel safe with no-one but me as company.' His light tone masked a question. She made up her mind. 'I'd like that, but you'll explain to Matron that I'm not a loose woman who's leading you both on.'

He burst into the first real laughter she'd heard from him since their arrival. 'You do have a lurid imagination. Believe me, if Mrs Wainwright thinks anything about it, it's that we men are the ones to blame.'

'In this case I'd better let her know that I'm aware that none of you has any intention on my heart or hand.'

His laughter stopped. 'There is no ladies' side-saddle. I should have thought of that.'

She trod into a hole; a burrow of sorts most likely. He took her arm.

'Careful,' he said. 'I'd hate to see you as my patient.'

'I'll promise you won't have to.' She smiled at him, happy to see their old companionship restored.

'Are you up for another stroll after lunch? And maybe Mr Kendrick could join us,' she said.

'What are you thinking of?'

'According to your new friend it's very unlikely that our murderer had come to town on horseback, but Fred stank like he'd slept in horse muck. If we hear a horse, or find a pile of manure between the hotel and the outskirts of town, towards the mountains, that would change things, wouldn't it?'

As soon as they'd returned to the hotel, the light breeze picked up speed, chasing dark clouds across a sky that minutes before had been the soft blue of periwinkles, dotted with white cloud puffs. Alyssa still untied her bonnet as the first heavy drops hit the metal roof.

She and the doctor had to squeeze in next to the wall, because the whole town seemed to have descended onto the hotel, where Nellie and Harriet brought out bowl after bowl of steaming stew. Susanna floated from group to group, ushering men to the table and hurrying eaters to finish up, all with the greatest ease.

Her husband stood behind the bar, watching her with obvious pride. Dr Bryson led Alyssa through the throng, until they'd reached the counter.

'Have we missed another party?' Dr Bryson planted his hands on the counter, practically embracing Alyssa to protect her from being jolted by the crowd.

'You've only got your own group to blame.' Mr Abbott filled another coffee-pot. He cupped his hands in front of his mouth. 'Sorry, boys, no beer until dinner.' The men moved back a little. 'Stand in line, and you'll all get some coffee. And you step away from my wife, Alfie Harper.'

Susanna blew him a kiss. A few of the men whistled, until they caught Mr Abbott's icy glare.

Alfie Harper. That must be Bert's brother, Alyssa thought as she watched a man back away from Susanna hastily enough to stumble over another man's foot. He certainly carried a strong resemblance to the dead man.

'Have we seen him before?' she asked the doctor. 'You can let go of me now, thank you.'

'Oh. Sorry.' He lifted his left arm off the counter. 'Seen whom?'

'Alfie Harper.' She nodded towards the man. Dr Bryson shrugged after a short consideration. 'Don't think so, but to my shame I haven't paid over much attention to anyone in good health.' He reached for the coffeepot. 'Can I have two mugs? And why is this congregation our fault?'

'What do you expect when you let the best cooks this side of the border take over the cooking? Five minutes after the first group had stuffed themselves like pigs, we almost had a riot on our hands,' Mr Abbott said.

'You're here to keep order?'

'You better believe that. And to keep an eye on my wife.' He chuckled. 'You don't think there'd be a drop left to drink if the boys didn't have me standing between them and the booze?' Again, he formed a funnel with his hands. 'Anyone trying to get behind this bar will be banned for a week, do you hear me?'

Alyssa suppressed a grin. Bert's whip would have been useful to keep the men at bay, but Mr Abbott's authority still carried enough weight to have one after another shuffle away, pretending they didn't mind.

Nellie and Harriet rushed in and out of the kitchen, with stew, dumplings and bread that steamed when the crust was torn open. The girls glowed with happiness, as they received grateful looks and words of praise from the hungry men.

They'd arrived, in the real sense of the word. Here they'd be accepted as equals, instead of being judged by virtue of birth and family connections.

Alyssa's stomach reminded her that apart from a slice of fried bread in the morning she hadn't eaten anything.

Dr Bryson followed her hungry gaze. 'How about taking some food over to the Osbornes? Unless they've already been here, Abbott?'

'No. I'd come with you, but I think I'd better – Fred Keller, don't you believe I don't see your rotten carcass. If you're hungry, eat. If not, come back in the evening.'

'What about my bottle?' Fred pounded an oversized fist on the bar counter.

'Good question. You want to tell me where you got it from?' Mr Abbott bared his teeth. Fred took a step back and stumbled into Alfie Harper, who'd just grabbed a bowl with stew. The hot liquid splashed over Alfie's leather waistcoat. He scowled at

Fred, who turned tail without so much as a moment's hesitation.

Alfie set the bowl down next to Alyssa, giving her a discreet glance. 'Mind if I eat here, Miss? Tom?'

Alyssa shook her head and moved a few inches closer to the doctor, to afford Alfie enough space.

'Not a problem,' Mr Abbott said. 'Why don't you come and help me here, once you're finished? After all, it's going to be your hotel.'

Fred dropped his spoon as Peg-Leg was pushed against him by a quartet of men that Alyssa had seen but dimly before. None of them had courted any of her friends, to her satisfaction. Most of the prospectors had taken care with their appearance and their manners, but if these four had more than a fleeting acquaintance with water and soap she'd be surprised.

True, she hadn't been able to see much of their faces, between the wide-brimmed hats and the beards that covered up everything between cheekbones and chest, but their clothes were stiff with sweat and dirt. That needed to change.

Dr Bryson must have read her mind, because he said, 'Maybe Matron could set up a laundry once she's done here.'

He beckoned over to Susanna, who expertly weaved her way through the crowd. 'Can you possibly make sure that we can collect a meal for us and the Osbornes? We'll come round the back door.'

Susanna fanned her flushed cheeks and nodded. 'Sure. Two minutes?' She sashayed away.

'Tell your wife thank you,' Alyssa said. 'I hope we'll see her later, once she has finished here.'

'That's what I hope too. Although – yes, boys you can have coffee, but that's all.' He shoved over the pot to Will Turner, the owner of the hardware store and probable seller of the crowbar used to break open Bert's strongbox. She hadn't talked to him yet, but this needed to change, she decided as the doctor clasped her elbow and steered her towards the door.

Hannah tapped three times on Rosie's door. Rosie's eyes lit up in her strained face as she sniffed in the aromas of the food bowls. She reached for the bread. Hannah slapped her hand.

'Manners!'

Rosie's eyes narrowed for a second, but she managed to say, 'Sorry.'

Hannah opened a cupboard and took out bone china plates and silver cutlery that would have befitted a gentleman's residence. 'Not bad for girls from Tin Pan Alley,' Hannah said with a hint of pride in her voice as she handed them to Rosie, who deftly laid the table. 'They're heirlooms, and there's two boxes full of things that Mr Osborne hasn't even opened yet.'

She took a silver bell from the mantel and shook it. Alyssa had expected a delicate tinkle, but instead the clapper clanged loud enough to summon Mr Osborne and Mr Kendrick.

'That's where you've been hiding.' Dr Bryson gave his friend a resounding pat on the shoulder.

'Some of us like to make ourselves useful. I'm pretty sure that Mr Osborne will tell you what an invaluable assistant I am.' Mr Kendrick lowered his voice. 'I didn't like the idea of one man alone with all this gold, and in charge of protecting two ladies as well.' He held out his plate for Hannah to fill up.

'If this tastes half as good as it smells, we're in for a treat.'

'It wasn't me who cooked this.' Hannah tasted a spoonful. 'Not bad, but I can do it as good. Although Rosie and I don't mind somebody else doing the work for us, do we?'

'How are things?' Rosie's eyes had lost most of their puffiness but dark circles spoke of a sleepless night.

'It's going to be fine. You trust Alyssa and us, right?' Dr Bryson used the calming voice he saved for patients.

Rosie nodded.

'It simply takes time. The important thing is, Mr Abbott believes in your innocence, and you're safe here.'

'He knows I didn't do it?' Rosie blew out a loud puff of air. 'Has he told folks?'

'No.' Alyssa wiped her plate clean with a piece of bread. 'As long as the murderer thinks that we have fallen for his ploy, he'll believe himself safe. It's our best way to catch him when he's off guard.'

Rosie shivered. 'Please hurry. Every time we hear as much as a footstep, I think they're coming for me.'

'We won't let that happen,' Mr Osborne said.

'To make it clear that this household has nothing to hide, you will have dinner at the hotel tonight with your wife, Mr Osborne,' Mr Kendrick said.

'Leave me all alone?' Rosie's pupils widened with fear.

'The doctor and I will stay here. Should anyone notice our absence, we're making a few shelves as a surprise for Mrs Osborne. We seafarers are famous for our practical skills, and there is no carpenter left in town.'

'What about me?' Alyssa asked.

'You'll be your charming self and get people to talk. I'm sure you have already discovered a few men who might prove of interest.' Mr Kendrick's smile warmed her heart.

Matron bustled around in the hotel kitchen, observing half a dozen girls scrubbing, scraping and slicing mountains of cabbage, onions, potatoes and large slabs of meat. She moved around in a constant, slow circle, a fond look in her eyes as she in turn praised her help-meets or reminded them not to waste anything.

The girls chatted away like starlings, to Alyssa's astonishment. Even Grace and Bertha, two red-haired sisters who barely spoke more than half a dozen words to anyone else and even after several months were hard for her to tell apart, giggled together with Nellie.

Alyssa grabbed a piece of sacking from a shelf at the back and tied it around her waist. Her wooden-soled boots echoed on the floor. Matron turned around, a tasting spoon with a few drops of a green soup in her hand. 'Alyssa?'

'Good afternoon. I'm here to help.'

Matron led the spoon to her mouth and moved her lips from side to side as she tasted the soup. Alyssa's lips twitched. During their sea voyage the girls had cooked for themselves, but their chaperone had never gone to such length to supervise their efforts. She must have set her heart on making sure that her flock presented themselves as wonderful matches to their potential husbands.

Matron dropped the spoon into a bowl filled with water. 'We're almost done with the preparations for tonight and tomorrow. A filling pea-soup, and another stew that can be reheated, we thought.'

'Would you like me to help with the serving?' Alyssa stepped closer to the soup pot that must have held at least two gallons.

Matron paused. It had become something like an unwritten law to excuse Alyssa from most chores, relying on her to teach them instead. Most of the girls could barely write more than their name when they left Australia. Now they read fluently, and although some of the still used their fingers to do their sums, numbers held no more fear for them.

Her different status allowed Matron to treat Alyssa as a confidante, but sometimes it could be a hindrance. Like now.

'Nellie? I'm sure I could be of use,' Alyssa said,

Nellie frowned.

'Please, Nellie, you don't think I'm useless.'

'Nah, it's –' Nellie swallowed, a rare sign of nerves. Alyssa gave her an encouraging nod, although she felt like shaking her. And Matron. It would be so easy if she could explain why she wanted to mingle with the Canadians, but she didn't dare. A word in the wrong ear, and the murderer would be on his guard.

'It's the men.' Nellie glared at the others, least they make joke. 'Some of them are – I got pinched at lunch. Twice.'

Matron gasped. The girls fell silent.

'You should have told me,' Matron said. 'Who was it?'

'Don't know. I don't have eyes in my back, do I?' Nellie sighed. 'That's how men are, Matron. I can handle it. But Alyssa –'

'I will be happy to give anyone a lesson in manners should the need arise,' Alyssa said. 'I would appreciate it, Matron, if you would let me take care of matters. We didn't come here to be treated with disrespect.'

'Indeed. I'll ask Mr Wainwright too, to keep his eyes open.'

'And Alyssa's beaus – I mean Mr Kendrick and the doctor will be there too.' Nellie winked at Alyssa, who decided to ignore that statement.

'Excellent,' she said. 'What do you want me to do?'

Nellie scrubbed the tables with soapy water. Alyssa wiped them off with a cloth that might once have been a sheet. But at least it was clean.

Together, they put stacks of plates, bowls, and cutlery ready, and placed a water jug on each table. It would hardly be needed, Alyssa thought as she saw Peg-Leg rolling a fresh barrel of beer behind the bar. She wondered where the beer was kept. If a storage room existed inside the hotel, the murderer could have hidden there until everyone fell asleep.

Peg-Leg wore a black armband over his left shirt-sleeve. Alyssa couldn't read his face, but every movement seemed to cost him an extra effort, and judging from the state of the sawdust he didn't have the heart to attend to his duties as if nothing had happened. Or maybe Bert's brother didn't want him to. Poor Peg-Leg; losing a friend and employer.

She counted the spoons and knifes automatically while her mind churned over the questions that needed answers.

'Eighteen, nineteen, we need another spoon here, Nellie.'

Nellie handed her one. 'You know it doesn't matter, right? They'll all squeeze in any old how.'

'Do we have any idea how many men to expect? Peg-Leg?'

He shrugged. 'I ain't keeping track of people.'

'But surely you're aware of how many men are in town and how many – never mind.'

Mr Abbott and Susanna came through the door, the sun on their back. It cast a halo over Susanna's head, and a few rays caught the small mirror behind the bar and sparked rainbows on its rim.

Mr Abbott took off his hat. 'Ladies.'

Nellie curtsied. 'Sir, and Ma'am.'

Susanna giggled. 'I always think you mean Matron, when you call me Ma'am.'

She linked her arm with Nellie's and squeezed it. 'Your turn next. Ma'am to be. But I better report to Mrs Wainwright for duty.'

Alyssa approached Mr Abbott. 'Could you make a list of the men remaining in town, so that we have estimated numbers for the cooking, and to make it easier to keep the tabs?'

'I should have thought of that.' He snapped his fingers. 'Pencil and paper, please, Peg-Leg.'

He put his hat on a table and pulled out a chair, his long legs outstretched in front of him, ankles crossed.

'Some of the men were asking me about her.' Peg-Leg squatted on the table, interrupting Mr Abbott's concentration. The nib on the pencil broke. Mr Abbott pulled out a pocketknife and sharpened the pencil, wood curls falling onto the ground

'Her. Oh, you mean Rosie.'

'Yeah, her. Seeing that we have no prison.'

Mr Abbott put the pocketknife away. 'It's taken care of.'

'Good.' Peg-Leg breathed a sigh of relief. 'I wouldn't want to be her if some of the lads found out where you've stashed her.' He waved his thumb at Susanna. 'You're not keeping Rosie close to Mrs Abbott, I hope. Can't be too careful.'

'I'll look after my wife, thanks, Peg-Leg. Now I'm sure you've got things to do.'

Peg-Leg shuffled off, dragging his bad leg.

'How bad is his injury?' Alyssa asked.

'He's got good days and bad days, but I'm no doctor. Speaking of which ...'

She squinted at the list. Depressingly long. 'The doctor and Mr Kendrick are busy tonight.'

He raised his eyebrows. 'Yes,' she said softly enough not to be overheard.

He checked his fob-watch. 'Almost six. You'll be busy any moment now.'

'Alyssa!'

'One moment, Susanna.'

'I'll have the finished list for you tomorrow morning.' Mr Abbott picked up the pencil again.

Susanna prodded the swing door to the kitchen with her foot. She too still wore the sturdy boots that for most of them were the single pair of footwear they owned, although her husband had presented her with the most impractical shoes Alyssa had seen in years, made of soft leather soles and blue silk uppers, beaded with glass pearls.

They fit Susanna's feet too, so Mr Abbott either had hidden talents, or he knew someone else who had. She'd have to ask him. Matron would love shoes like these, and her birthday was coming up in September.

'Are you listening?' Susanna asked.

'Sorry.'

'As I said, about ten seconds ago, if we prop the door open, it'd be easier to get in and out with the food, but then anybody could barge in and get under our feet.' She lowered her voice. 'Grace and Bertha'd have a fit. I wonder how they ever want to find a husband, if they can't even look at a man.'

'It's probably shyness. But you're right, we'll leave the door as it is.'

Two hours later her arms hurt from lifting heavy bowls high over her head as she made her way through the crowd. 'You'll soon get used to it,' Nellie said as she saw Alyssa rubbing her upper arms. 'This should be the last lot to feed, and then we'll have our own dinner.'

'Or we could have it now. There's enough space for us all to sit down.' She hoped it sounded casual. She'd caught snippets of conversation while serving the men, but now, with stew in their bellies and beer beside them, the Canadians loosened up.

'If you really think so.' Nellie hesitated.

'I'll ask Matron.'

She poked her head into the kitchen. Matron got up from an armchair that her husband had brought for her less than an hour ago. Alyssa folded her hands demurely in her lap. 'If you have no objections, Matron, now would be a good time for us all to eat. There's enough space, and we don't want to give the impression that we're domestic help, do we?'

Five minutes later, Alyssa dipped her spoon into the rich stew, while listening to the group at the table next to hers, with Alfie Harper at its centre.

Hannah and Mr Osborne resided at the furthest end from where she sat, chatting animatedly with Mr and Mrs Wainwright. Both couples made such a harmonious picture that Alyssa didn't wonder about the open and covert glances the bachelors gave them.

Mr Abbott strolled over with a glass of ale, while Susanna joined Alyssa.

'Already needing to get away from the missus?' A bear of a man chortled.

'A man can be happily married, and still be his own master,

Graeme.' Mr Abbott took a long swig. 'You'll find out soon enough.'

'Hear, hear.' A wiry blonde man gave Graeme a hearty clap on the shoulder. 'You never said that you'd bought your way into the pool.'

Alyssa and Susanna both listened as discreetly as they could, while they savoured their dinner.

'I didn't,' Graeme said. 'At least until some of the boys pushed off for good. We both staked our claim then, didn't we, Alfie? Anything wrong with that, Hans? Or are you afraid of a bit of friendly competition?'

He lifted his arm and flexed his huge biceps. The sleeve strained under its bulk.

Hans laughed it off, but Alfie's fist clenched.

He emptied his glass in one huge gulp and wiped the foam off his moustache. Under normal circumstances Alyssa took him to be a pleasant, easy-going man, who resembled his brother physically, but without the short temper. At this moment though, Alfie appeared troubled, and Alyssa wondered if grief really was the reason.

He marched over to the bar and pushed the glass towards Peg-Leg for a refill. A vein on his temple pulsed as he joined his friends.

'No harm meant, okay?' Graeme said. Alfie clasped his glass with both hands and stared into the dark liquid.

'Come on, Bert wouldn't have wanted us to get all tearful. He had a good life, he did.' Graeme looked around. 'Right?'

The men nodded.

'A toast,' Mr Abbott said. 'To Bert. A good man. We'll miss him.'

'If I lay hands on that bitch –' Graeme stared at his huge hands. 'I'll choke the life out of her.'

'That's enough.' Mr Abbott thumped the table. 'We will have justice, but we'll do it by the book. And don't scare the ladies.'

'Darn right.'

'I'm sorry,' Alfie said, as he helped Mr Abbott finish up behind the bar. Peg-Leg had already left, and with him Fred Keller's moonshine. Mr Abbott had ignored it, because he could understand if Peg-Leg wanted to drown his grief, Alyssa assumed.

Alyssa and Susanna stayed behind, to assist with the clean-up.

Mr Abbott said, 'We all are. We've never had anything like this happen.'

'No.' Alfie wiped his knuckles over his nose. Alyssa resisted the urge to offer him a handkerchief, but at least he didn't blow his nose into his shirt-tail. 'When can I bury him?'

'I've asked Hans to make a coffin. Mr Kendrick offered to help. Day after tomorrow?'

Alfie moved his head in a slow nod. 'I'll dig a grave under the cedar trees uphill. He liked to sit there.'

'I'll give you a hand.'

Mr Abbott wiped off the spigot of the beer barrel. Alyssa and Susanna rinsed the glasses, careful to be quiet.

'I should have been there,' Alfie said. 'I might have done something.'

'Don't. Don't do that to yourself.' Mr Abbott flung down the soft cloth he'd used. 'I did wonder why I hadn't seen you in a while.'

Alfie raked his fingers through his dark-blonde hair that hung down to his shoulders. 'We had a fight.'

Mr Abbott leant against the bar, waiting for Alfie to go on.

'He got mad with me for putting in the blunt for a bride. He didn't want me to get married.'

'Why? You're more than old enough at twenty-six.'

'He said, he's the oldest, so it should be him, having help in the hotel. A wife to do the cooking.'

'I didn't notice him showing any special attention to the ladies.'

Alfie shrugged. 'He was cautious, was Bert. Almost got hitched way back before we came here. Girl he met in Portland, but she only cared for his blunt. He said he wouldn't fall for that again.'

'Where've you been?'

'Hunting, with Hans. Two weeks we spent in the woods, going after moose and anything else with a nice pelt, and in the meantime my own brother gets done in.'

'Sorry you had to come home to that. How did you find out?'

'Fred came out to our cabin, a day's ride from here.'

'I thought there were no horses?' Alyssa clapped a hand over her mouth, but it was too late. Fortunately, Alfie took her interruption in his stride.

'Fred's got an old mare he got a little while ago. Sleeps in the stable too.' That explained the smell.

'Lucky that he found you.'

'He'd been there with us before.'

'But not this time.'

A shadow crossed Alfie's open face. He shook his head.

'Fallen out?'

'Look here, Tom. You got anything to ask Fred, you go and ask him.'

'Fair enough. You didn't see anyone else?' Mr Abbott lifted a hand, palm outwards. 'There's smallpox out there, and it's usually the tribes who get hit worst. See any Indians?'

'Hell, no.' Alfie gaped at Mr Abbott, and then Susanna and Alyssa. 'Pardon my words, ladies, but jeez, what's going on?'

'If you didn't meet anyone, there's no reason to worry. Especially now that we have a proper doctor in town, and a lady who's used to nursing.'

Alyssa rinsed the last glass. Susanna yawned.

'I'm all in,' Alfie said. 'Thanks for letting me get things off my chest.'

'Anytime.' Mr Abbott patted him on the shoulder. 'By the way, you're the first who forgot to ask if his gold is safe.'

'It should be.' Alfie scratched his head. 'Unless that curs – that girl broke into the bank as well.'

'Everything is accounted for. Why didn't you let Bert look after your nuggets?'

Alfie hung his head sheepishly. 'I lost a fair bit, a while back.'

'On the steamer, or in Port Victoria?'

'On the steamer. Big Joe struck it luckier.'

'You got fleeced?'

'I don't like cards. Crap's more my kind of game.'

'Well, it happens to all of us.' Mr Abbott winked at Susanna before she could utter a word. 'See you tomorrow.'

In the morning, the list of names had been whittled down to twenty. Mr Abbott had excluded the remaining eighty-six men in town, because they all shared living quarters with someone else. 'The way I see it, if someone had left during the night, and the next morning Bert is dead, I'd have heard.'

Alyssa had her doubts, but thought it best to keep quiet for now. Twenty men still were a large group. She studied the list, while Susanna sat with her back to the window, mending her husband's shirt.

Dr Bryson read the list, too. They'd heard most of the names by now, among them Fred, Big Joe and Barry, the old man at the pack train station.

'How do we find out where they were during the night in question? We don't even know at what time Bert died.' Alyssa realised with a growing sense of trepidation that they needed more than the conviction that Rosie had been set up, to save the girl.

Dr Bryson rubbed his chin. 'For all it's worth, I'd say that he'd been dead six to eight hours when I saw him, shortly before nine o'clock that morning.' He shot Susanna an apologetic look, but she smiled serenely and concentrated on her needlework. 'It's to do with the stiffening of the body.'

'The wedding party broke up close to eleven. That leaves two to four hours until the murder.' Mr Abbott reached for his list and scanned it, a slow grin forming. 'I didn't stay until the end, but a few of the boys were already a bit drowsy. They'd have been out of it for most of the night, the rate they were going.'

He pencilled crosses next to seven names. 'Down to thirteen.'

Alyssa's spirits rose. 'Now we need to find out when our man could have entered Rosie's room on the three crucial occasions.'

Mr Abbot and the doctor met her with blank stares.

'It stands to reason, doesn't it? He needed to obtain her dress, sweep over Bert's floor with it, put it back, and he needed the opportunity to plant the fool's gold under her mattress. Which brings us to the next question: Where did he get the fool's gold, if it's not commonly found around here?'

Susanna bit of the thread and smoothed over the mended hem of the shirt. 'Why don't you ask Rosie when she last saw the dress, or if something was wrong with her box?'

She put her sewing into a wicker basket on the window sill. 'I think we should pay Hannah a visit, but first we need to go and see Nancy. We've neglected her shamefully.'

If Nancy had felt neglected, she hid it well. She bustled about in her pristine home, showing off the built-in seat under the window which opened into a box for storing furs to keep out the winter cold, the cast-iron range with two hobs, and the rug-rag she was working on with all the enthusiasm of a small girl playing house.

Her husband was out at the back, digging over a new patch for autumn vegetables. At the end of their yard stood a sturdy outhouse, with a large heap of soil next to it.

'You're really going to become farmers, like Nellie?' Susanna admired the neat rows full of cabbages and carrots. Beans climbed up on frames.

Nancy nodded. 'Joshua has already found the perfect place, a few miles further down the river. He and George Potter are going to work together. They're cousins.'

'When are you moving?' Alyssa asked.

'Next spring. That gives us all winter to build a house, but we need to put a crop in this autumn, for a harvest in springtime.'

'Oh good, we're not losing you too soon.' Susanna clapped her hands.

'You'll come and visit, won't you? Both of you?'

'We all will.' Susanna reached out for Alyssa and Nancy and pulled them into a dance. They twirled around the room, until they stumbled over their own feet.

'We'll never ever leave each other,' Susanna said. Alyssa bit her tongue. 'But now we need to go and see how Hannah is doing. Unless you want to come along?'

Alyssa gave Susanna a signal to stop. The fewer people shared the secret of Rosie's whereabouts, the better, and they could not expect Nancy to lie to her husband. She let out a breath of relief when Nancy said, 'I'd love to, but I promised Joshua I'd help him. It's how we make our money after all.'

'He's done searching for gold?' Alyssa tied on her bonnet.

'He said, you need to know when to stop. It's fine to give a man a start, but it can turn your soul and make you greedy.'

'He's a wise man.' Alyssa gave Nancy a brief peck on the cheek. 'If you come to the hotel tonight, I'll make sure you get the best portions, and Susanna will grant you the best seats.'

'What are you talking about?' Nancy's eyebrows crept higher and higher.

'Alyssa and I have taken on proper jobs. We all have until Mr Harper's brother has figured out what to do.'

They found Hannah in a state of agitation. Three men had knocked on the bank's door and demanded it to be opened.

'I thank the Lord that Mr Kendrick had stayed the night. They pushed their way in as soon as Mr Osborne opened, and they shouted at him that they wanted to see their gold.' She bit her knuckles. 'Poor Rosie came close to fainting in her hidey-hole.'

She rang her silver bell. Alyssa could hear three bolts being lifted, before Mr Kendrick appeared. He quickly put on a cheerful mask, but his eyes had a worried look.

'Good morning, ladies,' he said. 'I'm sorry I couldn't join you last night.'

'What is happening?' Alyssa asked.

He gave her a helpless shrug. 'Somebody must be stirring up folks.'

'But who? And why?' Alyssa's mouth felt dry as sandpaper.

He closed the door behind him. 'I think it's to flush out Rosie. If you tell someone their money is in danger, they will shout for the thief.'

Alyssa grabbed hold of the table to steady herself. 'Will she still be safe here? And the Osbornes?'

A small cry escaped Hannah. 'Sorry,' she whispered. 'I – what about my husband?'

'I've got a pistol, and I'm an excellent shot,' Mr Kendrick said. 'But it won't come to this. Mr Abbott will need to be informed, and then we'll figure out how to calm down the situation. If Alyssa could be good enough to inform him? I daren't leave my post.'

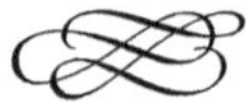

Mr Abbott flung open a wall cabinet hidden in a recess. Inside, two rifles stood upright in wooden rests. A pistol box sat at the bottom. 'Can you handle a gun?'

Dr Bryson whistled. 'A Henry rifle? I've heard of them.'

Mr Abbott handed him one and took a small cardboard box from the back of the cabinet. Several layers of copper cartridges caught Alyssa's eye.

'You load it like this. Open the loading sleeve. The magazine fits sixteen bullets.' He demonstrated it.

'The rifle that you can load on Sunday and shoot all week long.' Dr Bryson nodded. 'I've heard the slogan, down in San Francisco.'

'The reputation should be good enough to cool off any hotheads.'

The doctor put three cartridges in to the loading sleeve and closed it again. 'Anything I need to be aware of?'

'Just that you better be careful. The hammer's on the cartridge rim, so if there's any impact on the hammer, you might fire off a shot.'

Alyssa did not follow it all, but the doctor said, 'Got it.' He lifted the rifle and aimed at the door.

'Steady,' Mr Abbott said. 'I hope we can deal with the problem without using up my precious cartridges.' He put the rifle back into its rest, careful not to touch the trigger. 'Let's go and see the town folk.'

Susanna reached for her bonnet. 'What are you doing?' her husband said. 'I'm coming with you.' She linked her arm with Alyssa's. 'We both are.'

Her husband barred the door. 'It's not a place for a woman.'

'They won't hurt me. Not with everyone watching. It's much easier to grab me when I'm alone, to force you to give up Rosie.' She gave him a bewitching grin. 'You and the doctor will protect us.'

'She's right.' The doctor tested the weight of the rifle. 'I assume you want your boys to see the gun, and to understand that any questions will go to you, not Osborne.'

'That's the plan.'

Mr Abbott opened the pistol box. Dr Bryson whistled through his teeth. 'A Colt army revolver? Can I borrow this? I assume your folks wouldn't be happy with a visitor weighing in with a Henry rifle, but this beauty would fit nicely under my jacket.'

Abbott held it out to him. 'Six shots.'

The doctor opened the cylinder. It sat empty. He reached for the ammunition.

Alyssa and Susanna watched closely as he put in the cartridges. Alyssa wished she had a pistol too. Her father had taught her how to shoot, after he'd been threatened for speaking out against the inhumane treatment of prisoners on a hulk that had led to a murderous revolt in Melbourne.

Her mother however had balked at the idea of letting their daughter possess a firearm. She'd feared about the consequences for Alyssa's reputation. She'd had enough to overcome, simply by being the daughter of a civil servant who placed his own conscience over public opinion. What only Alyssa seemed to understand was that he did not condone murderers and thieves, but that he saw that convicts who were treated worse than animals tended to become degraded.

Alyssa's thoughts returned to the present. The doctor had closed a pistol holder over his hip. His jacket fell over the pistol.

Mr Abbott slapped his hat on.

Outside, a handful of men loitered on the main street, an unusual sight.

Mr Abbott clasped his rifle tighter. Susanna and Alyssa strolled behind him, with the doctor one step behind them.

They stopped at the half-built church. A steep ladder led to a bell chamber in which hung a huge bell, with a rope tied to the clapper. Mr Abbott signalled the doctor to pull the rope.

Three mighty tugs, and the bell rang out loud enough to be heard miles away. Within ten minutes, an assembled crowd stood outside the church, with the Osbornes and Rosie noticeably absent.

Alfie stood in the centre, leaning on a loamy shovel.

Mr Abbott moved forward. 'You all know me, boys, as far as the law is concerned, I'm in charge of this town.'

The men nodded their agreement.

'I've heard that some of you are worried about their gold. But let me tell you this, it's still there.'

'How can you be sure?' Graeme and a second man, with a barrel chest and trunks of legs, challenged the statement; Big Joe, Alyssa recollected.

'I got Bert's ledger, that's how. It all tallies up with what I found in Bert's strong-box.' He raised his left hand to quell any further interruptions. 'We're weighing every single pouch, and if you leave us in peace, we'll also record every single nugget. But you must let Mr Osborne do his job. If not –' He patted his rifle. 'I won't have the man harassed or threatened, do you hear?'

'But what about the female?' A slight, hat-less man with a mane of unkempt black hair spit on the ground. 'We all know she did for Bert, and she did it for the gold.'

'Then why is it still there?' Mr Abbott squinted in the sunshine that cast golden stripes over his face. 'Tell you what, I'll get your gold from the bank, and hand it back to you if you come to my office this afternoon.'

The men shuffled their feet.

'I trust you,' Peg-Leg said. 'I ain't got much, but if you say it's there, that's good enough for me.'

'Anyone else?' Mr Abbott scanned the crowd. The men shook their heads.

'Good,' he said. 'In that case, how about you all go back to your work, and I'll inform Mr Osborne that he can proceed with his task in peace and quiet.'

Alyssa and the doctor remained after everyone else had gone their ways. Alyssa fished in the hidden pocket sown into the folds of her skirt and took out a small purse.

'Would you care to accompany me to Mr Turner's shop?' she asked.

'With pleasure, but whatever for?'

'If I can purchase an additional shovel, you – or I – could help Alfie Harper with the grave-digging.' She lowered her voice. 'And the crowbar in the hotel looked new, without scratches or rust. I'd like a look at Mr Turner's ledger.'

They shared a tiny smile.

The store owner stood in his crowded shop, a square room with gold-pans, sluice boxes, knives and spades jostling with cast-iron trivets, hooks, pots, down to thick woollen socks and fishing lines. Barrels full of flour and dried goods lined one wall.

Two identical crowbars lay on a shelf, half hidden behind a stack of the flannel shirts half the town population wore.

The doctor ran his finger of the blade-rim of a long-handled spade.

'Nice workmanship,' he said. 'Yours?'

Mr Turner grinned, to reveal two missing front teeth in his lower jaw. 'Imported, from Oregon. Last blacksmith we had got the gold-fever bad. First word that Kamloops had turned up something, and he took off with the first pack train.' He gave Dr Bryson a shrewd look. 'Last spade, and it will be for a while now that we're cut off.'

'In that case I'd better have it.'

Mr Turner produced a black ledger from under his counter and searched for the right page. 'That's 40 cents.'

Dr Bryson handed over a few coins. The shop owner licked a pencil and wrote down; 'Spade to the Doctor, 40 cents paid.'

In the second line from the top, Alyssa could make out the word crowbar upside down, and the name next to it – the disappointment hit her like a physical blow – Bert Harper had purchased the crowbar, two days before his death.

Alyssa fetched a jug with beer from the hotel. She found Mr Wainwright behind the bar. 'Where's Peg-Leg?' she asked as he handed her the brew.

'Feeding the pigs.' He pulled a face. 'He's taken it hard, poor bloke, and the less time he spends here, while Mrs Wainwright is in charge, well ...'

'I see. Where is the beer kept, by the way?'

He pointed behind him. 'There's a storage room at the back, where it's coolest. We're down to four barrels but I gather Bert used to brew it himself, and Alfie has learned from him.'

'Can I have a look?' She put the beer jug down.

The room had a packed earth floor. When crammed full of barrels, a man would struggle to hide in it, but now it stood half-empty, and instead of a lock or handle, the door had a hole through which one could hook a finger to pull it open.

Mr Wainwright studied the door, too. 'Less than a dozen proper locks in this whole town. A locksmith would be sitting pretty here.'

'As would a cabinet-maker, or a grocer. Nancy's farm could supply vegetables, and the river is supposed to be full of fish.' She saw a speculative gleam in his eyes. If he really intended to settle down instead of leaving his wife at home for endless periods while he was at sea, she'd do her best to encourage him.

'Please tell your wife I'll be back in good time for my duties,' she said as she picked up the jug.

She found the doctor standing in a half-dug grave. Slender cedar trees cast their sparse shade over the spot. The land away from town rose gently, until it became the craggy outcrop of the Rockies. The sun dappled the grassy parts of the slope, and wild flowers dotted the green with yellows, bright reds and all shades of blue. Small birds stalked around in the grass, searching for worms or insects.

Alfie sat under a cedar, his back against the slim trunk. His hat lay beside him, and sweat beaded his skin. Alyssa handed him the jug. His hands trembled, and his lips showed cracks. He drank in hasty gulps, as if he'd been parched.

'Thanks,' he said, wiping foam from his moustache. 'Better get going again.' He stood up, slow and painful like an old man.

'No need,' the doctor said. 'It does me some good to do something else from loafing around.'

Alyssa said, 'I'm very sorry about your brother.'

Alfie stared with red-rimmed eyes at his boots. 'It's wrong, that's what it is. Him being gone like this.'

'Is he your only brother?'

'There's Tony, but he lasted less than a year here, when we came, back in 1858.'

'Is he looking for gold too?'

'Trapper. Sells to the Hudson Bay Company. Said he hated being cooped in like this.'

'But Bert and you liked it.'

'You get tired of pushing on and on, after a while. It was Bert put his foot down after our Ma died, so we all could get some schooling. Smart, he was. Generous too, but he didn't like being taken for a fool.'

The doctor flung shovel-full after shovel-full of heavy soil onto a growing heap.

'I've seen him with his whip,' he said. 'Anybody ever tried to cheat him, with a dud coin or anything? Mind you, they'd have to be braver than me.'

'Folks are honest around here. Tom Abbott sees to that. A man not toeing the line finds himself in mighty hot water otherwise.'

Alfie closed his eyes for a second. 'Only place to get swindled is when you fall in with the card-sharps on the steamer. There was this one time ...' He broke off, his breath growing shallow.

'Doctor!' Alyssa held on to Alfie as his knees gave in.

'Damn.' Dr Bryson heaved himself out of the grave. Alfie rested against the tree, his legs at an odd angle.

Alyssa took Alfie's wrist and counted the seconds under her breath. 'The pulse is weak.' She touched the hot, clammy forehead.

'Fever, too,' the doctor said. 'I'm afraid our ride needs to be postponed. We need to get him to my cabin. Can you fetch a few strong men? And a stretcher?'

Alyssa hurried as much as she could, all the while watching out for holes and burrows. The last thing she needed was a sprained or broken ankle.

She ran the last few hundred yards, knocking on Mr Abbott's office door. No reply. She rushed on to the hotel, hoping to find Mr Wainwright. Yes, there he was, comforting and reliable as always. Her heard her out, and told his wife to close the hotel until his return.

Alyssa had trouble keeping up with him. He grabbed the first man he saw by the sleeve; Little Joe.

'We've got an ill man in the woods,' he said. 'Do you have a stretcher somewhere? And I need two more men.'

Little Joe gaped at him.

Mr Wainwright shook him gently. 'It's urgent, man.'

'Tom's got a stretcher. Tom Abbott.'

'He's not in,' Alyssa said. 'If you two gentlemen could fetch the doctor's bag and go ahead, I'll find Mr Abbott and follow you.'

She didn't wait for an answer, silently praying that she would find the constable at home.

'He's at the bank,' Susanna said. 'We were so happy, and now – it's not smallpox, is it?' She pressed her hands onto her heart.

'No, it's nothing but a fever,' Alyssa said, crossing her fingers behind her back. 'Otherwise the doctor wouldn't have sent me here.' She prayed silently that this was true, but how could she be sure?

CHAPTER 14

Mr Kendrick stood in Hannah's back yard, sawing a thick oak board. Next to him stood an almost finished coffin. Alyssa averted her gaze; it hardly bore thinking about one brother to be lowered into this wooden box and hence be returned to the earth, while the other lay stricken with fever and who knew what else next to his brother's final resting place.

He stopped. 'Something has happened.'

'We need a stretcher, and Mr Abbott. Alfie's fallen ill with a fever.'

'He's inside. Why don't you sit down and have a drink of water while I fetch both.' He tapped a signal onto Hannah's door.

'Thank you. I don't dare go inside without the doctor's permission.'

'I see.' He left her standing, and returned with water. 'Mr Abbott will fetch the stretcher, and meet us here. I wish I hadn't sent Hans away, but he didn't look too good.' He pushed a lock of hair back behind her ear and adjusted her bonnet. 'We'll get through this.'

While they waited for the men to return, Alyssa and Matron turned an empty cabin – little more than a one-room shack really - into a makeshift surgery.

They set up two camp beds, acquired from William Turner and to be paid for by the town. Matron had frowned at the rough sheets his store offered, but kept her counsel. Alyssa scrubbed a card table they'd borrowed from the hotel. Peg-Leg had carried it over for her, while she boiled gallons of water. A kerosene lantern stood ready.

Matron sat down on one of the two rough-hewn wooden chairs the cabin had offered, hands folded in her lap. Next to her stood her small chest with bandages, laudanum and smelling salts.

Alyssa pulled the second sheet tight and folded the corners into perfect squares when the men arrived. Between them, on a seven feet long piece of canvas stretched between two irregular poles, Alfie lay prone, head lolling to the right side. Underneath his tan, his cheeks were flushed.

Mr Abbott, Mr Kendrick, Little Joe and Mr Wainwright lowered the stretcher onto the floor and heaved up Alfie by his arms and legs.

The doctor directed them to the bed next to the window. In the stillness of the cabin, Alfie's breath sounded magnified, leaving no space for anything else.

'That'll do for now,' the doctor said. He took of his jacket, rolled up his sleeves and dipped the flannel that Alyssa had put ready into the bowl with still hot water. He wrung it out and wiped Alfie's face and wrists with it.

Little Joe's gaze fell onto the pistol on Dr Bryson's hip. He pursed his lips, but Mr Abbott silenced him with a single look.

'If you gentlemen would wash your hands before you leave?' Matron handed her husband a bar of soap and a piece of cloth and pointed him towards a second bowl of water. Little Joe snorted, but fell in line as soon as he saw Mr Abbott scrub his hands hard enough to drown out Alfie's breathing.

Dr Bryson took his stethoscope out of his bag.

'I'll be back as soon as the doctor can do without me,' Matron said to her husband before she closed the door after him. Only she, the doctor and Alyssa were left with Alfie.

'What about Hans?' Alyssa asked while the doctor unbuttoned Alfie's shirt. Matron put a finger on her lips while the doctor listened to Alfie's heartbeat and lungs. Alfie coughed, a wheezing noise that brought up spittle.

Dr Bryson let the stethoscope dangle from his neck. 'Mr Kendrick will find him.'

Matron's unspoken question hung in the air. She sat down again, waiting for an explanation.

'I believe it's a kind of influenza. There are no symptoms of the smallpox, and the streams offer clean drinking sources, so the water wouldn't have been contaminated.' He worked up a good lather with the soap as he washed his hands. 'If it's contagious, Hans will have it too. They've been out there in the woods together for close to a fortnight.'

'It will spread.' Matron hugged her arms to her chest.

'We'll keep them confined.' He covered Alfie's body up to the chin with a blanket. 'He needs a drink.'

'Tea?' Alyssa knelt in front of a small fireplace and set a match to the kindling. From a trivet hung a pot with water. She stood up and joined the doctor at Alfie's bed.

He nodded and gave her one of those smiles that he usually reserved for occasions when they were alone. She beamed back at him.

Someone banged on the door; Mr Kendrick, with a dishevelled Hans at his side. He propped him up and led him straight to the second bed.

'I'm fine,' Hans said, but his voice lacked conviction.

'On the bed, and open your shirt.' Dr Bryson put in the ear-tubes of his stethoscope.

'What?' Hans' jaw dropped. He almost jumped back, eyes swivelling madly towards Alyssa and Matron.

Dr Bryson stifled a grin.

'I'm not getting undressed in front of ladies,' Hans said.

Alfie coughed, still barely half-conscious.

'Matron and I will turn around,' Alyssa said, to break the impasse. To her surprise, Matron rolled her eyes at her. Before her remarriage, she'd have blushed at the thought of an improperly dressed man in the company of a young, unmarried girl, Alyssa thought.

'You appear to be healthy,' the doctor said. 'Do you have a headache? Aching bones?'

Hans murmured something inaudible.

'Speak up, please,' the doctor said. 'This is important. And button up your shirt so the ladies can stop staring holes in the wall.'

'I might have had a drink or two too many.'

'But the liquor is rationed.'

Hans made circles with his boot-tip. 'Not if you know the right people.'

'Fred Keller,' Alyssa said.

Hans' clamped his mouth shut.

'Where's his distillery?' Dr Bryson wiped Alfie's feverish brow again.

'I ain't saying nothing.'

'Alright. But I warn you, that stuff could cause blindness if you're not careful. Still, you getting drunk doesn't explain Alfie's symptoms. Unless he drank himself into a stupor, and that doesn't make sense.'

'He didn't touch a drop. Bert'd have whipped him silly. Strictly beer, is Alfie's drink.'

Hans looked down on his friend's slack face. 'Could've been his tumble in the river.'

'What happened?'

'About five days ago, we'd spotted a wolf pack on the other side of the river. Alfie thought it'd be worth it to put out a few traps. Looked shallow enough, the water, with a couple of nice flat boulders to help you nip across.' He shrugged. 'Except he slipped, and in he went.'

'He got wet.'

'Soaked like an otter. One of the wolves must've heard something, because it doubled back and watched him, he said. Just stood there, staring, while Alfie didn't dare move a muscle.'

'You didn't help him?'

'I was at our cabin, getting a meal ready. We took turns cooking. Must have been in the water for two hours at least. Took days for his clothes to dry.'

'Didn't he get changed straight away?' Alyssa poured tea into the two mugs they had found in the new surgery. The water hadn't boiled properly, but the patient might scald himself with too hot tea.

'Why should he? Besides, he had but that one pair of pants.'

Dr Bryson lifted Alfie's head and shoulders. Alyssa held the mug to his lips. Alfie took a tiny sip. A few drops ran out of the corner of his mouth. She patted them away with a flannel.

'You need to drink,' she said. He took another sip. 'That's better. Take your time.'

Hans scratched his chin, his beard rustling under his fingers. 'Reckon it was the drenching that did it?'

'I hope so,' Dr Bryson said. 'Meet anyone up there?'

Hans' face took on a shifty expression.

'Spit it out, man.'

Alfie moaned as Alyssa lowered his head onto the rolled-up blanket doubling as a pillow.

'Fred dropped in one evening.' Hans rubbed his chin again. 'He had a bottle or two he wanted to sell.'

'He's got a distillery up there?'

'Don't know, don't ask. All I'm telling is who we saw.' His mouth set in an obstinate line.

'How long ago was that?' Dr Bryson took Alfie's pulse again. The sick man breathed easier now.

'About a week. Must have been right before the boat stopped running, or Fred would've hiked up the price.'

'Was that why Alfie and Fred had a falling-out?' Alyssa asked.

'None of the Harpers hold with moonshine. Their Dad got hold of a bad load when they were kids. Killed him.'

'But Bert sold spirits,' Alyssa said.

'Beer that he'd brewed himself, and liquor from proper distilleries, that's all.'

Dr Bryson took a small stoppered bottle of laudanum out of his kit bag. 'If you and Fred are in the clear, and you three were the only people out there, chances are it's not contagious.' He eyed Hans critically. 'I'll keep you over night, and if you're fine in the morning, you can go.'

A shrill whistle from outside made Alyssa start. The doctor gave her a quick smile as he jerked the door open. A stack of blankets appeared as if out of nowhere. On top of it rested a slipping bundle wrapped in a shirt.

'Hurry up, man,' a voice said as the doctor grabbed the whole load; Mr Kendrick's. 'Is it safe to come in?'

Mr Kendrick surveyed the situation with his usual swiftness. Alyssa handed him and the doctor tea in one of the mugs that had been contained in the bundle and helped herself to the rest. Her spirits rose, as always when both her good friends kept her company. 'I'll get you another camp bed,' he said. 'Unless you can do with my assistance tonight?'

'I'll stay too if you need me,' Alyssa said.

The men stared at her. Only Alfie lay still, with his eyes closed.

'That's not necessary,' Dr Bryson said after a shocked pause. 'Mr Kendrick will return you to your cabin, and we'll manage between us.' His voice softened. 'I'm grateful for your help, especially if you could arrange for some food for us?'

Mr Kendrick offered her his arm as they strolled towards the hotel. 'You scandalise those poor men,' he said. 'Hans came close to having a fit at the thought of having a woman around.'

Alyssa remembered the Canadian's panic when the doctor made him unbutton his shirt in her presence and chuckled. 'I hadn't expected a town full of men to be so –'

'Sensitive? But you must remember that most of them aren't used to female company. No mothers around, no sisters, and the ladies they might meet on the rare occasion when they go to a town are not – ahem ...' Now he showed signs of discomfort, too.

Alyssa took pity. 'I'm perfectly aware that not every female meets Mrs Wainwright's standards, usually due to unlucky circumstances.'

He wiped his brow. 'Thank you.'

Matron found them a clean canister to fill with hot chicken soup, from a recipe that had been in constant use at the Women's hospital in Melbourne where she had gained her nursing experience.

A few feathers stuck to Bertha's apron, clear proof of who had plucked the birds. Alyssa breathed in the soothing aroma of the spicy broth.

'It's not quite as I would have liked it,' Matron said after enquiring after the patient, 'but we'll soon have a kitchen garden created, and a few more hen-houses. It's a miracle how these men used to cope before we arrived.' Her face glowed with satisfaction as she looked around at the rearranged kitchen, with its row of washing-up bowls lining a long work-bench, and crockery and cutlery stacked on a table next to the swing door, ready to be carried inside the bar room.

Matron had found her place. Alyssa hoped for her sake that she wouldn't be wrenched away, as could easily happen to a sailor's wife.

Mr Kendrick received a basket with plates, spoons, and bread, without Matron bothering to stop her flow of words; another sign how comfortable she'd grown in her role.

'I'll return as soon as I can.' Alyssa said.

'I'd appreciate that.' Matron sighed. 'We'll do our best to make Mr Harper's funeral and wake worthy of such a sad occasion.'

A wake! That explained the dozens of dough-balls being kneaded while they spoke.

Mr Kendrick gave Alyssa a sign to hurry. She lifted the heavy canister by the wooden grip that covered most of the metal handle.

'Let us swap,' he said as soon as they were outside. Gratefully she obliged.

'Should I feel offended that Mrs Wainwright deemed it unwise to let me carry anything I might spill?'

Alyssa shook her head. 'More of a compliment to your elevated status that she doesn't want you to undertake a woman's task.'

'I see.' But clearly, he didn't. 'I'll explain the niceties of our class system as Matron observes it to you another day. Now we've got more pressing tasks at hand.'

With refreshments duly delivered, Mr Kendrick accompanied Alyssa to the Osbornes. Outside, covered with a dirty piece of old canvas that might once have covered a wagon, sat the coffin.

'I'll finish it. While Hans is confined,' Mr Kendrick said. He lifted the cover and ran his hand lightly over the rough edges. The lid needed another two or three boards. 'If Wainwright can be spared at the hotel, we'll have this done before sundown.' He winked at Alyssa. 'That way I can keep an eye on the place while the Osbornes go for dinner.'

Mr Osborne protested against handing over his guard duties, but his wife convinced him of the importance of showing themselves. 'After all,' she said, 'if we had a guest we'd be staying home.'

'That is exactly what I'd be thinking,' Alyssa said. 'It would also be interesting to see if anyone else approaches you about his gold, or Bert's ledger.'

Rosie cowered in a corner, unusually quiet. Her sharp features looked pinched in the feeble light cast by the kerosene lamp. Alyssa wondered how long they could get away with leaving the window shuttered in broad daylight. She rubbed her aching head as she mentally added this to her growing list of problems to be tackled.

'Are you unwell?' Hannah peered at her. 'It is a bit stuffy in here.'

'I haven't been sleeping well, that's all.'

'It's hard to stop worrying, isn't it?' Hannah put her hand upon her husband's. It shouldn't have been like this, Alyssa thought. Instead of creating a happy home together, they must spend every waking minute fearing a horde of angry men clamouring for Rosie's head. As for Rosie herself, she showed more courage and frankly, common sense than Alyssa had credited her with. She would have been so easy to set up as scapegoat, a young woman coming out of nowhere, without visible support or friends.

Another idea formed in her mind. Did it show more than simple avarice and disregard for human life, to pin a murder on a young woman? It certainly was easier to use someone whose character was unknown in town (at least as far as the Canadians were concerned), but framing her for a crime that might well be punished by death, felt vindictive.

'Has anyone made advances to you, Rosie?' she asked.

Rosie gasped, 'What do you mean! You know darned well that I've been following every word of Mrs Wainwright's instructions.' She almost spat out the name, proving that the Rosie of old still lived on in the frightened girl.

'I'm wondering if any of the men here, or someone you met on your way, has paid you any unwanted attention.' Alyssa sighed. 'Maybe somebody wanted to pay you back for being rejected. I'm clutching at straws here, but surely there is a reason why you were so obviously implicated.'

Rosie's brows drew together. 'There's always a fellow or two that's a bit free with his hands.'

'You should know.' Hannah clapped a hand over her mouth. 'I'm sorry.'

Rosie shrugged. 'I never said I've joined a convent, have I?' Her eyes flickered towards Mr Osborne, but he listened with the utmost tolerance.

Alyssa smiled. His character more than made up for his colourless appearance and his middle age.

'Was there anyone you rebuked?' she asked.

Rosie's stomach growled. Hannah pushed a biscuit tin over to her. 'We need to get more food in for you, but how we are going to do that without it looking suspicious is beyond me. At least you're eating again.'

'I'll think of something,' Alyssa said. 'Now, Rosie?'

Rosie nibbled a hard biscuit with her sharp teeth. 'On the steamer,' she said. 'One fellow tried to get me alone.' Her jaw muscles worked. 'Not again. I got a hat pin ready, like you told us before we arrived.'

'You stuck him with it?' Alyssa couldn't hide the satisfaction in her voice, and Mr Osborne nodded to himself.

'Too right I did. Yelped like a dingo, and off he went.'

'Would you recognise him? Is he here?'

Rosie nibbled some more on her biscuit, forehead creased in fierce concentration.

'He had a scratchy beard, and he stank of liquor.' She shuddered. 'Oh, and there was a scar on his left hand, like something slashed across it.' She held thumb and index finger two inches apart. 'About that long.'

'If he's here, we'll find him. If you remember anything else, tell us. Or anybody else.' Alyssa rose, signalling Rosie to return to her bolt-hole. Rosie obeyed, but her whole body slumped as if she had to drag herself forward. It must be hell to be stuck in there, for a seemingly infinite number of hours.

'We'll get you out of this,' she said. 'Have faith.'

'I should have stayed in Melbourne.'

'Nonsense.' Hannah pressed her hands on her hips, like a mother chiding her offspring. 'What did we have there? Rags on our backs and hardly enough to feed ourselves? You let Alyssa sort things out, and then we'll make sure you mend your ways. Do you hear me?'

'Maybe Susanna will hire me as maid.' Rosie forced her lips to curl upwards in an attempt at joking.

'You'd drive her batty in a week,' Hannah said. 'Nobody deserves that.'

'I already have something in mind,' Alyssa said. 'But now I really need to go.'

Mr Kendrick drove the final nail into the coffin as Alyssa left the house. He'd attached four six-inch lengths of rope to the sides, to serve as handles. Mr Wainwright smoothed down the edges of the lid with sandpaper. He'd shaped them tongue and groove style, so the lid would fit perfectly. His right hand worked the sandpaper forwards and back, in one continuous movement. A red crescent on one knuckle reminded her of Rosie's description. She'd never noticed Mr Wainwright's scar before, so chances were that Mr Abbott would say the same about his neighbours. They'd have to inspect all hands themselves.

Mr Kendrick agreed. 'It's familiarity that does it. If I asked you what colour Captain Moore's eyes are, you probably would have to guess, although you've seen him dozens of times.'

'Icy blue, in a red face,' Alyssa aid.

'That's true, but what about someone you see but don't notice?'

Alyssa agreed, recollecting her struggle to tell Grace and Bertha apart. 'Can you talk to Mr Abbott?' she asked. 'And the doctor?

Mark squatted next to his patient, who had fallen into a fitful sleep. His face was still flushed, and his breathing shallow.

Hans strolled around the cabin, the ill-effects of his drinking session wearing off without other signs of unwellness appearing. He stayed as far as possible from Alfie's bed, watching his friend from a ten-foot distance.

'He'll be right, won't he?'

Mark put a hot, wet flannel on Alfie's forehead and nodded with what he hoped looked like conviction. He didn't like this too sudden collapse with a fever that must have been raging on for days without too much harm. Probably the murder of his brother had proved to be the final bit that broke Alfie's otherwise iron constitution.

He wished he had more medication to help his patient, but laudanum to quiet him down and hot steam to help him breathe were among the strongest weapons in his meagre arsenal. Some doctors swore by mixtures containing Nux Vomica, but he distrusted anything that could just as well fatally poison the body as heal it.

Alfie gurgled. Mark wiped his brow and dipped the flannel into the hot water, wrung it and replaced it on the patient's forehead.

'Have you been here long, Hans?'

'Close on three years. Heard about all the gold waiting for a man to pick it up, and a nice little place to settle.' He peered through the window at the long line of cabins, and the bank and store, leading all the way up to the hotel. 'It can get lonely out there, if you're a trapper. It's better here, with neighbours all around you, but you still answer to no-one but yourself. You want to up and go, ain't nobody going to say a word.'

'Freedom.' Mark took Alfie's limp wrist into one hand and counted the pulse under his breath.

'Yeah. Mind you, old Tom is keeping everybody on a pretty tight leash when it comes to drinking and gambling, but that keeps out the rough ones. Used to be a few of them around in the early days, but Tom soon sent them packing across the border. It's a peaceful country, is Canada. Even the tribes are okay if they stay in their place.'

Mark doubted that the Indians would applaud this sentiment, but Hans meant well, and from what he had heard, Canada was indeed to be a better place for other races than his own native US, and Australia with its inhuman treatment of the Aborigines. And now there was a war raging, with slavery at its core, and instead of doing the work on the frontlines that he'd crossed the oceans for, here he was, stuck fast.

Alfie's legs trashed around, but his pulse was regular.

'Is it really that easy to find gold?'

Hans shrugged. 'If you're lucky. You go down to the river with your pan and sluice box, and chance is, you come home after a few days with a fistful of nuggets. River gold is usually small, but it's not as much embedded in rock, so what you see is the real thing.'

'And away from the rivers?'

Hans helped himself to cold coffee. His whole body became animated. 'Depends on where you are. Sometimes a pick-axe will do to chip away at the mountains. If there's ore, you'll see it. You won't know how much, but it'll be there all right. Sometimes a tiny seam, sometimes a big layer of gold, sitting there waiting for you.' He took a swill. 'It's a darn good life if you ask me.'

'And the rocks need to be properly assayed, to separate the gold,' Mark said. 'That's why you get lumps of stone, whereas the river gold glitters right away?'

'A finer sight you can't imagine. Sweet as the first trickle of beer from a fresh barrel, and the sunrays on your sweetheart's hair.'

'Sounds like you're ready to settle down.'

Hans chuckled. 'We'll see. I've got some good years out in the fields still left in me, and besides, if you've got a bit of money in your pocket, you'll always find a friendly lady for a dance or two.' He winked at Mark.

'As long as you don't get fleeced.'

'If you don't wager your equipment, you'll always make good again, if you try. Easy come, easy gone.'

That's what Mark thought as well, recalling several conversations. Although the existence of gold both in an almost pure state and embedded in rocks explained how the pyrite could be substituted, why would somebody commit murder over something that could be gained with relative ease?

Hans said, 'Say, doc, is it really necessary for me to stay overnight?' He licked his parched lips and glanced meaningful at the soup canister and the pot with coffee.

Mark grinned. 'Don't you worry, there'll be proper food and a jug of beer later. One night won't harm you.'

'What size jug?'

'Big enough. Put a little trust in my friends.'

CHAPTER 15

Alyssa found the preparation for tomorrow's wake completed when she reported for duty. Matron put a plump hand, hot from the kitchen fires, on Alyssa's forehead and cheek before she enveloped her in a hug.

The familiar scent of lavender soap washed over Alyssa. It had become rarer and rarer these days, as Matron's supply dwindled. Alyssa had managed to organise two bars when they'd stayed in San Francisco that she intended for birthday and Christmas presents for her friend, but after that they would have to get used to going without these luxuries. Unless – it surely couldn't be too hard to learn how to make soap, and scent and colour it with plants.

She sniffed the air surreptitiously. All their clothes needed to be washed soon, or they would rival the men's stench of sweat and stale beer.

Matron gave the swing door a quick push to see if anyone had arrived yet, but the lone figure was Mr Abbott behind the bar. On a stool sat his wife, chin propped in her hands as she regaled him with tales that included kangaroos, from what Alyssa could hear.

The swing door shut again.

'Ten minutes,' Matron said. 'You really had me worried for a while, Alyssa, but you appear to be as healthy as ever. This slight flush on your cheeks fooled me.' She frowned. 'Where's your bonnet?'

Alyssa's hand went to her hair. 'I must have left it at Hannah's.' She stepped aside, to let Harriet and Grace put two large soup canisters on a table, ready to be taken out any moment. The kitchen teemed with action, but in an oddly calm way. The girls had easily fallen into routines of doing chores together.

Alyssa pulled Matron aside. 'You have worked wonders already,' she said.

'If my girls are going to live in this town, we all need to do our best to make it a happy community.' She lowered her voice. 'It also makes everyone feel better, not having to live on the charity of these good men, but to work towards our keep.'

Alyssa nodded. 'I wish we had a laundry set up. Cleanliness is not high on the priorities of most bachelors, and if one or more of the girls don't marry straight away, we need to think of ways for them to earn a living.' She forbore to mention Rosie's name.

Matron's eyes lit up as she pondered the scheme. 'It would be quite simple, and –'

Susanna peeked in. 'They're coming.'

Alyssa flew back and forth with food, fighting the urge to check hands for tell-tale scars. If the man Rosie had fought off lived in this town, they would find him.

Mr Abbott filled beer jugs as if he had tended bars all his life. Susanna had taken over the collection of empty glasses, and Nancy insisted on doing the washing up, helped by her husband. Peg-Leg spent most of the evening sitting in a corner with the store owner and Fred, who kept his head down whenever Mr Abbott glanced his way.

Poor Peg-Leg, losing his friend and having his duties usurped by a band of strangers. Alyssa hoped that he would settle into the changed circumstances as soon as he had overcome his obvious grief for Bert.

The funeral was set for nine in the morning. Alyssa kept a close watch on all the men volunteering as pallbearers. Would a murderer be keen on seeing his victim to the grave, or would he fear the spirit of the dead man? If only she knew more about superstitions.

She shivered. The idea of being so close to a man dead from one's own hand should be repulsive to any but the most cold-blooded. But, if she thought about the ruthless way Rosie had been framed, the man they sought was cold enough to freeze her heart.

One more thing they'd learned about him – he reacted fast, planned thoroughly, and had no remorse. Bert's fate had been sealed the moment the discovery of the thefts was imminent. They were dealing with a clever, calculating man, who either disliked women in general or Rosie in particular; or he cared for nobody but himself.

Rosie pulled her thin blanket over her eyes and clutched her rag-doll. She could cope with daytime, when she could sit with Hannah for a few hours, but being hidden in this tiny room, like a hunted criminal, preyed on her nerves. With every sound coming through the walls she gave a start, and when there was silence, she imagined a band of men lurking outside, guns at the ready to demand she be handed over to them.

Silent tears rolled down her cheeks. She felt scared and sick, although food stayed down better lately. She was trapped, that's what she was. And Hannah and Mr Osborne – what would the townsfolk do to them if they found out that they kept Rosie hidden? If she could get away from this all, but what chance did she have in this horrible country, with its wild animals and wilder men?

Her only hope was Alyssa, but really, how much longer was she supposed to live in constant fear without losing her mind?

She turned around on the thin mattress and curled up into a ball.

Four men lifted the coffin. Wide-brimmed hats shaded their faces, and with beards down to their chests and up to their ears and the usual uniform of flannel shirt, leather waistcoat and leather breeches, Alyssa would have struggled to tell them apart anywhere. All she could say was that they were not among the group of suitors, or carried the scar that Rosie described.

The solemn procession led them up a gentle climb, towards the cedars stand. Peg-Leg walked right behind the coffin, in Alfie's stead, followed by Mr and Mrs Abbott, and the rest of the town, including Hans. Alyssa, with Mr Kendrick by her side, kept well back, the better to observe.

She'd wondered about the lack of a priest, when their own voyage had been organised between clergy here and back home in Melbourne, but the three graves she'd spotted behind the half-built church on her quay to the funeral probably answered that question. Or the priest had decided that the word of the Lord was easier to spread in bigger towns, with more amenities to ease a shepherd's burden.

The sun burnt down in what promised to be the hottest day since their arrival. Her shift already stuck to her legs, and perspiration soaked into the brim of the bonnet that Hannah had returned to her.

Beside her, Mr Kendrick looked enviably cool in his lightweight suit and bare head.

They'd arrived at the grave-site. The hole in the ground stood out like a gaping wound in the dark soil.

On a signal from Mr Abbott, the four coffin-bearers lowered their sad load. Matron sobbed, and Susanna wiped her eyes with a snowy lace handkerchief.

A lump formed in Alyssa's throat as she listened to Mr Abbott read a passage from the bible before he and Peg-Leg picked up the shovel and spade resting on the ground and covered Bert's coffin with earth. Load after load hit the wooden box with a muted thump.

She genuflected.

The mourners ambled back in a sedate fashion, as if everyone was afraid others might deem it unseemly if they hurried up. Alyssa snatched fragments of conversations, mostly about Rosie and her whereabouts, but nothing like the heated arguments that had forced Mr Abbott to open his gun cabinet.

He'd left the rifle at home today, but a bump in his jacket told Alyssa that he wore the pistol in a holster around his hip.

Mr Wainwright had handed his own navy revolver over to the doctor who'd stayed with his patient.

Alyssa's thoughts went to Rosie, for once alone and unprotected. Her foot caught on a protruding tree root. Mr Kendrick steadied her. That was what Rosie had lacked; the security of knowing that she had support and people she could lean on when she needed to.

Even during their long voyage, Rosie had mostly been at odds with the other girls, jealous of beauty as in Susanna's case, or Nancy's sweet nature, Hannah's cheerful practicality. That's how she ended up succumbing to that stoker instead of waiting to find her future husband here.

Once the recent dilemma was resolved – and Alyssa firmly disallowed herself to believe otherwise – Rosie needed to be reconciled with the others. Maybe this was the sharp reminder she needed, to stop alienating everyone and hurting herself in the process.

'Your brow furrows, and the Captain would pale if he saw the decisive gleam in your eye,' Mr Kendrick said. 'I assume your thoughts are not happy ones.' He gently pressed her arm. 'We'll see this through, however long it takes.'

'Yes,' she said, as another thought hit her like a blow. They'd been here for several weeks, and with them being cut off, what happened if Captain Moore received his orders to leave?

She asked Mr Kendrick who shrugged her worries off. 'He wouldn't sail without Wainwright and me.'

'But if the owners tell him to?' Despite the heat, goose-bumps formed on her arms. The idea of having to see him go forever hurt.

'Are you afraid we'd be marooned in Run's End? He chuckled. 'Mr Wainwright could think of a worse fate, I reckon. To be honest, so could I.'

Her goose-bumps vanished.

The wake at the hotel lasted less than an hour. While the men were still stuffing their mouths with the game pies, roast turkey and mountains of fruit tarts the girls had laboured over for two days, Mr Abbott informed them that Dr Bryson had set up a clinic and would invite the men over for an examination.

'You don't have to,' he said, making it sound anything but voluntary, 'but in the light of Alfie's illness, and when you remember how quick the priest and two others were taken in spring it sounds like a good idea to me.'

'What's going on with Alfie?' Fred asked, his eyes mere slits under his beetling brows.

'It's the smallpox,' another man said, causing an oppressive silence.

'Nonsense,' Mr Abbott said. 'It's a fever, that's all. Look at Hans, all rosy cheeks and clear eyes, eh? But go, ask the doctor.'

The store owner jostled Alyssa aside as he made for the door; followed by a surprisingly fast Peg-Leg, whose irregular gait hardly impeded him.

Mr Kendrick held out his arm to Alyssa. 'Shall we make our escape, or are we needed for the clean-up?'

'You've done enough,' Matron said, a glitter in her eyes as she observed the two together. 'Mr Wainwright and I have promised to sit with Alfie while the doctor holds his clinic. Why don't you two take some pie and go for a picnic?'

Alyssa's hand rested in the crook of Mr Kendrick's arm as they strolled along the back alley to the Osborne's home, a basket full of pie and tarts covered with a handkerchief swinging from his other hand.

Hannah gasped with delight as she saw the food. 'I smuggled out a tart in my dress pocket, but that's all I could bring for Rosie. I need to go down to the store soon.' She rang the silver bell.

Rosie's face lit up as she saw Alyssa, or it could have been the feast awaiting on the table. She snatched up a tart stuffed with apple, but before she so much as took one bite, she asked. 'May I help myself?'

'Yeah, of course,' Hannah said. 'I swear, your manners are getting nicer each day. Soon enough you'll put us all to shame.'

Rosie chewed as fast as she could and swallowed every crumb before she answered. 'Haha.'

'It was a compliment,' Hannah said. 'Honestly. We're proud of you, right Alyssa?'

'Yes.' Alyssa picked up a tart, too.

A slow grin brightened up Rosie's face as she saw Mr Kendrick's approving nod. For once she seemed content in their company.

Mr Osborne confined himself to a small piece of game pie, before he excused himself and returned to his work.

'How is it going?' Alyssa asked. 'You have assisted in the assay, haven't you, Mr Kendrick?'

'It's a slow process. Takes a lot of skill, and patience. I don't envy your husband this task, Mrs Osborne.'

'He wants to do it just right,' Hannah said with more than a hint of pride in her tone. 'It's his safety that I worry about. All this gold, and we're alone in this house.' Rosie gave a small shriek. Hannah patted her hand.

'No need to worry,' Mr Kendrick said. 'The doctor spends his nights in the surgery, but I've already arranged with Mr Abbott that I'll be your guest during the night. That is, if you'll put up with me.'

'That would be wonderful.' Hannah peered around her. The whatnot shelf, the range, table and chairs made her living quarters homely, but apart from the blank floor the offered no sleeping-space. They only had the one bedroom, and Rosie's hide-out.

'I'll set up in your husband's workroom. If anybody comes for the gold, I'll be ready and waiting.' He patted his revolver. 'If you need me, one shout and I'll be there. I sleep lightly.'

'You're too kind.' Hannah gave Alyssa what must be meant as a secretive wink. Matrimony had clearly gone to her head, if she saw a romance for Alyssa with every handsome, dashing – she called herself to order. By now everybody must see her friendship with Mr Kendrick and the doctor as exactly what it was – an easy communication between like-minded people, without any deeper attachments.

'I should probably go and offer the doctor my assistance,' she said.

Mr Kendrick chuckled. 'I assume that Hans won't be the only one with a delicate sense of propriety.'

Hannah gave her a questioning look.

'Our new neighbours prefer the comfort of having a man present at examinations instead of me.'

'That's stupid,' Rosie said. 'I mean, you're every bit as good as Matron when it comes to crook folks.'

'They'll come around when they have to.' Mr Kendrick checked the clock. 'But I'm sure Matron would appreciate being relieved, and then her husband could bring me my bedroll.'

'I'll tell him,' Alyssa said.

She passed a line of half a dozen men outside Mr Kendrick's cabin which for now served as a second surgery. Hardly anyone gave her a glance, in their anxiety to get a clean bill of health from the doctor.

Alyssa filled her lungs with the smell of cooking wafting from the hotel, pipe tobacco from the smokers and sun-baked soil. Despite the dark cloud hanging over Rosie, she felt lightheaded, simply strolling through town unchaperoned, uncensored and unshackled. This was the kind of freedom she'd longed for, the kind of freedom usually only granted to men.

If she really made good on her plan to return to the England she'd left as a toddler, she'd have to buckle under convention again. An unmarried woman of means would still be frowned upon, unless she found a respectable companion. An image flickered in Alyssa's mind; of a mild-mannered elderly gentlewoman, forever winding wool around her hands or working on her tapestry until the light grew too dim for her near-sighted eyes. A few months ago, even that seemed to be preferable to staying in Melbourne, with no chaperone or guardian, an outcast from society. Now her doubts grew daily.

As soon as she'd relieved Matron and asked Mr Wainwright to deliver the necessary things to Mr Kendrick, she was too busy to think about her future. Alfie's temperature had broken, but he tossed and turned on the creaking camp bed. His eyes were clearer, when he managed to prop them open, but mostly he seemed to be half-conscious, and aching all over.

Alyssa spoon-fed him broth and arrowroot. Alfie was willing enough to let himself be administered to. She cooled his brow and wrists. A bluebottle buzzed around his head, landing on the patient's cheek with unwavering persistence. Alyssa suspected that Alfie's sweat attracted the insect, but apart from swotting it, she was helpless to deter the intruder.

As soon as he had finished half a cup full of broth, Alyssa bade him rest. She pulled the blanket up to his chin.

'Too hot,' he said, the words coming out slurred. He tried to push away the cover but Alyssa held it in place.

'Doctor's orders,' she said. 'I'm sorry, but you will have to be uncomfortable a little while longer to get well again.'

'I need to get up. My brother –'

'Your brother would wish you to recover.' She pressed him gently back down. 'That is all you can do for him.'

'The funeral.' He licked his cracked lips. She needed to make sure he drank more.

'Mr Abbott took care of everything. Try to sleep for a while.'

He felt for her hand and clasped it. 'Thank you.'

Alyssa spent the afternoon sitting idle, with only her brain engaged. She soothed Alfie whenever he woke up, but it appeared that the sound of her voice alone sufficed to calm him down. Otherwise she thought about everything that had happened since their arrival, and most importantly, the murder of Bert Harper.

Firstly, why did he have to die? Because Mr Osborne would find the fools' gold as soon as he had assayed the contents of Bert's strong-box? But that would happen anyway. There was one explanation she could think of would make the murder necessary. The pyrite must be linked to one specific man, and Bert would have known. Otherwise the theft would have become obvious, but all the men would be suspect.

Why only two nuggets from each pouch? She tried to remember if Mr Osborne had checked them all, or simply a handful. The strong-box had held at least one hundred pouches. If the thief had stolen in equal measures from his neighbours, it showed a certain sense of fairness. How much would the missing gold be worth? And where did the pyrite come from?

Alfie groaned. His eyelids fluttered open. Alyssa rekindled the fire and hung the broth canister on a trivet. Sweat formed in her armpits, but Alfie needed the heat. Alyssa fanned herself.

The pyrite. And why not simply go out to the goldfields again and pan or dig or whatever it took to harvest those precious ores?

The door burst open, bringing with it a welcome breeze that lasted all of ten seconds until the doctor shut the door again.

'How's the patient?' he asked. 'And more importantly, how are you?' He set down his medical bag and sniffed the broth. 'How much has he had?'

'I was just about to give him his second mug. Would you like something?'

'I'll make the tea. You're doing enough.' He ladled broth into Alfie's mug and handed it to Alyssa before propping up his patient.

Alfie swallowed easier, and his skin looked a lot less flushed. 'Thanks,' he said.

'If you improve like this, you'll soon have proper food again.' Dr Bryson measured the tea and filled the pot with a surprising grace that he would not have learned in the Australian mining towns he used to practice in.

'I'm not hungry.' Alfie drank the last drop from the spoon and sank back.

'You soon will be.'

Dr Bryson took the teapot and motioned Alyssa away from Alfie's bedside. His manner exuded satisfaction.

'You've found something,' she said.

He poured the tea and spooned sugar in both mugs.

'Well?' She reached for her drink.

'The most important bit of news is, this is the healthiest place you could hope for.' He lowered his voice. 'Although I've suggested stricter hygiene rules, now that the wild and untamed times are over.'

Alyssa thought of the reek that had assaulted her nose at dinner, and agreed with all her heart.

'Until now, the only causes of death were accidents, and this spring a sudden fever that took a priest who's said to have had a weak chest, and two men whose constitution was weakened by their fondness for moonshine. Among them the oldest Keller brother.'

That explained the three graves Alyssa had seen. 'And the man with the scar? Rosie's assailant?'

'I've found him.'

His voice held a hint of triumph. 'It's Fred's older brother Michael, who spends his wealth more readily than he can acquire it. An unsavoury specimen, but there is no getting rid of him while we are under quarantine.' He grinned. 'He still sits down very gingerly, a result of Rosie's hat-pin if I'm not mistaken. She must have stabbed him good and hard.'

'He deserved it.' Alyssa's lips curled up. This would cheer Rosie up. 'Did he admit anything?'

'I didn't ask. The last thing I want is to make him or anyone else aware of our interest, or have them think about Rosie.'

'True, but how do we find out where he was during the night in question?'

'I've asked Abbott to chat with the men. There isn't much you can keep secret in a community like this.'

They sat in agreeable silence for a few minutes.

'I'll bring your dinner as soon as I can,' Alyssa said.

'That won't be necessary. I've arranged with Wainwright and Kendrick to take turns, so we all are seen without having to vacate Rosie's guard.'

Alyssa's gaze flickered to Alfie, but he snored gently. 'Thank you,' she said.

He walked her the five steps to the door. 'I'll see you at the hotel.'

Matron pulled Alyssa aside as soon as she saw her. 'How's Rosie?' she whispered. 'I really feel it's my duty to go and see her.'

Alyssa sighed. Mr Wainwright had told his wife; understandably, but the more people knew the harder it was to keep a secret.

'Your concern honours you,' she said, 'but it is paramount that we keep everything and everyone as quiet as possible. You already have so many pressing tasks that I could hardly look Mr Wainwright in the eyes and tell him that I did not prevent you from taking on even more.'

Matron appeared mollified; clearly her well-developed sense of responsibility had prompted her to ask for someone she could not care for. That also needed sorting at some stage, but for now keeping them apart would save Rosie additional aggravation, and lectures.

'But you can promise me that she is well looked after?' Matron peered at Alyssa with genuine concern.

'Yes.' Alyssa patted Matron's hand, satisfied that Mr

Wainwright kept Rosie's whereabouts a secret. 'But now we need to get down to work.'

Two hours later, while the first diners tucked into the leftovers from the wake and a stew of beans and salted pork, Alyssa wrote down the last names on the new schedule. As of tomorrow, the town would have a laundry service, and soon after a clothes repair shop. Matron had spotted sufficient frayed shirts and split seams to make that seem a valuable addition. In a short while the townsfolk wouldn't recognise themselves.

Matron hummed to herself, as she went over Alyssa's plan. They'd work on prices tomorrow, before taking in the first clothes for laundering. Mr Turner had come up with enough hard soap to last them for several weeks, even if every single man in town handed over his entire wardrobe.

Mr Wainwright and Mr Abbott would erect a few poles and string lines from them, for the drying, and the laundry itself would take over another unused cabin. Wash butts already stood ready by the river. Mr Wainwright had scrubbed four empty beer barrels with soapy water until his wife declared them clean enough.

He'd also remembered a recipe for soap making he'd learned as a seafarer. They only needed animal fat to give it a go.

'What are you and Mr Wainwright going to do, Matron?' Alyssa smoothed down the paper.

'I don't know. I really don't. Part of me wishes to stay here, but making Mr Wainwright stay ashore and cause him pain ...'

Matron's eyes clouded over for a split second. 'I'm sure everything will turn out for the best, especially once we've fed this lot again.'

Alyssa woke up to the sound of wooden boots stomping on the floorboards. Someone tugged on her blanket.

'The doctor sent for you,' Harriet said. 'Honestly, how he ever wants to do without you!'

Alyssa reached for her dress. Nothing; the hook on the wall on which she'd hung it sat empty.

'It's in the wash,' Harriet said and pulled out Alyssa's trunk. 'Will this one do?' She held up a pale blue muslin dress with a slight bustle. 'You'll look nice in this.'

'Thank you.' Alyssa stepped into the dress. Harriet did up the hooks for her. 'Especially for thinking about my dress.'

'Can't have you running around smelling like dirty feet, now, can we?' Harriet winked. 'We'll soon have this place licked into shape.'

Alyssa was the last to leave the cabin. Her friends made for the hotel, or the river to do the washing, while she set off for the surgery.

A quartet of men stood huddled into a corner as she passed them, among them Peg-Leg, Little Joe and Fred. Peg-Leg appeared to have quit the hotel altogether. He'd carried a bedroll and a large sack yesterday, she remembered. They'd have to air and clean his room, she thought, but that could wait.

The first thing she saw in the surgery was a bundle of clothes. Dr Bryson loomed over Alfie who struggled to get to his feet.

'Down, man,' he said, glaring his patient into submission. He handed Alyssa the bundle. 'Can you please take these to be washed?'

'Of course.'

'Give me back my pants.' Alfie reached out for the bundle.

'You won't need them for a day or two.'

Alyssa fled the scene.

The sun glinted on the river. Grace and Bertha stood side by side, dunking shirts into the suds-filled wash butts and twirling the plungers. They'd worked up a nice rhythm. Their bonnets shaded their faces, and they'd rolled up the sleeves to keep them dry. Harriet and Nellie took the clean shirts and rinsed them in the slow-flowing river. Hard to believe that a little bit further down bends and waterfalls turned this calm water into a dangerous torrent.

Alyssa handed over her bundle with stiff fingers. She'd carried it at arm's length, to avoid too close contact. Grace had less scruples. She dumped the pants onto a heap at the side, and dropped the shirt into the butt. Alyssa was glad to see that the bundle contained no underclothes; the doctor must have allowed Alfie to keep at least the most necessary garments.

She crouched and dipped her fingers into the cool water. The temperature had dropped a little, but the sun already warmed her skin. She should have put her name onto the list for laundry duty instead of suffering the kitchen heat in the hotel, or the fire in the surgery.

'This isn't half bad,' Nellie said. 'Fancy us earning our own money.' She held up a shirt and peered at it from every angle before she rolled it up and squeezed as much water as possible out of it.

Half a dozen dresses and skirts already fluttered on the washing lines. Alyssa saw with satisfaction that the girls had put their own clothes first; something they wouldn't have dared a few months ago. Yes, this enterprise has been a good idea.

'Where's Matron?' she asked.

'In the laundry cabin, with Hans.' Nellie noticed Alyssa's surprise. 'Somebody had to tell her who the fellow is we're washing for. Mr Abbott says as Hans is trustworthy.' She snickered. 'Maybe you should go and keep an eye on him.'

'I will, to make sure we get the book-keeping right.'

'You know what else you should do? Make more of those boiled sweets.' Nellie licked her lips. 'You could make a fortune with those.'

Alyssa laughed. Her bonbons, made from a recipe of her grandfather's, had turned out to be enough to win Nellie's reluctant friendship during the voyage. Maybe she should cook up a batch. A sweet or two might lift Rosie's spirits too.

In the laundry, piles of clothes sat in boxes. Hans identified the owners, and Mr Wainwright dictated the details to his wife – number of shirts, pants, socks, undergarments, and the colour. Poor Matron would be mortified if she handed over the wrong vest. There must be an easier way to do the book-keeping, but this would do for a start.

'Can you please add Alfie's name? One blue shirt, and brown pants.'

Matron's pen scratched over the page of a thin notebook. She looked all business as she painstakingly checked her entries. 'Done,' she said. 'But that is the last load we can take on today. Everybody else will have to wait a day or two.'

She handed the ledger to her husband.

Hans tipped his hat. 'I'll be off then.'

'Where do I find you when we reopen for business?'

He shuffled from one foot to another. 'I was kind of thinking of going back out again for a bit. I've been cooped up here now for a bit.'

'Two days,' Alyssa said.

'Two days with nothing to do. And with Bert gone – it's not the same.'

'You're getting restless.'

'It's not healthy, all this sitting around without so much as a proper drink.' He caught himself. 'All decent and civilised of course, Ma'am. Ask Mr Abbott.'

Alyssa found herself warming towards him. If she felt bored and restless when she had nothing to occupy her mind, how must this man suffer, when his very simple needs of physical activity, solitude and a drink with his friends were taken away from him? Alfie and he had been out in the wilderness when Bert died, so he wasn't a suspect.

'I'm sure the doctor and Mr Abbott will soon declare it safe to leave,' she said. 'In the meantime, there must be a few tasks for you.'

He wiggled his calloused hands. 'A man needs to have something to do.' Helping Matron identify customers obviously did not count.

'You're good with an axe,' she said. 'How about getting in a supply of firewood?'

Mr Wainwright smote him on the back. 'Excellent idea. I'll give you a hand, if that's alright with you.' He caught a warning glare from Alyssa. 'As soon as I've finished a few other things.'

Hans strolled off, a bit happier. They'd have to come up with a plan to identify the murderer fast, and to occupy the men trapped because of the smallpox threat, or they'd have a mutiny on hand.

Rosie looked like she could do with something to occupy her, too. She appeared pale and distracted, but denied that anything was wrong with her.

Hannah shrugged. 'I'd say it's cabin fever, only she was sick again this morning.'

'I'm fine,' Rosie said. 'It's nerves, that's all. Being trapped inside and listening, always listening.'

'I still think we should get Matron to have a look at you.'

Rosie clamped her lips together.

'Mrs Wainwright does worry about you,' Alyssa said. 'And she doesn't mean half the things she said to you.' A little white lie, she told herself, to comfort Rosie. Matron had suffered too much through Rosie's disobedience to forget and forgive easily. 'Shall we ask the doctor around?'

Rosie's hand went to her stomach. 'No.' Alyssa frowned. Usually the girl liked nothing better than male attention. 'You could at least talk to him, and if he wants you to be examined, he could tell me what to do, if you prefer that.'

Rosie hesitated for an agonising minute, before she nodded.

'That's settled,' Hannah said with a dangerous glint in her eye. Her patience seemed to wear thin, too. 'Let's get the men.'

Mr Kendrick broke into a wide smile as he saw Alyssa. 'You are a sight for sore eyes,' he said. 'Especially in a dress spun from patches of summer sky.'

Rosie and Hannah giggled as Alyssa felt blood rush to her cheeks. Even Mr Osborne's eyes twinkled as he said, 'You do your Welsh heritage proud, Mr Kendrick. You're as fine as poet as many of your countrymen. But he is right, Miss Chalmers, you look delightful.'

'Thank you, but I hope I'll soon be able to put away my finery for the proper occasion.' She broke off. 'You were informed that Mrs Wainwright has organised a laundry service for the town?'

'In the nick of time,' Mr Kendrick said. 'I'm down to my last clean shirt, and Mr Osborne can't fare much better.'

'You should have told me.' Hannah shook her head at her husband. 'I could've done the washing in a jiffy.'

'You had more than enough to cope with, my dear,' Mr Osborne said with a swift nod towards Rosie.

'Give me your shirts, and yours too, Mr Kendrick, and I will take them to Matron. I could do with a spot of fresh air,' Hannah said.

'The girls are up to their ears in work for today already,' Alyssa said. 'Tomorrow would be better.'

'Tomorrow?' Hannah narrowed her eyes. 'I'm not too fancy to look after my own family and guests, thank you very much.' She turned to the men. 'You've got five minutes to hand over your dirty clothes.'

Mr Kendrick gave Alyssa a quiet signal, that he needed to talk to her. 'Why don't you and Mr Osborne sit in the back yard for a spell, and then Alyssa and I take care of the laundry?' He gave Hannah his most charming smile, melting her resistance with barely a try.

'What about me?' Rosie stared at the door with unveiled longing.

He shook his head. Alyssa thought for a moment. 'She can't go out in daylight, of course, but if she borrowed my dress and bonnet, and sat outside with you for a few minutes at night, with her back to the street?'

'It's risky,' he said. 'You and Rosie aren't the least bit alike.'

'Please, Mr Kendrick,' Rosie said. 'Just for two minutes.' Her voice caught in her throat. Tears welled up in her eyes. For a moment, she looked like a lost child.

Alyssa put her hand on his.

'People might talk about us,' he said.

She shrugged. 'You've survived worse.'

'I was thinking about you.'

'I know, but this is for Rosie. And you'll keep her safe, won't you.'

'I will.'

~

Mr Kendrick carried the laundry bundle down to the river. The girls had taken a break and squatted under a tree that offered them a little relief from the midday sun.

Fish darted to and fro in the water as Alyssa spread out the shirts.

'What are you doing?' Nellie asked.

'We forgot to let the Osbornes and Mr Kendrick know that they can bring their washing.'

Alyssa soaked the first shirt in the clear stream, at the same time trying to keep her dress from getting wet. Behind her, she could hear Nellie sigh. 'I'll take care of it.'

'Have your break. It won't hurt me to do this.'

Nellie chortled good-naturedly and strolled over to Alyssa, who righted herself. 'First the suds, then you rinse them.'

'But if I put them in with other clothes, they might get mixed up.'

Nellie rolled her eyes. 'You can remember what things look like, right?' She nudged Alyssa aside. 'You go for a stroll with Mr Kendrick.' She gave them both a coy smile.

'Thank you.' Mr Kendrick's teeth shone white in his tanned face. 'We will. That is –' He creased his forehead as if in heavy concentration. 'I'm never too sure if I leave things in my pockets. Do you look them through first?'

'That's being done in the laundry cabin, when they take the clothes in. Matron's got a special box for that.'

'Commendable. Not that I'd expect her to find gold, but you never know.' He watched Nellie for a reaction, but she laughed.

'Chance would be a fine thing. Gold! Who'd leave that in his pocket?'

Mr Kendrick led Alyssa further down the river. A light breeze ruffled the long grass that here still stood lush and green. Mice scurried in and out of a nest.

'You wanted to tell me something,' she said.

'We've by now weighed and checked every single pouch from Bert's strong-box.' He flicked a pebble into the water, creating a ripple of rings that spread out in ever growing circles. 'The last two didn't contain any pyrite.'

'Maybe our thief had run out,' Alyssa said.

'Possible. Or he missed his chance because he only dared jemmy it open after the murder.'

'Who does this gold belong to?'

'Dave, the red-haired man who handed his riches over in the bar. And Bert.'

'He didn't prospect anymore.'

'But he took gold as payment.'

A dragonfly hovered over the water, tantalisingly close to a fish that jumped out, missing its prey by the span of a wing.

'If he'd missed his opportunity, it means that the thefts took place before, probably every time after a new deposit.' Alyssa grew excited. 'That means he needed easy access whenever the situation arose. And because a nightly prowl might become noticeable, we need to look at opportunities during the day.'

'I've asked Abbott. Although Bert usually stayed at the hotel and Peg-Leg ran his errands if you forgive that pun, our good publican would look after his brewing operation two or three times a week, and he'd always let the men know that he'd have something fresh for them the next night.'

'A perfect opportunity. But why did you want to find out if the girls turned out pockets?'

'I don't see our thief skulking about with a bag full of fool's gold,' Mr Kendrick said. 'I'd have put my two nuggets into my jacket, or pants. It's a long shot, but as crumbly as the stuff is, there might have been broken bits left in the clothes.'

The laundry cabin sat empty. Matron's chair was covered with a sheet, to save it from getting dusty. The fabric hung down onto the ground. Alyssa lifted one corner. Like she'd thought, Matron had used this to hide the box that Nellie mentioned. She pulled it out and started to rummage through it. A crumpled letter with faded writing, a pencil, stained handkerchiefs that she lifted with the pencil.

'What on earth are you doing?' a voice behind her asked. Matron and her husband, armed with a tape measure, charcoal and yet another ledger.

Alyssa looked for assistance to Mr Kendrick. He shrugged. She beckoned Matron closer. 'We need your help,' she said. 'If you find anything that looks like a speck of gold, please inform me or Mr Kendrick as soon as possible, but don't let anyone else know. It's important.'

Mr Wainwright gave his wife a small nod; he'd understood.

His left hand slid into his pocket, pulling out a speck of mineral, gleaming brassy-yellow.

Alyssa drew in her breath. 'Where did you find this?'

'In the laundry we took in from those Kellers and Peg-Leg. The state of those clothes bars description.' Matron shuddered. 'Suffice it to say that I would have had to turn away that man from the hotel, had he insisted on staying.'

She took the tape measure and held out one end for her husband. 'Little Joe's clothes were a lot cleaner, I'm happy to say. There's still hope for that young man, if he learns to keep better company.'

The Kellers. Everything led back to them.

'Can I be of any assistance?' Mr Kendrick asked. 'What are you planning?'

'I want a proper counter, with a section that I can open, and a few proper shelves.' Matron's eyes sparkled as she surveyed her surroundings. 'The girls are settling in well in the kitchen, and if I train two or three of them here, I can divide my time between hotel and laundry. I've already agreed with Nancy and her husband that they grow as much fruit and vegetables as they still can this late in the season, and start a hay crop for cattle.'

'You're a marvel,' Alyssa said, meaning every word.

Matron flushed becomingly. Her husband gave her arm a tender squeeze before he drew a charcoal outline on the floorboards.

'What next?' Dust whirled around Mr Kendrick's toes as they

ambled along the Main Street. They needed rain, and soon, Alyssa thought. The complete town appeared parched, with the weather-bleached wood of the row of houses, the pale grey of the soil, and the washed-out blue of the sky. Everything took on a uniform appearance in weather like this. She wondered how much sameness Mr Kendrick could suffer without becoming restless. For someone used to the endless horizons and the ever-changing scenery of the oceans, this must be as stifling as the ship with its narrow confines had been for her.

She asked him. He stayed quiet for longer than she'd anticipated, but after an interminable wait he flashed her one of the quick grins that had won him most girl's sympathies. 'I wouldn't want to stay here idle,' he said. 'But it's a nice change, and with a mystery to occupy our wits I can hardly say that I'm bored. And I grew up in a village.'

'With other families, and friends,' she said. 'This is hardly the same.'

'True, but I'm used to the company of men, with but a few of them my equals due to the necessary hierarchy. This is a holiday.'

'This is a bad business,' Mr Abbott said. Susanna squatted on a freshly turned patch of soil and planted a few wildflowers she must have gotten from the meadows. Violets were the only ones Alyssa recognised.

Susanna put aside her trowel and wiped her hands on the piece of sacking she'd tied around her waist to protect her skirt. 'Let's go inside,' she said.

'What can you tell us about the Kellers?' Alyssa asked as soon as they sat in the parlour.

Mr Abbott pushed his lips in and out as he thought about her question. 'Not our most valued neighbours, but none too bad,' he said. 'Apart from that still. I told Michael and Fred before, I'll close it down if they don't.'

'But the moonshine is the only thing you hold against them?'

Mr Abbott rubbed his neck. 'It's a free country, and we can't always choose who moves in. Why?'

'Would Fred or Michael be desperate for money?'

'They're both fond of a game of poker when they get out of town, but most men are. Michael fancies himself a bit too clever, but then again he isn't the only one.' He shook his head. 'There's enough gold out there for everyone, so why steal it?'

'That's what we wondered about.' Alyssa sighed. 'Why steal nuggets, kill a man and risk being discovered, when all you need is hard work and a bit of luck?'

'There's one reason I could think of,' Mr Kendrick said.

Alyssa nodded. 'If a man can't go out himself and prospect.'

Mr Abbott opened his mouth and shut it again with a loud snap. 'I'll be darned.'

'Yes?'

'Michael was laid low for a spell. All the Kellers were, this spring, but Michael and Fred pulled through alright.' His mouth set in a grim line. 'He's fond of cards, too, that's why he's a regular on the steamer.'

'How can he afford that, if ill health prevented him from looking for gold?' Alyssa tried to keep her hopes down, but Michael Keller shaped up well as a suspect.

'The still. Most of the boys get a bottle or two of moonshine before they set off.' He rubbed thumb and forefinger together. 'A lot cheaper than Bert's regular liquor, and a lot more potent.'

'Or dangerous,' Mr Kendrick said.

'That too, but you don't go into the wilderness if a bit of risk scares you off.'

'He needed money, he didn't like Rosie –' Alyssa broke off as she saw the bewildered faces. 'When she followed us, a man on board tried to take advantage of her, but she defended herself with a hatpin.'

Susanna clapped. 'Good girl!'

'Did she recognise him?' Mr Abbott's voice was dangerously quiet. Mr Kendrick nodded.

'The scar on his hand. And he would have limped a bit because she jabbed him in the backside with a hatpin.'

'Good grief!' Mr Abbott broke into laughter. He put an arm around his wife and pulled her close. 'Remind me when I get close to overstepping a line with you.'

Susanna gave him a quick peck on the cheek. 'I will, my dear, I will.'

'One thing that's been bothering me is the pyrite,' Alyssa said. 'If it's not found in these parts, where did it come from in such amounts?'

'A steamer.' Mr Abbot shrugged. 'Or one of the gambling dens in Port Victoria. It'd be easy to fool someone who's gullible enough. Take their gold or dollars first, and then you put your worthless stuff into the pot and let them win.'

'You wouldn't have to be that gullible. The pyrite looks real enough to take in anyone but an expert.' Mr Kendrick paused.

'You had a bank here before. Did the man in charge ever say anything?'

'He was more of a bean-counter,' Mr Abbott said. 'Happy to take in a couple of dollars and write a receipt, but that's about it. We'd never have expected someone like Mr Osborne, with this knowledge and fancy equipment, to be sent our way.'

His eyes crinkled at the corners as he grinned at this wife. 'Seems we're going up in the world, my love. I bet you a new hat this means they will build a railway along these parts, when they send someone like our friend Osborne into the wilderness.'

Susanna's dimples showed as she replied, 'Betting? You are a gambler, then, after all your talk about keeping the town clean?'

'From card-sharps and heavy gaming,' he said. 'And this bet was offered in the privacy of my own home, surrounded by friends.'

Their mutual affection was obvious. Alyssa hated to spoil the moment, but she had to. 'If Michael killed Bert Harper, how do we prove it? Can we get into his cabin, to search for pyrite?'

Mr Abbott shook his head. 'How? With him, Fred and now Peg-Leg sharing, there's bound to be someone in.'

'When everyone's at dinner,' Mr Kendrick said. 'If we find pyrite, or gold ...'

'Doesn't prove anything worth a damn. Pardon my language, ladies. No, he could always say it's his from last year, or Fred's.'

'Or Peg-Leg's.' Susanna's fingers twisted a strand of her hair in deep concentration. 'He hasn't been able to go prospecting since the accident.'

'He could claim he won it on the boat, couldn't he?' A sour taste rose in Alyssa's mouth. They needed to find a way to show everyone who the real murderer was. 'Would Peg-Leg tell a lie to protect a man who killed his friend and employer? Surely he owes the dead man loyalty?'

'Hard to tell,' Mr Abbott said. 'He and the Kellers have been friends for years, and Peg-Leg always put in a good word for them with Bert.'

'We need a way to make Michael talk,' Alyssa said.

Susanna's eyes lit up. 'That should be easy. He's a man, and men like to brag, right?'

Her husband and Mr Kendrick looked aghast. 'Most men, that is. Not you,' she said. 'We know that Michael is susceptible to females, so if somebody would show a little bit of appreciation for his rugged charm?'

'I'm not having you go near that fellow for all the gold in Canada.' Mr Abbott glared at her. 'Or another unprotected girl.'

'Not me. Don't be silly.' Susanna stroked her husband's arm. 'I thought, Alyssa could do it.'

Mr Kendrick sputtered. 'That's preposterous.'

'Is it?' Susanna showed him her most winning smile. 'Everybody's seen the two of you together, or the doctor and Alyssa, but no-one's claimed her yet, right?'

Alyssa chuckled. 'Because I'm not much for a fancy man, but like them a bit rough around the edges?'

'What do you think?' Susanna twirled her around.

'That's madness.' Mr Kendrick got hold of Alyssa's arms. 'Consider his behaviour with Rosie, and if he's a cold-blooded murderer and catches wind of what you're up to?'

'He won't try anything with half the town having seen us together.' Alyssa wished she could muster more conviction, but this plan was all they had. 'If you could see your way to restoring the bottle of moonshine to Fred and making sure that he and his brother have a glass or two, I could try to gain his trust for the evening.'

'He won't talk in the bar,' Mr Kendrick said.

'But he might on a stroll in the balmy night, down to the river.'

'No.' Mr Kendrick pleaded with Mr Abbott. 'This is your town. Stop her.'

'I'm relying on someone being close by. How good are you with your pistol?'

'Good enough to stop a man.'

CHAPTER 17

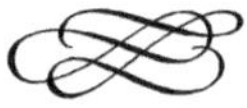

Alyssa returned to an empty home. All the other girls were busy in either the hotel kitchen or the laundry. A thin film of sand and dust covered he floorboards. She picked up the broom that stood behind the wall and swept in long, vigorous strides. The rhythm helped her think.

How could she get close enough to Michael to get his attention? Most evenings, the men shovelled down their food, to conclude the meal with a few beers and a chat with their friends.

The select group that had paid for the girls' journey, tended to sit for a spell with them after they had finished their work, under the benign supervision of the Wainwrights. Maybe a dance would be the solution.

The door burst open, slamming against her elbow. She dropped the broom and yelped in pain.

'I'm sorry.' The doctor grabbed her by the shoulders. 'Are you hurt?'

She rubbed the afflicted bone. The pain subsided.

He propelled her onto a chair. 'Kendrick told me about your crazy plan. You're not really intending to seduce Michael Keller in the hope to get him to confide in you?'

'Do you have a better idea? And I wouldn't call it seducing him. That sounds –'

'Exactly like what he's going to think.'

'Mr Abbott will protect me.'

'No, he won't,' the doctor said. 'Because I'm - '

'Do you play an instrument? The fiddle, or the harmonica, anything we could dance to?'

'Mr Kendrick does. As does Little Joe, if you remember.'

'How fortunate.' She patted the seat next to herself.

Half an hour later they still had no better idea, but at least the doctor had devised a scheme to keep her safe. On a string around her neck hung a tin whistle that he'd produced without an explanation. Alyssa secretly thought of it as a childhood souvenir, long since played with, but cherished for its memories. They'd practiced how to pull it out of her bodice and have it at her lips in a heartbeat.

Dr Bryson planned on loitering nearby, with Mr Kendrick. People were used to seeing them together, so Michael would think nothing of it. They'd also spike the moonshine with a mild sedative, too little to make the drinkers fall asleep but enough to dull their reactions.

The doctor had calmed down during their conversation,

although he still cudgelled his brain to come up with a better plan to discover the truth.

'I don't like it,' he said. 'I don't see why you of all people should have to put yourself in harm's way. Let Abbott deal with it.'

'He can't', she said with as much patience as she could muster. 'We should be glad that her Majesty's representatives have chosen a man of rare integrity to hold a position of power.' She touched his hand. 'How can I desert Rosie? Especially since I've got two knights in you and Mr Kendrick.'

He ruffled his hair. 'I'll borrow Abbott's pistol.'

'Thank you. How's your patient today?'

'Impatient, and a darn nuisance. He's been asking after you, but forbidden me to let you or Matron in before he's got his pants back. Wainwright is sitting with him.'

'I'm glad to hear that he's on the mend. Do you have a few minutes for another patient?'

Rosie scowled at Alyssa but meekly answered the doctor's questions, seconded by Hannah. Yes, she'd struggled to keep her food down for a bit, but that was better now. 'It's been all that upset,' she said. 'I was fine while we did our own cooking, right, Hannah? But the things they fed us on the steamer, why, smelling it in the kitchen did for me. I'm better now, and as soon as Alyssa has sorted this mess, I'll be good as gold. Honest.'

Alyssa took Rosie's pulse while the girl prattled on. Cold

sweat beaded her temples, although Hannah's house kept deliciously cool in the summer heat.

'You were also feeling faint,' Alyssa said.

Hannah nodded. 'She was that close to crumbling right here, doctor.'

Rosie opened her mouth but her hostess shushed her.

'I'm not an expert in these matters,' Dr Bryson said with an apologetic air, 'but I would strongly recommend, to consult Matron. If I'm not mistaken, Rosie, you are healthy enough for a young woman in your delicate condition.'

The last drop of colour fled Rosie's face. 'What?' Hannah dropped the shirt she was sewing.

Dr Bryson averted his gaze. 'It appears that you are expecting the first baby to be born in this town.'

CHAPTER 18

Matron blanched. 'Whatever next?' She grasped for Alyssa's hand, squeezing it hard enough to make Alyssa flinch.

'Rosie appears well enough,' she said, 'but I'm sure that she could do with some advice and moral support.'

'Moral! An alley cat has nothing on that one.'

'She's trying to improve,' Alyssa said. 'And how can we, who never lacked guidance or affection, judge her?'

Matron rubbed her temple. 'You're right, but she's been nothing like a trial to me, from the very first day.'

'Give her a chance to prove herself to you. For the baby's sake.'

Matron reached for her bonnet. 'Very well.'

Alyssa left Hannah, Rosie and Matron chatting about babies and their needs. Rosie had overcome the first shock and showed the proper respect and gratitude for any help. This should keep them all entertained until the evening, when Mr Kendrick would relieve the Osbornes of their duty.

Alyssa stopped in the middle of the street, causing Peg-Leg to stumble as he passed her.

'I'm so sorry,' she said automatically. If Mr Kendrick took up his place as Rosie's guard again, and kept his promise to sit with her in the open air for a few minutes, he could not play his part in their plans for Michael. Nor would anyone mistake Rosie for Alyssa, if they'd seen her a little while ago in the hotel.

She turned around, automatically heading for the surgery, to discuss these issues with the doctor. Twenty feet from the cabin another bit of information made her stop again and change direction, towards the river.

Nellie, Harriet, Bertha and Grace giggled over something Alyssa couldn't hear. They sat under a sheet they'd pegged up between two lines, to serve as sun-cover. Clean shirts and vests fluttered in the light breeze, and the girls folded and stacked heavy pants. At the side lay the garments Alyssa had dropped off earlier. She picked up Alfie's brown twill pants and rubbed a bit of fabric between her fingers. It felt dry enough, as did the shirt.

'Can I take these clothes?'

Nellie rolled her shoulders and stretched. 'Sure. Saves us the walk.'

Alyssa looked at the clotheslines that sagged under the weight.

Grace giggled again. Her gaze flickered towards a stretch further down the river where two men squatted, fishing lines lazily dancing in the water. 'They're waiting for us to finish, and then they'll carry the laundry for us.'

Bertha chimed in. 'They offered to do that every day, have the Joneses.'

Alyssa caught Nellie's wink. These must be the two brothers Alyssa had seen at the hotel. They must have made a big impression on Grace and Bertha, to render them loquacious. Nellie gave her a small nod and waved her away.

'Where's you suitor, Nellie?' Alyssa asked in a low voice as Nancy handed her the bundle.

'He'll be around for dinner, don't you worry. Every night after I'm done George takes me out for a walk, and we sit under the stars and chat.'

'I wish you'd introduce him. Properly, I mean.'

'I will, but you're constantly running around, busy as a bluebottle.' She lowered her voice, too. 'Tell Rosie I miss her.'

Alyssa put a warning finger on her lips but Grace and Bertha were caught up in their own world.

Alyssa waited outside while Alfie got dressed.

When she was allowed inside the surgery, he complained about being stuck inside, but with a lack of conviction that made Alyssa think that he realised it would take him awhile to get back on his feet.

At least he no longer needed constant care, and begged her for some proper food. 'A nice fat slab of meat.' He held his hands eight inches apart. 'Or a hunk of bread and cheese. Anything but the slop you've all been feeding me.'

'I'll see what I can get for you, if you refrain from repeating these words in Mrs Wainwright's presence. That nourishing slop was cooked especially for you, and it seems to have worked,' Alyssa said, after receiving a nod from the doctor.

Alfie blushed, but it no longer was the feverish flush that he'd shown the last few days. He must possess the constitution of an ox, Alyssa thought.

'Is there anything else I can do for you? What about you, Dr Bryson?'

'I'd appreciate bread and cold meat or cheese. Anything that's easy and can be eaten outside.'

Alfie perked up. 'Beer would help wash it down, Miss.'

Alyssa hid a smile. Alfie on the mend appeared to be a likeable young man. With properly trimmed hair and his open face, he might easily find favour with one of the few yet unspoken for girls. But he'd have to be quick.

The doctor opened the door for her. Alfie followed, stepping out into the sunshine. He squinted, as if the bright light dazzled him, and swayed slightly. The doctor pulled him back inside. 'Give it a few more days.'

Alyssa filled a basket with pies, bread, cheese and a few apples, when she spotted two leftover fruit tarts. She hesitated, before she took them both. Nobody paid her any attention. The girls were too busy getting yet another dinner of stew, beans and potatoes ready.

Mr Wainwright stood behind the bar and handed Alyssa a stoppered flask with beer.

She stopped at Hannah's place first.

Her friend shook her head as Alyssa unpacked half the food, including both tarts. 'I can look after my own family,' she said, while giving Rosie the signal to come out.

'I know, but it's nice for a bit to have someone else look after you.' Alyssa handed Rosie a tart. 'You need proper nourishment.'

Rosie sniffed the pastry. 'Oooh, it smells ever so good.' A tiny tear formed in her left eye. 'You're all so nice to me, and I've been such a cow.'

'Yes, you have.' Hannah gave her a chuck under the chin. 'But you're our cow, and that baby is family too.'

Rosie sighed as she bit into the tart. She chewed and swallowed properly. 'Thanks, Alyssa. And thanks for lending me your clothes so I can sit outside with Mr Kendrick. I swear, that's all that's keeping me from losing it up here.' She tapped her head.

Alyssa stifled a groan. She couldn't tell Rosie that her tiny taste of freedom had to be postponed.

Michael and Peg-Leg ambled past her as she rushed towards the surgery. Michael's gaze flickered over her shape as he and Peg-Leg tipped their hats. Alyssa forced herself to give them a quick smile and a curtsy, bearing in mind her future flirtation with the Keller brother.

Her hand went towards her hidden whistle. Michael stood six feet tall, with shoulders wide enough to fill a door frame, and huge paws for hands. Easy to imagine him knocking Bert unconscious with the pan and smothering him without breaking a sweat.

Peg-Leg and Michael entered Mr Turner's shop.

Alfie tore into his food as if he'd been on the brink of starvation. Alyssa and the doctor took their meal outside, sitting on a blanket he'd spread over the porch. For a few precious moments, Alyssa was at peace.

Until a shot rang out.

Men shouted.

Alyssa jumped up. Dr Bryson's hand went to the pistol on his hip as they ran towards the source of the noise.

Mr Abbott stood outside his house, pointing his rifle at a man who stood next to Susanna, a flimsy looking musket pressed into her side.

'Drop the gun,' he said. The man obeyed. 'Now step away from my wife.'

Susanna ran towards Alyssa and threw herself into her arms. 'They want Rosie,' she whispered.

Dr Bryson turned his head for an instant towards the bank. Big Joe, a crowbar in his hand, squared up to Mr Abbott. 'Nobody's going to hurt your Missus,' he said. 'All we want is the skirt that killed Bert.'

Peg-Leg and Fred slipped into the back of the small crowd.

'She's under lock and key,' Mr Abbott said. 'We will bring

Bert's murderer to justice, but like I said before, we'll do it the proper way.' He lifted his rifle. 'Last warning, for all of you.'

'What do you call justice?' Michael raised his fist. 'We're tired of waiting.'

'And I'm tired of warning you. The next man who threatens my wife, or anyone else, will be locked up.'

'Without a prison?' Barry stepped forward, shoving Nancy's husband aside to make way for him. He smelled of donkey and liquor. That explained why he'd come to town; to purchase drink from the Kellers. His swagger and slurred speech bore testimony of that.

'If you want to find out what I can come up with, you're welcome,' Mr Abbott said. 'I give you all two minutes to go your own way.'

They shuffled off, with muttered threats.

Susanna stumbled toward her husband.

'I'm so sorry, my love,' he said.

She touched his cheek with trembling fingers. 'It's alright. I don't think he'd have hurt me.'

'Nobody will lay a finger on you. I swear.'

'We need to get Rosie away from here,' Alyssa said.

'Impossible.' Mr Abbott patted his rifle. 'I wonder what set them off.'

'Or who.' Alyssa couldn't explain why, but something told her that this was all part of a plan. 'Why should they demand Rosie now?'

'The funeral?'

'That was two days ago.'

'It takes a bit for peaceful men to get their blood boiling,' the doctor said.

'But it wasn't,' Alyssa said. 'They caved in fast enough.'

'They threatened my wife.' Mr Abbott hugged Susanna, handing his rifle to the doctor.

'Who was that man? I've seen him at the hotel a few times.'

'Pierre Dubois. They call him French Pete. He used to help with the brewing when winter set in. Not too keen on roughing it in the snow, is French Pete.'

'A friend of Michael's?'

'He and Peg-Leg are buddies. So's Barry.'

Alyssa tucked the tin-whistle loosely under shift. By now she marvelled that the string hadn't broken, with being tugged out hundreds of times for practice. She could feel the tension rise. Luckily the other girls didn't notice anything amiss.

She smoothed down her hair and pulled out a few strands at the sides, to twist into ringlets. Pinching her cheeks heightened their colour.

Waiting for the men to eat and the drinking and music to start was agony. Her stomach had shrunk to the size of a marble, and bile rose in her mouth as she worked her way closer to Michael.

He leant on the bar, his eyes slightly unfocussed as he poured a shot of brown liquid from Fred's bottle into his beer.

Mr Abbott gave Alyssa a quick nod. Susanna stood next to him, serving beer and coffee. She'd promised her husband to stay by his side, after this afternoon's incident. Her smile was a little bit too brittle, and her hands unsteady, but Alyssa felt the same.

She moved up to the bar where Little Joe made a few more inches space for her.

'What can I get you?' Susanna asked.

'Not water.' Alyssa tried to think of how Rosie would behave. 'Do you have something with a bit more flavour to it?' She looked at Michael's glass. 'What this gentleman's having looks good.' She rested her hand on the bar, less than an inch from his elbow.

He looked up from his glass. His pupils were dilated. She attempted a coy smile. He ran his gaze over her figure.

Mr Kendrick moved past, waiting for her signal to play his fiddle. She slowly shook her head. Michael didn't look too steady already, and the last thing she needed was for him to keel over on the dance floor, or push into others and start a brawl.

Susanna shoved a glass of water towards her. 'You know I can't give you a drink.' She lowered her voice to a conspiratorial whisper. 'The doctor would kick up an almighty fuss. Remember last time?'

'If he thinks that's the way to a girl's heart.' Alyssa slid Michael a sideward glance. 'A real man treats her differently.'

'Maybe someone could, you know, take you for a stroll?' Susanna winked at Michael, who appeared to have trouble concentrating. 'What do you think, Mr Keller?'

'What?' A fleck of spittle appeared on his lower lip. Alyssa shuddered inwardly, but she forced herself to touch his hand.

'You wouldn't know where a thirsty girl could get a drink in private, would you?' She batted her lashes at him.

Susanna leant forward. 'The walk towards the river is lovely at night, if you're not dressed too warm.'

Bit by bit the words sank in. Michael leered at Alyssa. 'You'd like that, wouldn't you?' He smoothed his hair and slid his tongue over his lips. 'My bottle,' he said to Susanna. She glanced around, as if to make sure she was unobserved. She passed him his moonshine. There was less than half left. 'For your lady-friend,' she said as she passed him another, firmly stoppered, small bottle.

Alyssa grabbed it before Michael could get hold of it. She couldn't risk him finding out that it contained coloured water, with a rum-soaked cork supplying the necessary smell.

She sashayed out of hotel, uncomfortably aware of Michael's proximity, and of several pairs of eyes hefted on her back.

Michael tried to put a hand around her waist, but she eluded him by increasing her pace.

'You're in a real hurry,' he said, with a hint of a slur.

She half-turned. 'Don't you want to get away from all the stuffiness?' She batted her eyelashes again, hoping the sunset would wait long enough for her protectors to see them clearly. 'All these petty rules.'

'Rules.' He spat on the ground, in what seemed to be his habitual mode of expressing distaste.

'I bet you're much too clever to let them spoil your fun.' She let him catch up with her, careful to stay on his right side, so he couldn't touch her without dropping his precious bottle first.

'No-one's telling me what to do, that's for sure.'

'I can see that.' They were coming up to the riverbank, where a new, roughly hewn bench sat close enough to the wash butts for the girls to take a break from their chores. A few yards away, the well-faked call of an owl echoed from a cluster of maples. Alyssa smiled to herself; the doctor had arrived.

She lowered herself onto the bench and raised her bottle. 'To your health.' Michael took a swig from his bottle. His pupils dilated. Not much more, and he'd fall asleep.

'Why don't you sell your liquor at the hotel?'

'Not good enough for Bert, was it. That's what he said, Michael, he said, take our filthy rotgut away and have a proper drink on the house.' A hiccup shook his frame. 'Bloody good man, he was. Best friend I ever had.'

'But he wouldn't let you sell your moonshine. That must have made you angry.'

Michael tapped his nose. 'Didn't matter. Enough men happy to get a quart or two from Fred and me.' He took another swig, stoppered the bottle and slid it in his pocket. His left hand wandered onto Alyssa's knee.

'You're so smart,' she said. 'I bet nobody could put one over you with dud coins, or fool's gold.'

He broke into a guffaw as his hand squeezed her knee. It took all her self-control to keep her hat-pin hidden in her hairdo, or he would have received another painful reminder to keep his hands to himself.

'You bet, sweetheart. Ain't no-one fooling me, not like that stupid old sod. Thought we wouldn't hear about it, did he. Took him for all his hard cash, and then let him win. Taken in by all those shiny bits.'

'Poor man,' Alyssa said. 'Who was it?'

Michael brought out his bottle. 'A toast to good old P –' His eyes crossed, and the moonshine fell from his hand.

Alyssa moved out of the way before he could fall into her lap.

Instead, he sank onto the ground, his back resting against the bench.

The doctor left his hiding-place and pulled up an eyelid. 'He'll spend the rest of the night in Morpheus's arms. Shall I take you home?'

Alyssa shook her head. 'I've got one more stop to make.' She sniffed her clothes. A faint whiff of Michael's liquor and pipe tobacco lingered in the air, but her dress smelt clean.

Alyssa's dress was two inches too long for Rosie, and a little too wide in the shoulders. Hannah pinned it up while Alyssa arranged her bonnet so that Rosie's face was hidden to anyone but the closest observer. She'd only walk a few steps, to sit with Mr Kendrick in the back yard, but a girl tripping over her own hem might tip off any observer, and even in the last vestiges of dusk, nobody could mistake their two faces, or the difference between Alyssa's dark hair and Rosie's fair braid.

The doctor peered through Hannah's newly sewn curtains. 'They're alright,' he said. Alyssa sat hard against the wall, in the unlikely case anybody caught a glimpse through the window. Instead of trying to squeeze into Rosie's dress, she'd wrapped herself in a thick quilted dressing gown loaned from Mr Kendrick. 'How did it go with your admirer?' Hannah asked.

'I should have known it wasn't Michael,' she said. 'None of the Kellers have the cunning, or the cool head to come up with such an elaborate plan of stealing the gold and then implicating Rosie.'

'It was all for nothing?' Hannah pulled a face. She drummed her fingertips together, clearly itching for something to occupy her hands, Alyssa thought. Her husband put his hand on hers and clasped them. Hannah leant her head against his shoulder.

'Michael had one important bit of information,' Alyssa said. 'He told me about a man who's been fobbed off with pyrite, after losing all his money.'

'Who?' The doctor let the curtains fall in place.

'Unfortunately, he succumbed to his doctored drink before he could tell me. I think the name starts with a P, or a B, but his speech was too slurred to be sure.'

'Abbott should be able to help out,' the doctor said. 'He knows everyone, and more importantly, he would be aware of anyone prone to heavy gambling.' He peeked through the curtains again. 'Poor Kendrick, sitting as silent as a statue.'

'We can't have Rosie talking, and anyone figuring out it's not my voice.' Alyssa wished she could have a peek too, but that would be imprudent. 'How is Rosie?'

'Quiet and subdued, for once.' He paused. 'I pity her, you know.'

'So do I.'

'She'll be alright,' Hannah said. 'We'll keep an eye on her.'

Her husband nodded, but his face looked grave. 'I don't know how much longer we can keep the townsfolk quiet.'

Footsteps crunched on the gravel, and two short knocks, followed by two long signalled Rosie's return.

Mr Kendrick gently ushered her in and pushed the door close behind them. He shot the two bolts across.

Hannah led Rosie to her own bedroom, to get changed.

'Did anybody see you?' the doctor asked.

'I didn't dare turn around, but I heard a few men go past. French Pete, I think, and Big Joe. Peg-Leg and Fred too, but their quarter lies in that direction. Quite a bit of traffic you have here, Mr Osborne.'

The banker pondered this. 'It seems a lot for this hour, but then it's hard to tell under these unfortunate circumstances what is normal and what should put us on the alert.'

'True,' Mr Kendrick said. 'But I'm glad to say that your charge behaved as shy and well-mannered as you could wish for.'

Rosie entered the room as he spoke his last words. She held out Alyssa's dress, and they swapped places.

Alyssa changed into her dress. Hannah took out the pins and sat down on her four-poster bed. A faded quilt covered the mattress, and the whitewashed walls shone. Two candleholders and a wash set stood on a dresser. A folded cloth sat underneath the ewer.

The picture of an elderly woman hung on the wall. Her white hair set off her kind, dark eyes; Mr Osborne's mother, Alyssa presumed.

Hannah patted the space next to her. Alyssa sat down. 'They can't hear us, can they?' Hannah's glance wandered towards the door.

'No.'

'The baby – what are we going to do?' Hannah's eyes were troubled.

'I'm still thinking about it.' They both knew that an

illegitimate child brought not just disgrace upon the mother's head, but was already born with a stain upon its name. This couldn't be allowed to happen.

'Are you going to be our school teacher?'

Hannah's question threw Alyssa off-balance. 'Pardon?'

'Rosie's baby won't be the only newcomer these next few years. Who's going to teach them, like you taught us?'

Alyssa groaned. 'Let us sort one problem after the other, please. My head is spinning already.'

'Sorry. It's just that you always have the answers.' Hannah tugged at Alyssa's dress waist. 'All done.'

Mr Kendrick and the doctor flanked Alyssa on the short walk home. With only the moon to illuminate their steps, the doctor had borrowed a lantern to light their way. The night air was still, with an occasional hoot from an owl breaking the silence. The hotel lay in darkness, and the streets were deserted.

'We've been going about this all wrong,' she said.

'Why?' The doctor swung the lantern around.

She blinked in the sudden light. 'Whatever we do, we need evidence.'

'The fool's gold –' the doctor broke off. 'Darn.'

'It doesn't prove anything.' Mr Kendrick rubbed his neck. 'We can't prove that gold nuggets have been substituted, we can't prove that Rosie was set up, we can't prove anything.'

'We need to flush the culprit out.' Alyssa's heart hammered against her ribs. 'A properly baited trap is our one hope.'

They halted ten steps from Alyssa's door. 'When is Alfie fit to be released from your care?'

'With any luck, tomorrow.' A slow smile spread over Dr Bryson's face, thrown into sharp relief by the lantern. 'We're going to use him to spread some disinformation?'

'If we can come up with something convincing. Good night, gentlemen.'

She watched them both depart, the doctor towards his surgery, Mr Kendrick towards the bank. Soon they'd all go their separate ways, and with them a lot of her happiness would leave her life. Something painful formed in her chest, like her heart was being squeezed.

She knocked on the door. 'Who is it?' Harriet asked from inside.

'It's Alyssa. I'm sorry for the late hour.' A bolt scraped over the door, and a key turned noisily.

Alyssa slipped inside. Harriet looked at her with puffy eyes, a candleholder in her hand. The candle gave off enough light to make out the outlines of the furniture within a few feet range. 'Does Matron know you're out half the night?' she whispered.

Alyssa tried to think of an excuse, but nothing came to mind. 'It was important,' she said.

Harriet rolled her eyes. 'I bet. No, don't explain. I can't tell what I don't know, can I? And I don't want to lie to Matron, if I can help it.'

'Thank you.'

Harriet led her to Alyssa's bed. Gentle snoring filled the room, together with the rustling of blankets and straw-stuffed mattresses when one of the girls turned in her sleep.

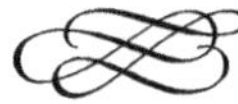

CHAPTER 19

The girls must have sneaked past her, to attend to their chores at the new laundry and the hotel, Alyssa thought when she woke up at the scandalously late hour of nine o'clock. It felt strange and lonely to be on her own in the log-house. Usually she relished a few moments of solitude – they were far and few between since she joined fortunes with Matron's flock - but today she'd have appreciated the company and idle chatter, to distract her.

She made herself some tea, and spread some wild honey on a slice of corn bread left for her on the table.

The honey was a new addition to their stores, thanks to Nancy's husband. The girl had made a good choice, Alyssa reflected. Joshua seemed as resourceful as he was kind, and if he could keep a hive or two on their future farm, they could not fail to be successful. As soon as Rosie's name was cleared, she'd start to make proper plans for all her friends. This town could see them all prosper. But first she needed to catch a murderer.

She filled a small tin with a few spoonful of the honey. This, together with some cold meat and bread from the hotel, would make a welcome breakfast for the doctor. He'd probably wonder where she was by now.

Alyssa needn't have worried. She found her friend and his patient feasting on fried potatoes with dripping, cooked over the fire by Mr Kendrick who eyed the honey with interest. She handed it to him, together with the bread.

'I'm sorry to be so late,' she said.

Dr Bryson waved her apology off. 'As you see, we can fend for ourselves if we have to.'

'That's his version,' Mr Kendrick said as he dripped some honey onto a piece of bread. 'I'll have you know that it was me who provided the provisions, and me who cooked them to perfection. The doctor may know his way around the surgery, but when it comes to operating pots and pans, he's useless.'

Alfie chortled. 'That's true, Miss. Now, you should've seen my Dad, or Bert, in the kitchen. Proper marvels, they were.'

'I thought Peg-Leg did the cooking.' Something stirred in Alyssa's memory.

'Stirring the porridge or a stew, more like it.' Alfie pulled a face. 'Not that I'm much use. I can tell a skillet from a coffeepot, but that's about it.'

'Then you're still doing better than most men,' Mr Kendrick

said. 'I'm sure Mrs Wainwright will see to it that the hotel kitchen is properly staffed. Unless your neighbours do object to having a wife work outside the house?'

Alfie shook his head as he wiped his mouth with a rag that doubled as handkerchief. A cough racked him, but instead of the barking of the last days, this sounded like the remains of a cold.

He fumbled for the pipe in his shirt pocket. 'May I?'

'If you've got any tobacco,' the doctor said. 'I'm out.'

'There's always tobacco at the store.' Alfie perked up. 'I'll just –'

'I'll go.' Alyssa signalled the doctor to stay quiet. 'In the meantime, the doctor can give you a final examination. Isn't that right?'

'I'll accompany the lady.' Mr Kendrick reached for his hat and put it on at a rakish angle. 'Cheerio.'

Outside, half the town appeared to be about. Hooves clattered on the hard-baked soil. Barry, astride one of the animals Alyssa had met during her visit to the pack station. The mule flicked its tail to ward of flies.

A pained expression in its eyes, as Barry overtook them, reminded Alyssa of an amateur performance of Hamlet she'd seen in Melbourne ages ago. Two other mules followed, led by a long rope that Barry had tied to his saddle.

Barry nodded in all directions, like a dignitary greeting his subjects after a long separation. Alyssa smiled. The first mule came to an abrupt halt. Its company skittered on for a few steps, raising up a dust whirl that flew in Alyssa's face.

She pulled away, sputtering.

Barry half-turned in the saddle. 'Morning, Sir, Miss.' He gave her a shrewd look. 'I got them mules the doc was after for a ride. If he still needs them.'

Alyssa gave him her sweetest smile, adamant not to let herself be irked. 'Good morning to you, too.'

Mr and Mrs Wainwright came out of the hotel. The ledger under Mr Wainwright's arm indicated their being headed for the laundry. Matron gave Alyssa a cheerful wave and a pointed look towards Mr Kendrick, but the lady was far too busy to stop for a chat, or just as likely, a warning about her taking too many liberties for an unmarried woman.

Alyssa marvelled again at the selection of wares in Mr Turner's store, and the haphazard way of displaying them. Where the shovels stood during her earlier visit, strings of onions hung from hooks. The bolts of fabric were wrapped neatly with a flannel sheet though, and far removed from anything that could spill, or was overly fragrant. Alyssa thought it likely that Matron had paid the storekeeper a prolonged visit.

She picked up a wooden box that would make a perfect container for the doctor's cigars. He rarely smoked, but one rare occasions both he and Mr Kendrick indulged.

'Three ounces of pipe tobacco.' Mr Turner took a set of scales from behind the counter. He sat two tins in front of Mr Kendrick. 'Which shall it be?'

'It's for Alfie Harper.' Mr Kendrick shrugged. 'You give me whatever you think he prefers.'

'I see.' Mr Turner dipped a small wooden shovel into the

smaller tin and heaped three ounces of coarse tobacco strands onto a piece of waxed paper that he turned into a screw. He handed it to Mr Kendrick, opened his ledger and moistened his thumb with his tongue before turning the pages.

'Three ounces pipe tobacco,' he wrote down in his spider script. 'Alfie Harper.'

Alyssa caught her breath. 'You always write down who something is for?'

'Sure.' Mr Turner gave her a weary glance. 'Seeing as he's the one paying for it. Why?'

'Nothing. I just admire your business sense.' Alyssa picked up the tobacco and tugged at Mr Kendrick's sleeve.

He followed her outside with his usual alacrity. 'Something important has occurred to you?' he asked.

'Oh yes. Let's just see Alfie off, and then we'll talk.'

Alfie pounced with glee onto the tobacco. 'I feel like a new man, doctor,' he said as filled his pipe and took the first puff. 'How about you, gentlemen?' He held out his tobacco pouch.

'Thanks.' The doctor produced his rarely used pipe. 'I've got one for you as well, Kendrick,' he said as he rummaged in his bag.

Alyssa kept well away as the three men sat together. She'd have liked to open the window to let out the whirling smoke, but decided against it, to prevent any eavesdropping.

'I'm good to go?' Alfie's voice held a tinge of hesitation. His sudden illness had shaken him more than he liked to admit,

Alyssa surmised. That, together with his brother's death and an inheritance he felt himself ill-equipped for, must be daunting for anyone.

'If you take it easy for a few days. No felling trees or jumping into rivers.' The doctor blew a languid circle of smoke, followed by ever smaller circles.

'I assume that Peg-Leg will return, now that you're in charge,' Alyssa said.

'Don't think so. He's never taken to me that much, has Peg-Leg. Probably thought I'd get between him and Bert. Funny guy.'

'But at least he's taken care of the pigs.' Mr Kendrick chuckled. 'Wouldn't let anyone get into the sty, Mr Wainwright said. Not that there'd be competition for the mucking out.'

'Bert loved his pigs.' Alfie's jaw worked as he tried to hide his grief. 'Good of Peg-Leg to take care of the sty.'

'Yes.' The doctor yawned. 'Anyway, no need to keep you any further.'

'Which reminds me.' Alyssa fished in her skirt pocket for a hazelnut-sized nugget. The yellow layers of pyrite embedded in a bit of rock gleamed bright enough to catch Alfie's eye. 'This was found in the laundry, after Mr Kendrick and I delivered your garments. I assume it's yours, Mr Harper?'

Alfie whistled under his breath as he took it. 'I wish I could say yes, but it ain't mine.'

'Oh, well, I'm sure you'll find the rightful owner at the hotel. Shall we take you over there to introduce you to your new kitchen staff?'

They handed Alfie over to Mr Abbott who'd just been on the way to check up on the patient and returned to the surgery.

Alyssa stripped Alfie's mattress of its sheet and bundled up the blankets, ready to be washed.

Mr Kendrick took them out of her hand. 'Sit down,' he said. 'You've been waiting long enough to share your revelations.'

She took a deep breath. 'You remember, doctor, how puzzled we were to find that the crowbar used to break open Bert's strong-box was purchased by himself?'

He scratched his chin. A bluish shade on his normally clean-shaven skin made him look dishevelled, in an endearingly boyish way.

'How could I forget? That was a blow.'

'Except, we don't know if it was him.'

'His name was in the ledger.'

She waited. Mr Kendrick's eyes lit up. 'Because the item was billed towards his account. Anybody could have said, it's for Bert up the hotel, and Mr Turner would dutifully put that down.'

'And who's the most likely candidate to do that without Mr Turner raising an eyebrow? Who would have thought of using a frying pan as a weapon to implicate Rosie? Even you two wondered if she could lift it, but our culprit knew.'

She let her words sink in. 'Tonight, gentlemen, you'll set a trap. Make sure word gets around that Alfie is celebrating his recovery. Every man in town must be there.'

Mark Bryson wished that Alyssa could be there, to watch their plan unfold, but all the ladies had been barred from the hotel bar for tonight. He was sure that celebrations would not get too rowdy, under Abbott's watchful eye, but they needed to loosen tongues as much as possible.

Abbott stood behind the bar, opening a second barrel of beer. Alfie had good-humouredly offered to take over his duties as the new publican, but he'd accepted the no with heartfelt gratitude.

Wainwright and Kendrick had served up stew and beans, which the men shoved down their gullets at an unparalleled speed, to get on with the evening's festivities. Boxes full of food-stained tin plates and mugs sat behind the counter, forgotten for the night.

Kerosene-filled sconces were lit as the single source of light now that the sun was setting. Mark silently applauded Abbott's decision to remove candles and other flammable objects from the tables.

Little Joe held a fiddle in his hands. Alfie accepted a second beer, obviously intent on following Mark's recommendation to moderate his drinking.

Others didn't feel the same restriction. It had taken them less than half an hour to empty the first barrel of beer, and several flasks implied that the Keller's moonshine was in appearance, too.

Little Joe moved the bow across the strings and listened with a cocked ear to the sound. He grunted and twisted the tuning pegs before giving the instrument another try.

'Give us a tune,' said French Peter. He downed the remains of his beer in one gulp, sat down the mug and clapped a rhythm. Peg-Leg, Big Joe, Alfie and Hans picked it up. Little Joe started to play, a Scottish reel if Mark remembered the song correctly.

Big Joe and Hans broke into a dance. The other men formed a wide circle. Hans held out his hand to Joshua and pulled him into the dance. Other men followed, including Mr Kendrick. Within a few minutes, the stomping of hobnailed boots and clapping of hands made the music a mere background noise.

Mark joined Abbott behind the bar. Abbott's left foot tapped in tune with the music.

'I'll take over if you want to join in the fun,' Mark said.

'Five minutes.' Abbott swung himself over the counter, in an effortless move, missing three mugs by inches.

'Make way for the big man,' Alfie shouted. The circle opened. Abbott linked arms with Kendrick, flinging his legs with as much gracefulness as the nimble Welshman.

Mark helped himself to a beer. A few more minutes, and the men should be ready for a break.

Hans was the first to falter. He dropped against the bar counter and held out a weak hand, sweat beading his face. Mark set down a row of freshly filled mugs. By now they were running out of clean mugs and glasses, and if people took someone else's drink, it wouldn't hurt them.

Little Joe dropped the bow. Some of the men protested, but he shook his head.

'We haven't had this much fun since the end of the snow in spring,' Hans said. 'How are we for beer, as long as it's on the house?'

'All good,' said Alfie. 'Don't you worry.' He pulled out the pyrite lump and tossed it into the air, catching it in his left hand. 'Anybody leave something in their laundry?' He held the pyrite up into the light. 'It's not mine, more's the pity.'

Mark thought he heard a sudden intake of breath. He glanced under lowered lashes towards Peg-Leg and French Peter.

'I wouldn't mind having that,' Barry said. 'What god darn idiot leaves gold in his pockets?'

Mark crossed his fingers behind his back. This was developing as hoped. If only Osborne played his part well.

The banker caught Mark's sign. 'May I see this?' He took the nugget.

'Not a bad size, eh? Enough of those, and you can buy yourself some really good times.' French Peter elbowed Peg-Leg in the ribs.

'The size is impressive,' Osborne said as he carelessly dropped the nugget onto the bar. 'The rest I'm afraid is not.'

'What are you talking about?' Barry's shot a greed-filled glance towards the nugget.

'It's pyrite,' Osborne said. 'You may have heard of its common name, fool's gold. It's only value lies in its property to strike a fire I'm afraid.'

'I don't believe you,' Barry said. 'I've never heard of fool's gold being found around here.'

'I thought it was quite common.' Osborne managed a weak smile. 'I've found more than one piece of pyrite in your offerings, gentlemen, and I've barely started the assay.'

A hush came over the hotel.

Abbott broke the painful silence. 'As long as you're not saying all we've found is fool's gold.'

'Dear me, no. I can't tell you in dollars and cents, but you should all be worth a decent amount.'

'In this case, I'd say we have another round.' Abbott pressed the pyrite into Barry's hand. 'And you can have this. You might find a use.'

'Yeah, find a mug for a card-game,' Fred muttered. His brother shot him a dark glance. Fred shut up.

Abbott joined Mark and pulled out something from underneath the bar; a dust-encrusted bottle of whisky. 'Last one,' he said. 'but if ever there was a moment to toast Bert's memory then this is it.'

The furious peel of the church bell broke through Mark's heavy sleep. He grabbed his clothes and ran out onto the street as soon as he could, still buttoning his shirt. A faint glow in the distance, coupled with an acrid smell in the air, would have told him where to go, even without the assistance of other men, running in the same direction. He stopped for a second, before he turned heel and fetched a bucket.

Back on the street, Osborne joined him, carrying two wooden pails. The banker panted already, but kept at a clipping pace.

Further ahead, Mark noticed Wainwright's broad back and Abbott's towering figure. He pressed on, towards the raging fire. For an instant, he thought he'd heard furtive steps in the back alley, going in the other direction, but they didn't matter. Nothing mattered but the flames that needed to be stopped before they could engulf the town.

Alyssa's first instinct was to head towards the source of the alarm. The other girls huddled around her, anxious for directions.

'Go to Matron's house,' she said. 'Stay there until the alarm is over.' She stepped outside and glanced around. Wisps of smoke curled up into the azure of the sky. 'Lord, no,' she said. 'It's a fire.'

Grace shrieked. Bertha hugged her to her chest, tears already rolling down her round cheeks. No-one who'd grown up in Australia underestimated a bushfire. In the hot season, a single flame could spread in the blink of an eye to ravage miles of country.

'There must be something we can do.' Nellie looked around.

'The men will know how to deal with it,' Alyssa said. 'We would get in the way. Please, go to Matron's until we receive news.'

'What about you?' Nellie put her hand on Alyssa's sleeve.

'I'll prepare the surgery. I hope it won't be necessary, but –' She let the sentence trail away.

On her way to the surgery, another thought hit her. Hannah and Rosie must be frantic for news.

She tapped the signal on the door. Hannah opened the door and embraced her, as Alyssa felt a painful shove between the shoulder blades. She fell into the room, taking Hannah down with her. The door slammed shut.

CHAPTER 21

Alyssa and Hannah scrambled to their feet. Alyssa opened her mouth for a scream, but a knife pointing at Hannah's throat silenced her. The light caught the wide blade, so she could see every detail. She'd never seen anything like it. Ten inches of vicious-looking steel with a double-edged blade that came to a curved point made her drop any idea of resistance. This was less of a knife and more of a sword.

'Where is she?' Peg-Leg's eyes gleamed with evil. Hannah's gaze darted towards Rosie's hideout.

Peg-Leg kicked the door. He wobbled slightly as his weight rested on his damaged leg. 'Come out, or I'll skin your friends alive.'

He shot the bolt across the back door.

'I'm counting to five,' he said.

Rosie inched out of her storage room. Fear turned her face

into a mask, with her skin drawn tight over her cheekbone and her pupils dilated into black discs.

'Why are you doing his?' Alyssa asked.

He pointed the knife towards Alyssa and slapped her with the back of his left hand. Hannah took a step back, her hand covering her exposed throat.

'Thank that banker for this,' he said. 'What harm did it do, take a bit here and there? But he had to come and meddle, didn't he. As for the little bitch here, making eyes at Bert and shaking her hips at him, she's getting what she deserves.'

White spittle formed in the left corner of his mouth. A spider-web of veins crisscrossed his cheeks and nose. Alyssa marvelled at the detachment with which she noticed these details about a man who held her at knife-point.

If only Mr Osborne had been around, or even better, Mr Kendrick with his pistol, she would have dared tackle Peg-Leg, but not on her own. And not with Rosie and Hannah in danger as well.

'We won't say a word if you just leave.' Time. She needed to gain time. Under her lashes she looked around for a possible weapon. She thought with regret of the hatpin, left in the girls' house. She still carried the tin-whistle, but with all the men gone, it was useless.

'Everyone will be attending to the fire for hours,' she said. 'You set it, didn't you?'

'Bit simple, is Peg-Leg, that's what you were thinking, right?' He slashed the knife through the air, relishing Rosie's flinching, and Hanna's sobs.

'I think you're very smart.' Alyssa's mouth felt dry. She willed herself to sound admiring. The longer he talked, the better her chance at finding a way out. 'No-one will suspect you.'

He giggled, a high-pitched noise that unnerved Rosie completely. She sank to the floor, mouth opened in a silent scream.

'Get up,' Peg-Leg said. 'Don't forget, one sound and I'll slit your throat.' He jerked his head at Hannah. 'Open the door.'

She moved toward the exit, like a wind-up toy. Peg-Leg's left hand shot out and grabbed her. 'The door to the bank.'

'I don't have the key.' Hannah voice shook, but she stopped sobbing.

'Smash it. Use the poker.'

Hannah picked up the long iron and struck at the door, but her feeble efforts made no difference.

'Stop it.' Peg-Leg's right eye twitched.

'Your knife,' Alyssa said. 'If you wedge it into the door-jamb, you might pry it open.'

'You do it,' he said, laying down his knife. In the next breath, he'd clasped both hands around Rosie's throat, thumbs digging into her windpipe.

Alyssa picked up the blade and slid it into the crack. She wiggled it back and forth. She could feel something give and wedged it in deeper.

'The poker, please,' she said to Hannah. With all her might she struck down the iron rod onto the handle of the knife. The door flew open, and the knife clattered onto the floor. Please let him pick up his weapon, she prayed. She had no qualms about hitting him with the poker, to save their lives.

But instead he said, 'Give me the knife.' His chokehold on Rosie relaxed a bit, but not enough.

Alyssa handed him the weapon. She rested the poker against the wall, beside her.

'Now get me the gold.'

'All of it?'

'You've got bags, don't you? Fill them.'

Alyssa and Hannah rushed to obey. 'We must keep him talking,' Alyssa whispered as they emptied unassayed gold, pyrite and buttons into hessian sacks.

They weighed enough to make them buckle.

'Take another bag,' Peg-Leg said. 'Put the fool's gold in.'

Hannah opened her mouth. Alyssa trod on her foot, to warn her into silence.

'I don't understand,' she said.

'Osborne would have set it apart.'

'But you told us to put everything into the bags. That's what we did.'

He shot her a glance of pure venom. How they could ever have taken him for a nice, if rough-mannered man, was beyond her. The menace he exuded made her skin crawl. Poor Rosie looked close to fainting.

'We can empty the sacks, and you show us what it looks like,' she said.

They didn't dare dawdle with the sorting. Still, any minute they spent was a minute less until at least one of the men would come back.

'Enough,' Peg-Leg said as three quarters of the gold had been put back into the sacks. He'd relinquished his hold on Rosie and resorted to wielding his knife again. 'Come back here.'

'What are you going to do now?' Alyssa's heart pounded against her ribs. Breathing was painful.

'I'm going to catch a murderous bitch.' He bared his tobacco-stained teeth in a snarl and mimicked slitting his throat. 'Too bad I didn't get her before she killed you both.'

Rosie's face blanched even further. She pressed both hands on her belly. Hannah's breath came in rasping bouts.

'Here? In this room?' What was supposed to sound firm came out as a whisper. Alyssa dug her fingernails into her palms to help focus her mind.

'Right here.' Peg-Leg ran a loving finger over the blunt side of his knife. 'Ever seen a Bowie knife? This little beauty can skin a deer and cut the carcass, bones and all, before you can say a Hail Mary.'

'You'll be covered in blood. No-one's going to believe your story.'

'They goddamn will.' New spittle flecked his beard.

'And how are you going to get away with the gold, and Rosie?' By now surely the fire must be extinguished, and the men on their way. She moved so the poker was behind her back.

'What are you saying?'

'We'll help you, if you let us go. You've got the gold. No-one will come after you, if we say we saw someone covered in pustules along the river.'

'A redskin?' A cunning look spread over his features. 'Go on, then.'

'Barry's mules,' she said. 'He left two tethered behind the

surgery. We'll load the sacks onto them. Hannah and I will lead it, and you take Rosie on the other animal. Tie her hands together, so she can't run away.'

'How can I trust you?'

'You've got all the cards in your hand.'

His eyes were small slits as he pondered Alyssa's suggestion.

'Get the mules,' he said. 'Don't try anything, or else.' He touched Rosie's throat with the knife-point.

'I won't,' Alyssa said. 'I swear it on my mother's grave.'

'You've got three minutes. If you're not back, bye-bye bitch.'

She ran towards the surgery, praying the mules were still there. For once she was lucky. There they stood, with their nose in a feedbag and saddles on their back. She pulled the saddle belts tight und untethered them, but they wouldn't move. Tears sprang up in her eyes as she pulled with all her might. 'Please,' she said. The smaller mule looked at her. 'Please,' she said again and stroked its soft muzzle. It sighed and started moving, as did its friend.

Alyssa barely had a chance to draw a crude arrow with her foot in the earth, to point in the direction she intended to take. Now all she could do was hope that her friends would see it and come to her aid.

She craned her neck. Smoke still curled up in the air. She clenched her hands until the knuckles turned white. She would not give in to despair, and let Hannah and Rosie down.

The mule gave her a hurt look as she and Hannah hefted the two sacks onto its back and tied them onto the saddle. A few dozen nuggets, most of them pyrite, were spilled on the floor of Mr Osborne's room, to make it look like the bank had been ransacked.

Alyssa helped Rosie onto the other mule. Rosie swung her leg over the saddle as Peg-Leg roughly tied her hands to the pommel.

Alyssa and Hannah led the first mule, striding as fast as they could away from the town. They kept to the back of the houses, in the unlikely case that apart from the girls in their house far behind them, anybody else was home.

No one dared say a word until they were a good two miles away from the last dwelling.

Rosie swayed. Peg-Leg raised his blade.

'Let her walk for a bit,' Alyssa said. 'You don't want her to fall off and delay us.'

'Bitch.' He slapped Rosie's face, but the girl kept still. A sharp blow with the knife, and Rosie's hands were free. The length of rope fell onto the ground.

Alyssa marched on. Together with the hoof print, that rope should be enough for pursuers to follow them – if there should be any help coming.

Rosie bit her knuckles as she trod with her bare feet onto sharp pebbles. None of the girls had ever gone without shoes in a land where the bite of a spider or a snake could kill in a matter of minutes. Alyssa cursed herself for allowing Mr Abbott to take

Rosie's shoes, to prevent her running away, but that couldn't be undone.

She slowed down to let Rosie chose her path with care and found herself next to Peg-Leg. She firmly kept her gaze away from his horrible weapon.

'What I don't understand is, why kill Bert? Nobody would have suspected anything.'

He yanked his mule to a halt. 'The bastard deserved it.' He spat out again. 'Peg-Leg, that's what he made me.'

'Bert injured your leg? I thought it was an accident.' Alyssa dropped the rein, only to pick it up as quickly as she could, together with a sharp-edged rock she slipped into her pocket, and got the mule going again. One tiny part of her brain wanted to believe that she'd heard faint noises not far behind them, noises not made by small mammals scurrying in and out of burrows or birds wheeling through the sky. If anybody was out there, the clatter of hooves and their own breathing should mask any sound.

'We shouldn't have gone up the mountain in the rain,' Peg-Leg said. 'I slipped, didn't I? Crashing down those blasted rocks.'

'I heard he carried you back.'

'I'd have done the same for him. And I'd have made him partner in that hotel he built while I was laid up in that stinking tent he'd dropped me in.' Peg-Leg shook with anger. 'I've been nothing but his god darn servant ever since. He even took my name from me. Ain't nobody ever call me anything but Peg-Leg since.'

'I'm sorry,' Alyssa said. Real or imagined, the wound must

have festered in Peg-Leg's soul until it poisoned him. 'What is your real name?'

'Daniel,' Peg-Leg said. 'Daniel Cole.' He wiped his nose. 'You know what he did when I got taken for all I had, on that steamer? He laughed at me. He laughed so hard he spilt his drink down the front of his shirt.' A malicious gleam came into his eyes. 'He's not laughing now, is he. And I put that fool's gold to good use.'

'You were ingenious,' Alyssa said, giving Hannah and Rosie small hand signals behind her back to keep quiet. The longer Peg-Leg talked, the better their chances of rescue. How long had they been going already? An hour? Two hours? The sun stood high in the sky. Mr Kendrick would be able to tell the time simply by glancing at it, but Alyssa had no idea.

But Peg-Leg's mood had soured. 'Shut up,' he said to Alyssa. 'Shut up, all of you.'

The noise in the background became louder, but it wasn't what Alyssa had dreamed of. Instead of footsteps, her ears filled with the drumming of water beating down on rocks and the whooshing of a torrent. They'd reached the dreaded cascades.

Peg-Leg pointed the mule towards the river. Alyssa's breath caught in her chest. She shook her head.

Peg-Leg raised the knife with the same hand he held the reins with, and grabbed Hannah with his left. Alyssa obeyed.

'Good,' he said. She turned her back to him, fumbling out the tin-whistle. They were ten feet from the river's edge. Before her, the water foamed white as it whirled around boulders and crashed into them with a violence that made her shudder. If they went into the water, they'd die.

CHAPTER 22

He gave Hannah and Rosie a violent push, towards the edge. 'I want to see you all together,' he said.

Alyssa hid the tin-whistle in one hand, her other hand around the rock.

'There's no need for this,' she said. 'We're no threat to you.'

He smiled, for an instant transformed into a happy man. 'You should've been nicer to me.'

'Then do it,' Alyssa said. 'It's so easy to be brave when you've got your Bowie knife to deal with three unarmed women. Or when you smother an unconscious man.'

For a heartbeat she thought she'd taunted him too much, but instead of coming after her with his blade, he put his knife into its sheath and inched closer, step by lurching step. The long march had taken its toll on his leg.

'Down,' Alyssa said sharply as she brought the whistle to her lips and blew in it with all her might. For one blessed moment

Peg-Leg froze, as the shrill noise assaulted his ears. Rosie and Hannah threw themselves to the ground and rolled away from the river bank and Peg-Leg as far as they could.

Peg-Leg reached for his knife as Alyssa threw the rock at his temple and kicked out at his kneecap. Her hobnailed boot made crunching contact with bone. She threw herself out of the way when a shot rang out, and with the blade whizzing past two inches from Alyssa's chest, Peg-Leg keeled over and feel into the water.

The last Alyssa saw of him, were his wide-open eyes, and the red tinge of the water swirling around his body.

'Thank God,' Mr Kendrick said as he pulled her close to him. 'I thought we'd lost you.'

Mr Abbott lowered his revolver. His jaw clenched as he stared at Peg-Leg's body as it got caught in the currents and smashed against the rocks. He genuflected before he gave Rosie and Hannah his attention. They still lay on the ground, uncomprehending that they were safe.

'Are you hurt?'

Rosie shook her head, tears streaming over her face. Alyssa knelt beside her and stroked her hair. 'It's fine,' she said. 'Everything is fine.' Hannah joined them, and hugged Rosie so hard the girl winced.

'She did it,' she said. 'Alyssa did it.'

'Mr Abbott saved us all,' Alyssa said, her voice shaky with relief. 'And Mr Kendrick.'

'You looked as if you had it all under control.' Mr Kendrick pulled her up. 'Sorry the cavalry took so long, but the fire distracted us all, and with everyone milling around, I didn't notice Peg-Leg's absence till after a goodish while.'

'But you came.'

'As fast as we could. We couldn't risk taking Abbott's horse, because of the noise, so we walked. The doctor would have joined us, except that Fred ran into the burning building and got himself badly hurt.'

'Peg-Leg set the fire.' Alyssa's knees felt weak. 'What building? Is everyone else safe?'

'No need to worry.' Mr Abbott tethered the mules together. 'He lit a gunpowder trail more than a mile to town, which led directly to the Keller's still. Saved me the trouble of shutting it down. Now, which of the ladies would prefer a ride?'

'Rosie. Her feet have suffered enough without shoes, and Hannah.' Alyssa smiled at Mr Kendrick. 'The nightmare is over, isn't it? Rosie is no longer a suspect?'

'No.' Mr Abbott shook his head, his sadness over Peg-Leg's duplicity forgotten. 'It was clever of you to get him to talk so freely. I wish I could have taken him down sooner, but I couldn't risk hitting any of you.'

She had heard correctly, then. Mr Kendrick gave her a quick wink. Of course; he was a superb shot, but if he as a newcomer had killed Peg-Leg, there might have been doubts about his version of events. But Mr Abbott as constable was beyond any doubt.

They stumbled more into town than anything else. Only the

mules seemed fresh, despite having to carry the gold as well as Hannah and Rosie.

The latter grew frightened again as soon as they spied the first person on the street, but Mr Abbott gave her a reassuring pat on the shoulder and made a point of walking right next to her.

As they moved closer, Alyssa recognised Matron. She carried a covered basket which she dropped where she stood, before rushing towards them.

'I've been so worried,' she said, stretching out both arms.

'We are all safe and sound,' Alyssa said.

Matron clapped a hand over her mouth as she noticed Rosie's unnatural paleness, and the dried blood on one sole where she cut herself on a rock. She helped the girl off the mule with infinite care and kissed her on the cheek. 'My dear, dear child,' she said. Hannah and Alysa shared a surprised look.

'Doctor!'

He came barrelling out of the surgery before Matron's call had finished. Mr Kendrick took a step back as his friend grasped Alyssa by both shoulders. 'You had me grow grey hairs today,' he said, looking her over with an unwonted tenderness mixed into his professional demeanour. She smiled at him, for once lost for words.

'Where shall we take Rosie?' Matron asked. 'She cannot be treated in the surgery while Mr Keller is laid up there.'

'Does she need special care?' Hannah frowned. 'Otherwise she's more than welcome to stay with us.'

'Or with us.' Alyssa gave Matron a quick nod. 'With our first brides married, there is more than enough space.'

'I don't see any reason why Rosie shouldn't decide herself,

once we've made sure that she is physically well.' The doctor lifted the surprised girl. 'I can walk,' she said in a feeble attempt at protesting.

'Not until I've cleaned and bandaged your feet. If Alyssa could fetch my medical bag and Mrs Osborne would be so good as to let us use her home again, you'll soon be free.'

'Free!' Rosie's eyes grew huge. A small sob escaped her.

The cuts were superficial, and a meal and some rest restored all three girls. The closest to a serious patient the doctor had, apart from Fred with his burns and a broken arm, was Mr Osborne, Alyssa thought. The poor man had almost suffered a heart attack when he discovered the danger his beloved wife had been in. His nerves had to be steadied with brandy from a bottle the doctor mysteriously produced.

CHAPTER 23

When the bell rang again the next morning, Alyssa grabbed the sheathed knife she'd insisted on having. She hid it in the folds of her skirt as she followed the other girls to the bell tower. The doctor and Mr Kendrick joined her, both as composed as she'd ever seen them. Her heartbeat steadied.

Mr Abbott, dressed in his best suit, stood outside the church, next to Alfie and Susanna. The other men formed an irregular half-circle.

Alyssa found herself led to the front, next to Hannah and a trembling Rosie. Several hostile glances were fastened onto the poor girl, but she held her head high.

'Come here, if you please,' said Mr Abbott, reaching out his hand to Rosie. Hannah gave her a little nudge. Rosie trudged forward, where she found herself embraced by Susanna.

'We all owe this young lady an apology,' Mr Abbott said. 'We've been foully tricked by a murderer and thief in our midst.'

'What are you saying?' Little Joe's mouth gaped open. 'Are you saying the skirt –'

'Miss Thatcher,' Mr Abbott said, a dangerous glint in his eyes.

'Miss Thatcher is innocent?'

Alfie nodded. His hands clenched. 'It was Peg-Leg,' he said. 'The murderous swine stole our gold and killed my brother.'

'Our gold!' The men turned as one man towards Mr Abbott.

'Hold your horses,' he said. 'Thanks to Miss Chalmers and her friends, we have retrieved every single nugget.'

'How do you know it was Peg-Leg?' Michael asked, his brows beetling together.

'Because I heard him with my own ears,' Mr Abbott said. 'And because he tried to kill the young ladies. Let me ask you this, Michael. How many men knew where your still is?'

'Me and my brother. French Pete. And Peg-Leg.' Understanding swept over his face. 'The bastard. He burnt down my still.'

'He needed to create a distraction, to break into the bank and take hostages.' Mr Abbott held out his hand to Rosie. 'Let me apologise again, Miss Thatcher. We'll make it up to you.'

Rosie shook his hand and curtsied, her gaze on the ground. 'Thank you, sir.' She limped towards Hannah, her bandaged foot still causing her pain.

'Our gold is safe?' Big Joe repeated.

'Yes.'

'All of it?'

Mr Abbott nodded.

'Yeehaw!' Big Joe threw his hat in the air and caught it before it fell onto the ground.

Alyssa kept quiet, but she wondered if it had occurred to Mr Abbott that although they had retrieved the gold from the bank, the originally stolen nuggets were still unaccounted for, possibly because Peg-Leg had intended to kill the girls, hide the gold and return as a hero, only to escape with his loot as soon as the boat took up service again. But where would he hide the stolen gold?

She tried to get out of the crowd, bumping into Hannah in the process. Michael blocked her way. He seemed to have suffered no ill-effects from the sedative, she noticed with a relieved conscience. He leered at her, to be met with her iciest stare. Unperturbed, his hand grabbed her waist.

'Hold it,' the doctor said. Michael stared at his hand, which was removed from Alyssa with a vice-like grip. 'I think you mistake the lady for someone else.'

Michael's brows moved together as he looked closer at Alyssa. His breath smelled of onions, and tobacco. She tilted her head away.

'But weren't you and I walking out?' he asked in a surprised tone.

Mr Kendrick pulled Alyssa away. 'Highly unlikely, wouldn't you say? I thought it was common knowledge that Miss Chalmers is already spoken for.'

Michael scratched his beard.

'I'm sure if you apologise nicely, the lady will let it go. If I were you, I'd stay clear of moonshine.' Mr Kendrick gave Michael a dazzling smile. 'Coming, doctor?'

'Thank you, both of you,' Alyssa said as soon as they were out of earshot.

The men exchanged a strange look, almost as if they were challenging each other. 'Say no more.' The doctor took her arm. 'Or rather, let us in on the secret of your sudden flight.'

'I may be mistaken, but I think I know where the missing nuggets are.'

'Mr Abbott will be glad to hear that. Shall we surprise him?'

Alyssa wrinkled her nose. 'I believe Susanna would prefer him to be a bystander.'

When Alyssa pointed out where the men should search, Mr Abbott pushed aside the idea of volunteers and instead asked his wife for one of the shirts she'd selected as future rags. She gave in with good humour and, after a few words with Alyssa, added a flannel and a piece of hard soap to the bundle.

'Let me know if you need more,' she said, kissing him on the cheek.

'I'll see you as soon as I can.' He took the clothes and disappeared into their bedchamber.

'Oh, we're coming along,' his wife called after him. 'I'm sure we'll be fine if we cover our noses.'

The four hotel pigs squealed with surprise as Mr Abbott slung his long legs over the fence of their run. A layer of straw covered the ground, and Mr Abbott trod with as much care as he could muster, a pitchfork in his hand.

One of the pigs looked at him with deep distrust in its eyes as he made for the sty. It lowered its head and butted Mr Abbott in the legs. Susanna gasped, but it appeared the pig was simply in a playful mood.

Mr Kendrick tapped a metal pail against the fence, and as one the pigs trot towards him. He tipped the contents of the pail into a trough on the other side of the fence. A mix of vegetables and corn came out, to the animals' delight. They jostled each other for position to get at the feast.

Mr Abbott disappeared in the sty, a solid construction made of logs and sealed with mud. Muffled swearing made Susanna giggle. If she heard correctly, Peg-Leg had done a less than thorough job with the mucking-out, Alyssa thought. The poor animals. That would have to change, too. If her list of needed improvements kept on growing at this pace, she'd really be here long enough to teach the first children.

Mr Abbott bolted out of the sty, pitchfork in one hand, a tightly rolled sack in the other. He kicked the sty shut behind him and made for the fence.

'Not here, darling.' Susanna pinched her pretty nose and nodded towards the farthest end. 'We'll see you when you're clean.'

Even after half an hour's bath Mr Abbott kept a prudent distance from the guests in his house. They'd counted one-hundred-and-seventy-two nuggets in the stash from the pig-sty. Some of them were as small as a grape, others as big as an apple, with flecks of gold in what looked for the most part solid rock. But whatever their monetary value, Alyssa doubted they were worth the price of Bert's life. Or Peg-Leg's.

Mr Abbott echoed her thoughts. 'He was a decent man once. Funny how you can see someone every day and not realise he's gone to rot. If I hadn't heard and seen him, I'd never have believed it.'

'I would.' Alfie sat perched next to Mr Kendrick, trying hard not to spill his tea or display any bad manners. 'He's always been the jealous sort, sucking up to Bert and kicking out when nobody else saw him. I thought it was because he liked to be number one.'

He lifted his cup with both hands until he saw how Mr Kendrick lifted his by the handle. 'How's the poor girl?'

'She'll recover,' the doctor said. 'All she needs is some rest, fresh air and feeling safe.'

'What a rotten thing.' Alfie shook his head. 'Doing in my brother is one thing, but trying to get an innocent lady hanged – if you ask me, he came off lightly.'

'Anyway,' Susanna said, 'that's all in the past. For now, I suggest we celebrate.' Her gaze travelled from Alyssa to the doctor and Mr Kendrick. 'I'm sure we'll find a reason.' A dimple showed as her smile deepened. 'This afternoon, at four o'clock sharp, in the hotel.' She touched Alfie's hand. 'I hope you don't mind.'

He gaped at her, enchanted. 'No.'

'Good.' She sniffed the still slightly pungent air. Her husband shifted away a little further. 'It's not too bad, I reckon,' she said. 'It's much nicer outdoors anyway. Let's stroll to the river.'

'I think we should look in on Rosie,' Alyssa said.

'I'll come with you, if that's alright.' Did Alfie change colour? It was probably simply the light, but his compassion pleased her.

'We'll bring her to the hotel,' she said swiftly.

Rosie sat inside, with Hannah. Her face had lost that pinched look, but she fidgeted on her seat.

'Shouldn't you sit outside, take in the air?' Alyssa asked.

Hannah sighed. 'That's what I keep on telling her.'

Rosie's shoulders slumped. 'I don't want people to see me?'

'Why ever not? You've got nothing to blame yourself for.'

Rosie's hand covered her belly. 'Easy for you to say. You know what they call females like me.'

'Yes, I do.' Alyssa lifted Rosie's chin. 'They call them widows.'

'What?' Rosie snorted.

Understanding dawned in Hannah's eyes, and, more importantly, in Mr Osborne's. He gave her an encouraging nod.

'Mr Osborne, your furnace should be hot enough to melt precious metals.'

'Most of them, yes.'

Alyssa felt a tiny pang of regret, as she nestled out the precious locket with her mother's picture she kept around her neck. From the locket chain hung a signet ring that had been her father's. The one thing she had to remember him by. She'd taken it out of her box this morning with its purpose fixed in her mind.

'Can you melt this down and form it into a wedding band?'

'I need a mold.'

'I can make one.' Mr Kendrick jumped up. 'Between us, we should have everything in your workshop to do a stellar job.'

'Thank you.' Rosie's bottom lip trembled. 'But who's going –'

'Who's going to wonder why you wouldn't shout out your bereavement? Nobody, I hope, otherwise Matron will give him a piece of her mind. After all you've been through, nobody would dare. And if they ask, tell them. Tell them how you went for a picnic by the river, and how your new husband, well ...' Alysa paused.

'He slipped, fell into the water, and you never saw him again.' Mr Kendrick warmed to his theme. 'When you heard of a group of young females, naturally you followed them. What initials shall we carve into the ring?'

'R and W.' Rosie's eyes gleamed wet, but Alyssa saw hope in them, too, and trust. Rosie had found a home.

'Consider it done. Allow me to measure your finger.'

Matron presided over a marvellous spread. Alyssa counted half a dozen different pies and pastry. The girls must have worked without a moment's break since the morning. Her husband stood beside her, beaming with pride. The girls clustered around them, with Rosie in their midst. She wore the wedding band not on her finger, but on a thin chain around her neck. The chain had belonged to the late Mrs Osborne, and although it should rightfully have been

Hannah's, it had given her and her husband the greatest joy to gift it to Rosie.

Matron gave Susanna a nod. Susanna clasped her husband's hand and cleared her throat.

'I've never held a speech before,' she said. 'All I really want to say is, thank you. Thank you to the men who let us come, to all the neighbours who welcomed us, and most of all, to Mrs Wainwright, who took care of us.'

A few men at the back of the room whistled and cheered.

Susanna's dimple made another appearance. 'I wish we had more than beer and tea to toast you all, but it'll have to do.'

With the party in full swing, and Rosie enjoying herself with the other girls, Alyssa decided that her work was done.

She slipped out to the back, where the pigs lay on their sides, sunning themselves. She rested her elbows on the fence. There was something peaceful about the animals, something soothing that calmed her worries. Soon enough she'd have to decide her next steps, but for now she was content.

'Deep thoughts?' Mr Kendrick asked. She gave a small start.

'I wouldn't call them deep,' she said.

'No?' Dr Bryson ambled over, hands behind his back.

'We've done it, haven't we?' She tilted her face towards the comforting sun. She'd forgotten her bonnet again, but it didn't matter. 'Solved the murder, and Rosie's problems?'

'Not much left up in the air,' Mr Kendrick said. 'Except for the future.'

A pig rolled over, moaning in the process.

'Maybe we should find a more congenital spot,' the doctor said, hands still hidden behind his back.

They strolled down to the river bank. The water lay becalmed, with a tiny ripple here or there speaking of movement. The sun glinted on the surface, sparking golden lights. What a difference to the torrent that had claimed Peg-Leg's body. Alyssa shuddered.

'Do you regret coming here?' the doctor asked.

She shook her head. 'It's a good place, and even if it weren't, the friendship I've found would make up for a thousand hardships.' She looked from one man to the other. 'At least I hope so. It makes me less afraid for the future.'

'Don't be afraid.' The doctor laid a bulky parcel into the grass and reached for her hand.

'I've phrased this badly,' she said. 'It's – part of me wants to stay here, and watch my friends be happy, and watch their children grow up, but I know I don't really belong. Maybe I never will.'

'You're scared of standstill.' Mr Kendrick reached for her other hand. 'You weren't made for a small life, no matter how satisfactory it may be for others.'

'Thank you. But what shall I do? What can I do?'

'You could marry me. Or the good doctor.' Mr Kendrick pressed a kiss onto her palm. 'It's entirely up to you. We'll always be your friends, no matter how you decide.'

For once, she was lost for words. Luckily, the doctor made up for it. 'We realise we're both not ideally situated. If I go to the battlefields, I'd have to leave you behind for who knows how long, and our good Kendrick is no more his own master as a seafarer.'

She opened her mouth but he shushed her. 'Think about it.'

Mr Kendrick breathed another kiss onto her palm before he let go of her hand. Her heart fluttered. 'Of course, I could follow Mr Wainwright's example and ask Captain Moore to release me as soon as he can replace me.'

'You'd settle down?' she asked.

'If we can find a place that suits you. There's a lot I can turn my hand to.'

'You're the kindest, most considerate men I've ever had the fortune to meet, both of you.' Something muffled her voice.

'No tears.' A gentle finger wiped away the treacherous trickle on her cheekbone. The doctor smiled at her. 'You don't have to answer now. We've waited long enough to ask you, we'll survive waiting for your decision. In the meantime, we've got something for you.'

He picked up the parcel. 'From both of us. In the interest of fairness, we decided a few weeks ago not to act behind the other man's back where you are concerned.'

'It is your birthday, isn't it? At least, according to Captain Moore's list,' Mr Kendrick said.

She nodded, but instead of opening the parcel, she put it down again and hugged Mr Kendrick. His body felt solid and comforting, and slightly disturbing. She let go of him and hugged the doctor, an altogether pricklier experience as his cheek touched hers. 'I should have shaved better this morning,' he said.

'I don't mind,' she said.

She reached for the parcel and undid the string. Inside the

brown paper, she found four novels, each of them calling out to her to be read at once.

'A Christmas Carol.' She touched the embossed words on the leather. 'Pride and Prejudice. A Tale of Two Cities. The Black Tulip. I don't know what to say.'

'Happy birthday,' the doctor said. 'My dear.'

She cradled the books in her arms. Thoughts whirled in her mind. Marriage. But to whom? Mr Kendrick, with his reliable, steadfast character, quick wit and charm, or the doctor, with his ever-changing temper which hid a kind heart and passionate nature?

'I'll think about your words,' she said. 'But for now, I'd like to be alone.'

CHAPTER 24

She sat by the window, while the other girls milled around, chatting and giggling. Rosie's newfound status as widow found widespread approval, and since the lady in question had joined them to give Hannah and her husband some privacy at last, she once again was the centre of attention.

Alyssa only caught every tenth word. The doctor, or Mr Kendrick. Their faces appeared unbidden in her mind. Both so very dear to her, and if she was honest, both essential to her happiness. The healer and the explorer.

She reached for a book, opening it at random. 'You must allow me to tell you how ardently I admire and love you,' she read. Love. That was the answer surely. But how did one find out?

'Alyssa? Are you unwell?'

'Pardon?'

Harriet bent over her. 'We've asked you twice about what we'll do now.'

'Do now?'

Harriet put her cool hand on Alyssa's forehead. 'Shall we call the doctor?'

'No! I mean, no. I'm sorry if I was distracted.' Alyssa put a proprietorial hand on her stack of books. What a thoughtful present.

'Leave her be,' Rosie said. 'Alyssa'll tell us if she needs something done, right?'

Alyssa nodded, hiding her amazement. Maybe the new Rosie would surprise them all.

'Come on then,' Harriet said. 'I'm hungry.'

'Again?' Nellie rolled her eyes. 'You had more pie than the rest of us together.'

'I also worked harder than the rest of you together,' Harriet said. 'Leaving me with half the town's laundry.'

Nellie poked out her tongue. Harriet laughed. Alyssa joined in. With all the bickering among the girls, she could sense the affection.

This wilderness town would not do forever, but at least for the time being while she was needed she, too, had found a home. And she realised something else, too, something her heart and head had found out between them.

She smoothed down her skirt and took out her hairbrush. 'Give me five minutes,' she said. 'Or I'll follow once I'm done.' After all, she wanted to look her best when she informed Mr Kendrick and the doctor about her decision.

~

The moon and the sun both stood high on the firmament as Alyssa and Mr Kendrick left the hotel. The doctor had stopped by briefly for his meal, because his patient's condition had worsened. Although he did not fear for Fred's life, he felt the need to sit with him until the latest dose of laudanum had taken hold.

Alyssa and Mr Kendrick walked in a silence that would have been uncomfortable with most people. Their steps harmonised well, as did their minds, she thought. She smiled up at him.

Mr Kendrick poked his head into the surgery.

'One moment,' the doctor called out.

When he came out the door, Alyssa blinked twice. He'd outdone himself, with his best suit, and slicked back blonde hair. A twitching nerve on his temple betrayed his nervousness.

'Shall we get down on our knee?' he asked.

'In this dirt and dust? Matron would never forgive me if I let you both ruin your suits,' she said. 'My dear friends.'

'Well, Alyssa?' Mr Kendrick's voice lost his usual steadiness.

'You've both done me the greatest honour.' She touched Mr Kendrick's hand. 'But how could I accept the kind of sacrifice that you would make if you gave up the sea? It's not a partnership if it diminishes one half of it.'

'I see.' He attempted a smile, but she could feel his sadness.

'The same goes for you, doctor.'

'Don't ...'

'Hear me out,' she said. 'I will marry you, if you promise to let me be part of what you do. I will not be left behind, or put aside.'

She held her breath while she waited for his answer.

'If I were you, Bryson, I'd say yes. Otherwise my offer still stands.' Mr Kendrick's light tone did not mask his hurt.

'I can't take you to a battlefield,' the doctor said. 'Impossible.'

Mr Kendrick said, 'What's wrong with staying here for a bit? I understand you want to do your bit in your own country, but doesn't a Canadian life count as much? Not to mention Rosie and the other ladies who might need more support than Matron can give.'

The doctor stood stock still.

'Think about it. A doctor's skills are needed everywhere.'

The doctor went down on one knee and clasped Alyssa's hand. 'Will you marry me and be my nurse and partner in crime and life?'

'Yes. Yes, I will.'

While he got up and patted the dust off his pant leg, Alyssa embraced Mr Kendrick and whispered in his ear, 'You see, he needs me, and you, my darling friend, don't.'

'That's what you think,' he said and kissed her on both cheeks, long enough to make her wonder if she'd made the right decision. Then her groom reclaimed her, and every conscious thought fled her.

They broke apart after what seemed like a lifetime, when Mr Wainwright hurried down the street.

'Incredible news,' he shouted.

Alyssa tried to step away from the doctor but he pulled her close again.

'What's so momentous that a man can't have some privacy?' he asked.

'The whistle,' Mr Wainwright said. 'Hans said he heard the

steamer whistle when he checked on his traps. He said the boat should be here tomorrow.'

'You're leaving? And your wife?'

'Mrs Wainwright will stay here, and so will I after I've spoken to the captain. He'll just have to promote someone.' He beamed. 'Don't you see? No smallpox. We're free.'

The End

The Case of the Missing Bride

It was supposed to be the start of a happy, new life ...

1862 - a group of young Australian women set sail for matrimony in Canada. Their presence is withheld from the male passengers and all but a select few members of the crew. But their worlds collide when one of the gentlemen stumbles over the women.

When one of the intended brides goes missing, only Alyssa Chalmers, the one educated, wealthy woman in the group, is convinced the disappearance is no accident. She sets out to find out what happened.

Has there been a murder?

Alyssa is willing to move heaven and earth to find out the truth. She is about to discover that there is more to her voyage into the unknown than she bargained for ...

False Play at the Christmas Party

December, 1928. Jack Sullivan plans a charity party in his new night club in aid of his fellow war veterans to celebrate his arrival in Adelaide. But some party guests have plans of their own how to benefit

...

A Matter of Love and Death

Adelaide, 1931. Telephone switchboard operator Frances' life is difficult as sole provider for her mother and adopted uncle. But it's thrown into turmoil when she overhears a suspicious conversation on the phone, planning a murder.

If a life is at risk, she should tell the police; but that would mean breaking her confidentiality clause and would cost her the job. And practical Frances, not prone to flights of fancy, soon begins to doubt the evidence of her own ears - it was a very bad line, after all...

She decides to put it behind her, but it's not easy. Luckily there is the charming, slightly dangerous night club owner Jack. Jack's no angel - six pm prohibition is in force, and what's a nightclub without champagne? But when Frances' earlier fears resurface, she knows that he's the person to confide in.

Frances and Jack's hunt for the truth puts them in grave danger, and soon enough Frances will learn that some things are a matter of love and death...

KEEP IN TOUCH

You can follow Carmen Radtke on Bookbub:
https://www.bookbub.com/profile/carmen-radtke

and on Twitter: @carmenradtke1